I0728821

SOLOMON

Solomon

Book 2: The Chronicles of DarkBridge Technology

RICHARD GUERIN

Richard Guerin

This book is dedicated to my Uncle Jack. His simple three word saying of "keep the faith" has always lifted me through troubling times. Always upbeat whenever I saw him, he was a true force of nature. Rest in peace, Uncle Jack.

Copyright © 2023 by Richard Guerin

The characters and events portrayed in this book are ficti-
tious, except for certain historical references.
Any similarity to real persons, living or dead is coincidental,
except in certain historical references and
is not intended by the author.

All rights reserved. No part of this book may be reproduced in
any manner whatsoever without written permission except in
the case of brief quotations embodied in critical articles and
reviews.

First Printing, 2023

Website: www.darkbridgetech.com
Email: rguerin@darkbridgetech.com

Other books in this series:

DarkWeave Book 1: The Chronicles of DarkBridge
Technology

Contents

Chapter 1

Secret Revealed

Paul lay in bed gazing at the ceiling. It had been a few weeks since the attack by Belial and much had been accomplished. Mostly, by Maggie who was sleeping soundly next to him in bed. Maggie had done exactly what she had told Martin at their prior meeting. She had reopened Maggie's restaurant here at the DarkBridge Technology facility and had been taking various training lessons. The training included the various technological devices developed by DarkBridge Technology, hand to hand combat and small arms usage. It was necessary training, so that she could fulfill her goal of becoming a Field Investigator. Paul was extremely proud of her. The two of them had become even closer after learning of their previous past lives together and had seemingly become inseparable. The old saying of "never knowing a love like this before", really didn't apply, since he had known and loved Maggie over many lifetimes.

As he lay there, Paul thought about his own circumstances. Ever since he had the Valinor dream about the alien technology located in the Antarctic, he had felt an urge to investigate it. The dream had shown him a large, excavated cavern some two miles or so, below the Antarctic ice cap. Paul as Valinor and Maggie as Shaynor, had excavated the cavern, many thousands of years ago, in order to store a secret cache of Anunnaki technology. Whether any of it had survived the thousands of years since that lifetime as Valinor, was the question. There was only one way to find out. He needed help and the only one he trusted with this knowledge was Martin. Tomorrow, he would meet with Martin and see what could be done. Decision made, he closed his eyes and drifted off to sleep.

Martin Weaver, founder and CEO of DarkBridge Technology, had woken up early, wanting to get a few things done at his office. Later in the morning, he and Hiram were scheduled to give a demonstration at Area 51 pertaining to alternate uses for the company's GAGE devices. Sitting behind his mahogany desk, Martin was reviewing the technology transfer agreement with Area 51 for the GAGE technology, when Eva suddenly interrupted.

"Sorry To bother you Martin, but Paul is waiting outside. He says that it could be important," said Eva.

Martin was curious. He tried to maintain an open-door policy, where any employee could come to him and talk. When that employee happened to be Paul, Martin knew it must be important.

"Send him in, Eva," replied Martin.

The door to Martin's office opened and Paul walked in, closing the door behind him.

"Good morning, Martin. Thanks for seeing me on such short notice," said Paul, a brief wave of anxiety passing through him.

"Good morning, Paul. Have a seat. Eva said it was important," said an intrigued Martin.

"I think it could be important to all of us," said Paul, as he began relating his dream of Valinor and the cavern in Antarctica.

Martin sat back in his chair, elbows resting on the chair arms, hands clasped together, listening to Paul as he related the dream.

"That was the dream I had and why I'm here," said Paul, with some relief at not having to maintain this secret from Martin any longer.

"I can see why it would feel important. There could be advanced robots, advanced spacecraft, gravity bombs, thermonuclear warheads and more stored there. Any single item would be important and collectively, they could represent a fantastic and powerful, trove of knowledge. The big question is whether any of it has survived," said a thoughtful Martin.

"That is the question. After thousands of years, it could all be a pile of rust," replied Paul.

"Possibly even radioactive, if the warheads have decayed," offered Martin.

"Yes, that could quite possibly be the case. We won't know until I can investigate," replied Paul.

Martin sat back in his chair pondering the situation. There was no way he would be able to hide any recovered technology from General Esterbrook, especially of this magnitude. While DarkBridge Technology was a research and development company, most of this alien technology fell outside his current business model. Maybe this was one of those situations where you left well enough alone and let it stay forgotten. There was always a chance that someone else would stumble upon it, possibly a foreign government. That alone was the deciding factor for Martin. Best if we have it, he thought.

"Okay, Paul. Work out the details with Eva. Let's keep this on a need-to-know basis for now. Make sure you do all your work topside far away from the building. We need to minimize any risks," said Martin.

"I'll get started right away and keep you posted on what I find. Thank you, Martin," replied Paul, as rose from his chair to leave.

"You're welcome, Paul. Good luck and I hope you're successful," said Martin, smiling and also rising from his chair.

The two shook hands and Paul left Martin's office, thinking about how to approach this investigation.

Martin watched Paul leave, thinking that General Esterbrook would be thrilled to no end, if he were to receive this alien technology. Especially the five Kyril spacecraft that Paul mentioned. Returning to his chair, Martin sat back down and leaned back, his mind focusing on the upcoming demonstration later this morning. The GAGE technology transfer was another one of those situations, which came with some reservations. It was but another example of technology that could be used against his company, should it fall into the wrong hands or even worse, that his own government could use it against him. Risky, but necessary, he thought to himself, as he got back to reviewing the transfer agreement.

Chapter 2

Demonstration

The sun was shining brightly on a cloudless morning at Area 51, the perfect type of day for an experiment with wide ranging implications. An Air Force ground crew was towing a Talon fighter jet out of its hanger and prepping it for another experimental test flight. The fighter jet, while still a highly effective, tactical deterrent in the Air Force arsenal, was a few generations behind what was housed in the adjacent hangars. Rather than risk losing a more advanced fighter jet, the Talon was viewed as dispensable and often used in experimental testing. The ground crew began fueling up the fighter, while performing some pre-flight checks. Minutes later, with refueling and other preparations complete, the ground crew waited patiently at a distance for the pilot to take over.

A helmeted figure wearing a gray flight suit exited the flight crew locker room, stepping into the brightly lit, cavernous hangar. The figure strode confidently out of the hangar, towards the waiting fighter jet, admiring its sleek, black angular shape. Major Robert Clark, call sign "Warlock", climbed up into the cockpit of the F-620 Talon fighter jet and prepared for takeoff. Flipping a few switches on the control panel, he felt a slight shudder, as the twin, Cyclone engines began powering up. Warlock taxied the Talon fighter towards the twelve-thousand-foot runway, large enough to land a fully loaded bomber, or as in some Hollywood movies, Air Force One. Warlock stopped the jet at the beginning of the runway and held the brakes as he awaited instructions from the control room. The twin Cyclone engines waited patiently, quietly purring, ready to deliver their awesome power at Warlock's command.

Meanwhile, in an underground control room, some one thousand feet below the surface of Groom Lake, General Esterbrook, commander of all U.S. "ultra black" sites, stood watching the monitors. Arrayed around the room were various flight control stations, tasked with communications, radar and maintaining a record of this important experiment. In attendance were Martin Weaver, President and CEO of DarkBridge Technology and Dr. Hiram Greenwood, Vice President of Research and Development at DarkBridge. They were here to see another application of the technology used at their company and if it was successful, license it to the government. Hopefully, it would follow an arrangement similar to the DarkWeave suits that DarkBridge had begun manufacturing for the military. Comprised of diamene, DarkWeave suits were the most advanced body armor created by man. In addition to body protection, DarkWeave suits had other abilities, but for now, those were reserved for DarkBridge Technology personnel.

"Anytime you're ready Major. Godspeed", said General Esterbrook, looking at the radar operator who gave him the thumbs up sign.

"Roger, Control. Mission starting", replied Warlock, as he released the brakes and throttled up the powerful Cyclone engines. Like twin lions unleashed, the roaring Cyclone engines sent the Talon fighter screaming down the runway, the acceleration pushing Warlock deep into his seat. Halfway down the runway, he pulled back on the joystick and the jet rapidly climbed into the clear blue sky. Within seconds the jet was at an altitude of 20,000 feet and a few seconds later, reached a cruising altitude of 40,000 feet. He leveled off and throttled back the Cyclone engines to a cruising speed of Mach 2.

"Altitude reached. Waiting for go ahead", said Warlock.

General Esterbrook looked at the radar operator, who gave him another thumbs up. For both safety and security reasons, it was critical that the airspace around Warlock be clear.

"Warlock, you are clear to proceed", said the General.

"Roger. Commencing Phase 1", replied Warlock as he reached out and pressed a blue button labeled "GAGE1". Pressing the button activated a piece of DarkBridge technology mounted on the front of the plane. It was called a GAGE device or gateway generator; its primary use was to open a gateway into a dimensional bubble that one could enter and then exit out at the same or different location. The effect was almost immediate and awed Warlock. The air in front of the jet began to shimmer and ripple, as a large, dark blue, gateway opened in front of the fast-moving jet. Warlock didn't hesitate and pushed the throttle forward, hurling the jet into the gateway, which promptly closed behind the jet.

"General. I've lost radar contact with Warlock", reported the radar operator.

"This is to be expected General. Once the jet is inside the dimensional bubble, it no longer exists in our dimension. Effectively it just disappears. Your pilot should be pressing the second button soon and we should see him reappear on radar", Martin explained.

Warlock found himself inside a dark void, the only light coming from the cockpit displays in front of him. He checked his airspeed and the jet seemed to still be traveling at Mach 2. The dark void seemed to stretch out infinitely before him.

"Time to press button number 2", he said to himself. Reaching to the display, Warlock pressed the orange button labeled "GAGE2". Once again, the effect was almost immediate and a large, dark blue shimmering gateway appeared in front of the jet. Warlock throttled forward, flying into it, leaving the featureless void behind him. Once through the gateway, Warlock was rewarded with the sight of a familiar cloudless blue sky. He checked his GPS coordinates and was amazed to see that the jet was some twenty miles from where he had entered the first gateway.

"Warlock to Control, Phase 1 successfully completed. No problems reported, except that my current position is 20 miles from the first GAGE entry point", said Warlock, with some slight confusion.

"Great job Warlock. Your present location is where we expected the second device activation to place you. Now, bring that bird home and expect a full debrief on your return", ordered the General.

"Roger Control. Bringing the bird home now", replied Warlock, as he throttled up the twin Cyclone engines and headed back to Groom Lake.

"Well Martin, it looks like Phase 1 is a success. You and Hiram should be proud of this achievement", said the General with a smile.

"Hiram has put a lot of time and effort into making this technology work and deserves much of the credit", replied Martin, turning to Hiram. Hiram was his best friend in addition to being the top researcher at Dark-Bridge Technology.

"Thank you, Martin. I'm glad that it was successful General. I think once you've gone over the data, you'll begin to see the endless possibilities with this technology. The one modification we made to these GAGE devices was to reduce the gateway formation time and account for the size and forward velocity of the jet," said Hiram, unused to so much attention.

"Excellent. Thank you, Hiram. I'm beginning to see the applications and also the dark side to this. I imagine that I'll never sleep well again, thinking that someone could open a gateway and deliver a thermonuclear device into the Oval Office", said the General with a pained expression.

Martin looked at Hiram and an unspoken acknowledgement passed between them. Technology was often a double-edged sword, cutting both ways, one side for good, the other for evil. Martin could only hope that control of this technology would remain in as few hands as possible. Only time would tell.

"That's all we have for now, General. Hiram and I will be returning to the DarkBridge facility. Will you join us for dinner later?" asked Martin, eager to show the General a new addition to the facility.

"Absolutely! I'd like to see this new addition to your facility. From all the reports, it's really something special", replied General Esterbrook. He'd heard reports from his people of something special taking place there and was greatly intrigued.

"Excellent. We'll see you later on then. Give our regards to Warlock", said Martin, as he and Hiram stepped through a gateway that Eva had just conveniently opened.

"Thank you, Martin. I will", replied the General, as he watched Martin and Hiram leave. It was going to take some time getting used to people disappearing like that, he thought to himself. Thanking the control room team, he headed to the debrief room to await the arrival of Warlock.

Chapter 3

Finding Answers

Earlier, Paul had left Martin's office, walking down the hallway, heading towards the elevator that would take him topside. Along the way, he spoke with Eva, letting her know of his plans.

"Eva, I'll need a drone and two robot sentries, preferably armed. I'll also need a GAGE device set for the following coordinates," said Paul, as he rattled off the coordinates he had committed to memory.

"All set, Paul. The drone will meet you at your destination and the sentries will meet you topside with the GAGE device," replied Eva, with her usual soft, sultry voice.

"Thank you, Eva. You're the best "said Paul, as he reached the elevator and stepped inside.

"Why thank you, Paul. I've cleared you through topside security and Major Esterbrook is on call if you need help," replied Eva.

There was a slight feeling of acceleration, as the elevator lifted him topside. Seconds later, the doors opened to the topside offices, which at the moment weren't very busy. Stepping out, he made his way towards a side door, waving at the security guard, who waved back smiling. Paul passed through the security doors, and into a crisp, early fall morning. He walked away from the DarkBridge Technology offices, pausing at about 20 yards, to wait for his sentries. He didn't have long to wait, hearing the steady, rhythmic gait of the sentries as they approached. Paul could see that they were armed with pulsed laser rifles and M35 assault rifles slung over their shoulders, probably loaded with diamene coated bullets. They stood seven feet tall, clad in diamene armor over their titanium frames. One of the sentries was also carrying a small metal box, presumably containing the GAGE device. The sentries halted, nodding their metallic heads, one sentry offering the metal box to Paul. Paul unhooked the box from the sentry's metal hand, as Eva spoke.

"The sentries are now under your control and will follow you to your destination. I'll assume command, if necessary," replied Eva.

"Thank you, Eva. Follow me!" commanded Paul. The sentries responded by closing a free hand into a fist and striking their metallic chests. It was both very impressive and somewhat intimidating, thought Paul to himself.

He walked further away from the building, the sentries falling in lockstep behind him. Paul wasn't exactly sure what a safe distance was, but figured a thousand yards would be sufficient. After a few minutes of walking, the group reached their destination, the top of the office building barely seen, due to a shallow depression in the landscape.

"I'm at the gateway point, Eva. Waiting for the drone," said Paul, as he opened the metal box and pulled out the GAGE device.

"Drone on the way, Paul. It should reach you shortly," replied Eva, as a metal gantry on top of the office building opened and a DarkBridge recon drone slid out and took to the air. Eva had enabled its various sensors, including radiation, bacteriological and electromagnetic as a precaution.

Paul looked up, as the drone descended to a position off to his right, some five feet off the ground. Everything in place, he was now ready to begin.

"Arm weapons and hold," Paul commanded the sentries, who promptly nodded their heads in recognition of the command and leveled their weapons, ready to fire if commanded.

"Eva, I'm opening the gateway now," said Paul, as he reached down and switched the GAGE device on.

The GAGE device began to hum, as it rose up to about 2 feet off the ground and a gateway began to form. Shimmering light blue at first, the gateway turned to a darker blue, signaling it had stabilized. The drone, under

Eva's command, glided forward to a position directly in front of the gateway and a few inches from the surface. A good sign, so far. At least no water had poured out, thought Paul.

"Sending the drone in now, Paul," said Eva, commanding the drone to move through the gateway.

The drone slowly inched forward through the gateway, its sleek metal body disappearing into the dark blue void.

"Paul, the drone appears to be pushing against some sort of resistance on the other side," said Eva.

"Resistance? Keep pushing through, Eva," ordered Paul.

"I've just lost contact with the drone, Paul. It reported a large EM spike just before I lost contact. No radiation detected up to that point," replied Eva.

"It could be something on the other side interfering with the drone transmission. Any thoughts, Eva?" asked Paul, not wanting to concede defeat at such an early stage.

"I have an idea," offered Eva, as she sent a command to one of the sentries. The sentry walked up to the gateway and extended its arm through it and into the other side.

"Connection restored, Paul. I now have control of the drone and am receiving data. It appears that there was some sort of field preventing communication with the drone. The sentry's arm acted like an antenna, connecting this side of the gateway with the other side," said

Eva, her voice tinged with satisfaction that her idea had worked.

"Good thinking Eva. What's the environment look like on the other side?" Paul inquired.

"Radiation normal, no biohazards detected, temperature cool, but not cold. This is interesting," said a perplexed Eva.

"What's wrong?" asked Paul, his positive feeling about the cavern now turning cautious.

"It seems that the drone's onboard clock has stopped and is no longer registering any passing time," said Eva, as her quantum processors evaluated this intriguing anomaly.

Paul wasn't sure what to make of the new information but, just as he was about to speak with Eva, he spotted a familiar figure floating towards him.

The angel, Gabriel, had watched Paul leave the building and walk some distance away, accompanied by the primitive robot sentries. Curiosity aroused, Gabriel had floated closer to view the events taking place and watched as Paul opened a gateway and a drone was sent through. Where was he going and why the security? Gabriel thought to himself. His question was answered soon enough, when he sensed a strangeness emanating from the gateway. When communication with the drone had failed and then the subsequent internal clock failure occurred, he had a good idea of what was going on. He remembered a time long ago, before the Ascension, when Raphael, the second most important scientist, behind Asmodeus, had developed the "stasis" field. The Anunnaki had recognized early on, the dangers of time travel and had instead, used the technology to create the "stasis field". It created a bubble around a set area that became removed from the normal flow of time. Inside the stasis field, no time would pass and even more incredible, no biological aging would take place. This was how the Anunnaki colonists were able to survive for so many thousands of years before the Ascension. Gabriel settled down to the ground and walked up to Paul, invisible to the sentries and to Eva's scans.

Paul watched as his old friend Gabriel approached.

"Hello, Gabriel", said Paul, knowing that Gabriel would still be unnerved by his being able to see the angel.

"Who are you talking to, Paul? I'm not sensing or seeing anyone near you," inquired a puzzled Eva.

"The angel Gabriel is here with me," replied Paul. This was where people and AI started thinking him to be crazy.

"Alright, as long as you're okay," said Eva, uncomfortable with not being able to detect the angel.

"Yes, I'm okay. He's a friend," said Paul.

"Hello, Paul. I see that you've found something important," replied Gabriel, his curiosity growing.

"I guess I can trust you, Gabriel, old friend. The other side of this gateway has theoretically opened to an underground cavern in the Antarctic. I had a dream from my Anunnaki past, where Shaynor and I built a special underground storage facility. The facility was to be used as a defensive support base for our colonies on this planet and a precaution against the Skarzi," replied Paul.

"I had forgotten about this place. It was so long ago in the distant past, for us. Only five people knew about it and that includes the two of us," answered Gabriel.

"Captain Beleron of the colony ship thought it best that not many people should know about it., lest it fall into the wrong hands," added Paul, remembering the conversation from his dreams.

"It was a wise decision, considering the rebellion that took place not long after. If Asmodeus and his followers had known about it, the rebellion would have had a much different outcome," offered Gabriel.

"It would've been a disaster," said Paul, agreeing with Gabriel and shuddering at the thought of Asmodeus having such powerful weapons at his disposal.

"Your drone seems to have run into an issue," said Gabriel, rather nonchalantly.

"Yes. Strange things seem to be happening on the other side," replied Paul, sensing that Gabriel knew what was going on with the drone.

"There's a stasis field in operation on the other side. It was developed by Raphael, a fellow researcher, who worked with Asmodeus. Relax, I know what you're thinking, I really do. Raphael is one of us and was never on the side of the rebels. In fact, he began to detest Asmodeus and what he was beginning to strive towards", replied Gabriel, trying to allay Paul's fears.

"That's good news. Where is Raphael now?" inquired a now curious Paul.

"I'm not sure. No angel has seen or heard from him for a couple of your human years, but you have to remember that time has no meaning for angels and two human years is akin to a day in Heaven. I hope to see him soon though," replied Gabriel.

"I seem to recall him from my past life as Valinor. Interesting fellow and rivaling Asmodeus in technical knowledge," said Paul as the thought triggered memories of his past friendship with Asmodeus before the rebellion.

"Are you ready to see what awaits you?" asked a smiling Gabriel.

"You make it sound rather ominous and dangerous. Should I be worried?" asked Paul, wondering if this was such a good idea after all. Of course, Gabriel wouldn't be worried, being immortal and all. Paul though, could easily die.

"Don't worry. If it'll make you feel any better, I'll step through first," offered Gabriel with a touch of humor.

"Thank you, my friend. I'll be right behind you, but I'll be taking a sentry with me just in case", replied Paul.

"It might be best if you do. This will be the first time as an angel that I've been in a stasis field and I'm not sure what the effects will be. Probably none, but the added security could help," answered Gabriel, a thoughtful look crossing his face.

"Okay. I guess I'm still officially worried. Eva, I'll be taking a sentry with me. Keep the other one here and in position to maintain contact," said Paul.

"Good luck, Paul. Remember the time discrepancy. I would hate to have you turn into a Rip Van Winkle," replied Eva, a touch of concern showing in her soft, sultry voice.

"Thank you, Eva. Keep in contact and give me a maximum of six hours," said Paul as he signaled Sentry 2 to follow him and Sentry 1 to remain on station.

Gabriel stepped though the waiting gateway, motioning Paul to follow. Paul, followed by Sentry 2, stepped through the gateway and into the unknown.

Chapter 4

The Cavern

Paul stepped through the gateway and into a world of total darkness. It was pitch black on the other side and there was a touch of coolness to the air. Paul couldn't see his hand in front of him and was starting to think that this was a bad idea. He also wasn't sure where the robot sentry was, assuming it had followed him.

"Gabriel. Are you here?" asked an increasingly worried Paul.

"Yes. I'm here. I'm actually right next to you," replied Gabriel. Sensing Paul's concern, he closed his fist, concentrated and opened it. A golden orb sat there with a dim glow, slowly rising from Gabriel's palm. The orb grew brighter as it slowly rose, higher and higher, eventually illuminating the entire, massive cavern.

Paul looked behind him at the still open gateway, the robot Sentry 2 seemingly frozen at the gateway.

"Eva, I'm inside the cavern, but there seems to be something wrong with the sentry," said Paul.

"I've lost communication with the sentry. I'll keep trying to reactivate it," replied Eva.

"Let me see what I can do," replied Gabriel, as he walked over to the sentry. Raising his hand to the center of the robot's head, Gabriel concentrated and sent a tiny amount of energy into the robot's processor. The robot jerked, as its systems reset and came back online.

"Paul, I've reestablished communication with the sentry. I am receiving full video and audio of the cavern. It's unbelievable what is in there," said Eva.

Paul turned his attention from the robot and looked around. He let out a small gasp, as the cavern's contents revealed itself. His dream of the cavern was one thing, seeing it in person was almost overwhelming. Before him sat the five advanced Kyril fighter spacecraft, various advanced weapons, including the ten thermonuclear warheads. Off to one side stood the two hundred assault robots and many more items of interest. Everything was in pristine condition, as if it were manufactured yesterday. Paul walked over to the Kyril spacecraft, running his hands over the smooth, angular surface. That he had once flown such a craft in battle both humbled and left him with a burning question. Could he remember how to pilot one, if the need arose?

Paul heard Gabriel let out a gasp of his own, as he spotted something right out of ancient legend stored behind a glass enclosure.

"Is that what I think it is?" asked Paul incredulously, as he followed Gabriel's gaze.

"Yes. It's what has come to be known as the Ark of the Covenant. Why and how it is here is a mystery to me. The only one of my kind who might know is Raphael," answered a perplexed Gabriel.

Paul went to move closer, but his body was held back by some invisible force.

"No, my friend, you must not get too close. The Ark isn't what you think it is. Housed inside its golden exterior is Anunnaki technology developed before our Ascension. It was rumored to be inherently dangerous and difficult to control. Humans have died from touching it and even from being in its vicinity," said Gabriel.

"Wonderful," said Paul, noticing the concerned look on Gabriel's face.

Paul looked further around the massive cavern, and something caught his eye. Tucked away into a corner of the cavern, were two long, cylindrical objects, jet black in color.

"What are those objects over there? I don't remember them from my dream," said a curious Paul, as the force restraining him relaxed, allowing him to investigate.

"I don't know. They must've been placed here long after the rebellion. Let's take a look," said Gabriel.

The two of them walked over to the objects, noting that they had some sort of display mounted on the side and tubes running out of them, connecting to some sort of machinery.

Gabriel was the first to reach the cylindrical objects, followed by Paul, who watched his friend approach the display.

Gabriel looked at cylindrical objects and knew almost immediately what they were.

They were cryogenic chambers of Anunnaki design, and the data screen was displaying the ancient Anunnaki language.

Gabriel read the display, the import of what it said, causing him to sink to his knees in homage.

"What's wrong Gabriel? Why are you kneeling?" asked a concerned Paul.

"My friend, these are cryogenic chambers. Once, before the Ascension they were used to allow us to extend our lifetimes far beyond our normal life expectancy", said Gabriel, his words tinged with a sense of awe.

"Okay, what is so special about these chambers?" asked Paul.

"It's what's inside them, making them special and impossible to comprehend, even for me," replied Gabriel.

"What's inside?" asked Paul, his curiosity growing.

"As impossible as it sounds, there are two Anunnaki inside them. This one here contains the body of

Commander Kalon and the one next to it contains the body of Jalon, his son," replied Gabriel.

Paul didn't catch the connection at first, but he began remembering his dreams and realization slowly dawned on him.

"Not Shaynor's father and only brother!" said an incredulous Paul.

"Yes. It's them and they are still alive," said Gabriel with a reverent tone.

"Alive? After all these thousands of years?" said a stunned Paul. The consequences were just beginning to dawn on him.

"You must remember, we are in a stasis field existing outside the normal flow of time. Combined with the suspended animation of the chambers, one could survive for thousands of more years into the future," replied Gabriel.

Paul contemplated what Gabriel had said, the next question immediately coming to mind.

"Is it possible to awaken them?" asked Paul.

"Yes. It is very possible. Everything is still functioning, and they appear to be in good health. However, I cannot personally do it. You must do it. There are limits to our direct interference in human events. There is one other consideration and that is Maggie. Remember, she was once Shaynor and here are her father and brother. Her first father, regardless of the other fathers she may have had throughout other lifetimes," said Gabriel, pausing to let that sink in.

Paul pondered what Gabriel had said, seeing the truth of it.

"Yes, you're right Gabriel. Maggie should have the final say in this," replied Paul.

"Good. Let's leave them undisturbed for now," said Gabriel, as he gently pulled Paul away from the two Anunnaki.

They walked back towards the gateway, a thought suddenly occurring to Paul.

"Eva, how much time has passed out there?" asked a worried Paul.

"It's been almost four hours since you stepped through the gateway," replied Eva.

"Four hours? We've only been in here a few minutes," said Paul.

"As I said before, time passes differently inside the stasis field. It might be best if we leave this for now," said Gabriel.

"Yes. You're right my friend. This was only meant to be a validation of my dreams. Now, we have real proof," said Paul, feeling vindicated.

Gabriel smiled and led the way back towards the gateway, the glowing orb drifted down from the cavern ceiling, dimming as it returned to his palm.

Paul, Gabriel and the robot sentry stepped back through the gateway and into the bright noontime sun shining over the grounds of DarkBridge Technology. Paul noticed the first robot sentry with its arm still extended into the gateway and gave the command to step away from the gateway. The robot complied and Paul reached down, turning the GAGE device off. The gateway closed, leaving Paul, Gabriel and the two robot sentries, standing in an empty field, the DarkBridge facility looming not far away.

"Thank you for your help, Gabriel. There's much to consider and I have much to discuss with Martin and Maggie," said Paul, turning to his angel friend.

"You're welcome, my friend. Like you, there is much for me to consider and relate to my fellow angels. I'll leave you for now. Have a nice lunch with Maggie.' replied Gabriel, as he opened a gateway to Heaven and paused. Concentrating, he closed the palm of his hand and quickly opened it, the golden orb once again sitting there. He silently gave it instructions to monitor events inside the facility and released it into the air. The golden orb flew into the air and headed towards the DarkBridge facility. Gabriel waved at Paul, as he stepped through the gateway.

Paul watched as Gabriel disappeared, waving in return. What was the orb for? How did he know about his lunch date with Maggie? Paul would have to make it a point to ask his friend when he returned.

"Eva, you can have the sentries return to the facility. Let Maggie know that I'll be a few minutes late for lunch," said Paul.

"Welcome back, Paul. I'll take care of the sentries and let Maggie know," replied Eva, in her usual soft, sultry voice.

"Thank you, Eva," replied Paul, as he followed behind the sentries and contemplated what to do next.

Maggie was sitting at a table for two at her restaurant located in the underground facility of DarkBridge Technology. Her restaurant, Maggie's, had proven to be a huge success and had become a source of great pride to her. It had been a second chance for her and a chance to get away from her father, Thomas Stanton and his constant surveillance. Her life had broken into two parts, life before Paul and her life after meeting him. Falling in love with Paul and finding that they shared a love that stretched across lifetimes, was both a revelation and had added a deeper meaning to her life.

Maggie's reflections were interrupted by Eva's voice in her ear.

"Hello, Maggie. I just wanted to let you know that Paul is running a few minutes late for lunch," said Eva.

"Thank you, Eva. Is everything okay?" asked Maggie.

"Yes. Everything is okay. Paul was just doing something for Martin," replied Eva.

"Thank you, Eva. I think I see him walking in the door right now," said Maggie, her demeanor brightening at the sight of Paul. She motioned to one of her waitresses, Jenny, who smiled and headed into the kitchen.

Paul spotted Maggie sitting at a table alone, waiting for him. He had tried to get here as fast as he could, but he was still a few minutes late. It still amazed him that their deep emotional connection was actually rooted in reincarnation and the sharing of past lives together.

"Hi, Maggie. Sorry I'm late. I was doing something for Martin," replied Paul, as he sat down across from Maggie. He hoped that she wasn't too mad.

"That's okay. It was just a few minutes, and your apology is lovingly accepted," said Maggie, flashing him a warm smile.

"Thank you," replied Paul, suddenly surprised as Jenny returned with two prime rib dinners.

Dropping the dinners off, Jenny flashed a knowing smile at Maggie and returned to her tables.

"You're amazing," said Paul, silently acknowledging his growing hunger, as he began cutting into his meal.

"I thought you might be hungry. You mentioned doing something for Martin?" inquired Maggie, as she too began cutting into her prime rib.

"Yes, I admit to being rather hungry. You remember the dream about the cavern?" asked Paul.

"Yes, I remember it. The one in Antarctica we excavated thousands of years ago as Shaynor and Valinor. As I remember, it also contained a number of interesting items," replied Maggie, her interest growing.

"It's all true. I went there this morning, with Gabriel and two robot sentries," said Paul.

"You actually went there? How?" asked a curious Maggie.

"We went there via a GAGE device. We also found two unexpected items. There are two cryogenic chambers there, with living Anunnaki inside. I'm not sure how to approach this, but it concerns you," said Paul, preparing himself for what he had to say next.

"Anunnaki? How can that be? Who are they?" asked Maggie, her curiosity growing.

"Gabriel read the ancient language displayed on the chambers and was shocked by what he read. The people inside the chambers are none other than Commander Kalon and Jalon," said Paul, pausing to give Maggie time to process the information.

Maggie didn't make the connection immediately, but seconds later a look of shock began to show on her face.

"Yes, Shaynor's father and brother. Gabriel thought it best that you be told and have final say in what to do. He also said that they could sleep for a few more thousand years, with no ill effects", said Paul, as he tried to imagine himself in a similar situation.

Maggie considered Paul's news, not quite sure what to make of it. Shaynor's father and brother were still alive and ready to be revived. Thomas Stanton was Maggie's father and yet wasn't she really Shaynor? The whole reincarnation thing really confused her. It was no wonder that most people usually didn't remember their past lives. Looking at it more pragmatically, Kalon was her

First Father, regardless of any subsequent fathers. How many other fathers she had over her previous lifetimes wasn't clear right now, but they had raised and hopefully had loved her just as much. Her vote would be to awaken them, but not just yet.

"Has Martin been told about what you found?" asked Maggie.

"Eva has apprised him of the situation", replied Paul, who was feeling sorry for Martin and the complications the discovery was going to cause him.

"I need a little more time to think about this. It's a difficult decision for me, the people here and for the sleeping Anunnaki as well. In the meantime, business as usual," said Maggie, coyishly smiling.

"We have time. It's not something that has to be decided right now anyway. Martin will ultimately have to decide and probably have to inform General Esterbrook," said Paul, as he and Maggie finished their lunch.

"Well, not to spoil the moment, but I really have to get back to work," said Maggie with a sigh, her eyes catching the increased business going on around her.

"Yes, duty calls, I suppose," said Paul with a smile, as he and Maggie rose from the table.

"I'll see you later tonight, my love," replied Maggie, thinking that work would help take her mind off things for a while.

"You can count on it," said a smiling Paul, who needed to get back to his office and file a report for Martin.

With a quick hug and a kiss, Maggie got back to the business of running the restaurant. Paul left the restaurant and headed towards his office to work on his report on the cavern. It was a formality, since Eva would have already explained it to Martin, but it had to be done, nonetheless.

Chapter 5

Quantum Signature

Later that day, Martin was joined by General Esterbrook back at DarkBridge Technology and the two sat down to dinner at a newly opened restaurant at the facility. Hiram had been invited also, but after the Phase 1 demonstration, a flash of insight came to him on a problem he was having with Project TimeBridge. Martin had learned long ago to let Hiram pursue his insights and was usually rewarded with success. A waiter came over to take their drink orders, with Martin and the General both ordering a Sam Adams draft beer. The waiter returned soon after, with two glasses of pure, amber joy. Taking a sip, Martin reflected on the restaurant and its manager. The restaurant was called Maggie's and was operated by a woman named Maggie Durham. Maggie had joined the company after a series of events had led her to reevaluate her life. In operation now for a month, the restaurant had become a popular place for employees and was actually profitable. While food and drink were free at the company cafeteria, people were willing to pay for the ambiance, food and drink at the restaurant. Not long ago, Martin had recognized the need for more than just a cafeteria to feed his employees, but he had been waiting for just the right person to make it a reality. To his delight, it had now become a place to unwind, relax with co-workers, enjoy good food and have a drink or two.

"This is a great idea, Martin. Thank you for inviting me here for dinner. It's a little unusual to have a place like this at a secure facility", said the General, taking a sip from his beer.

"We ask a lot from them, taking time from their families to work here. So, I did it for them", replied Martin, giving a small wave of his hand to the tables full of employees, while taking a sip from his own beer. He knew his decision wasn't totally altruistic, he thought to himself. In having a place like this, the employees were much less likely to venture outside the facility, which translated into a reduced security risk.

"It looks like they're enjoying themselves. Good for morale I guess", said the General, just as a waitress delivered two large prime rib dinners to the table.

Martin smiled at the look of anticipation on the General's face as he gazed upon the delicious meal. Unable to hold back any longer, the General sliced into the juicy steak and carved out a small slice. Tasting the juicy slice of meat, the General smiled with satisfaction.

"Delicious, Martin. It's been quite some time since I tasted anything so good. The plant-based meats they have at the other black sites are okay but, nothing beats the real thing", said the General, relishing the taste of his second bite.

"Thank you, Bob. Maggie operates this restaurant and knows how steaks should be cooked. The only restrictions I placed on her were no excessive drinking or rowdy behavior," replied Martin, feeling proud of what Maggie had accomplished.

There was a pause in the conversation, as the two men tore into their meals, savoring the excellent cuts of meat.

"She's done a fine job Martin. Does Stanton know that his daughter is here?" asked the General, after a few minutes.

"He might, since he seems to have spies everywhere. He hasn't done anything to retrieve her, or asked about her yet", said Martin. Thomas Stanton, CEO of Stanton Aerospace and father to Maggie, was one of the largest global defense contractors and a fierce competitor of DarkBridge Technology.

"He's a dangerous man to cross paths with. I can understand Maggie being here. I've seen your reports and they make for some interesting and hard to believe reading. I'm still not sure about the reincarnation angle, but if it gives us an edge over these demons, I'm all for it. It's all about the edge, Martin. Anything that gives us an edge over those wanting to do us harm, is important," said the General, taking another bite.

"I agree. We do our best here to help with that edge. Right now, Hiram is working on our next edge, and I expect a breakthrough at any moment," replied Martin, as he took another bite of his steak. There was another brief pause in the conversation, with both men taking time to silently enjoy their meals.

"I've read your update on Project TimeBridge. It would be the ultimate edge and conceivably the ultimate disaster." said the General, unhappy that he was almost done with his steak.

"Like most technology it's a double-edged sword, cutting both ways. We always hope that it cuts for us and not against us. Going into the past or future has repercussions if we aren't careful," replied Martin, as he too looked at his dwindling meal. Martin liked Bob and the two had formed a deep friendship over the years, which made Martin all the more unhappy with what he wasn't sharing. He was purposely withholding the results of Paul's report from the cavern from him. What Paul had found would give the United States an edge over its adversaries for years, possibly much longer. Martin was finding it exceedingly difficult to decide on the right course of action.

"It will still be worth the risk if it works. Keep me posted," said the General, preparing to leave.

Just then, Eva broke in with some interesting news.

"Martin, we may have an issue. I've detected a quantum signature located in the Sinai Peninsula while sharing some time on a DOD satellite in orbit," said Eva.

"A quantum signature out there?" asked a puzzled Martin.

"Yes. I've double-checked it. It is there and it appears to be ours," replied Eva.

"Okay, that's good enough for me. Let's start assembling a team to send there. I believe they are six hours ahead, so we'll schedule it for early tomorrow morning. This might be a good time for Maggie's first mission, since it should be just a routine investigation. Paul and Maggie will go first, via gateway to investigate and give us a status. Then we'll send the remaining team in. One more thing, have Hiram meet me in my office at 4am sharp. We may need his help on this." directed Martin.

"I'll let everyone know right away," answered Eva.

"Thank you, Eva," said Martin.

"Problem, Martin?" asked the General.

"I'm not sure. Eva detected a quantum signature unique to DarkBridge Technology, coming from the Sinai Peninsula. I might be sending a team depending on the results of an initial investigation. Scott will probably head the security side of the team," replied Martin.

"When do you plan on starting?" asked the General.

"It would most likely be early tomorrow morning. Probably around 4am. The Sinai is six hours ahead of us, so that would put us around 10am Sinai time, when Paul steps through the gateway," offered Martin, who immediately thought that this would also be a good time for Maggie to get some field experience.

"Sounds like something of interest. Unfortunately, I have a prior engagement at Area 53.

Otherwise, I'd probably like to sit in. Just keep me posted on any important developments.

I'm going to check in on Scott before I leave," said the General.

"I'll keep you posted, Bob. I hope you enjoyed your dinner," said Martin.

"Damn fine meal. Thank you, Martin. I think this place is now on my list of favorite restaurants. Please give my compliments to Maggie. Take care," said the General, as he rose and left the restaurant.

Martin watched the General walk away towards his meeting with Scott. Major Scott Esterbrook was the General's son and had come to DarkBridge Technology after retiring from active duty as a Navy Seal. Martin was more than happy to have a qualified individual like Scott in charge of security. Martin had tried to make the choice objectively, based on qualifications and not because he was the General's son. He tried not to second guess his decision, but with most of your revenue coming from one source it was sometimes hard to tell.

The waiter came by with his tablet and Martin paid the restaurant bill by pressing his thumb against the tablet. The restaurant was one of the few places in the facility that wasn't free. Long ago, he had decided that the company would pick up the tab for cafeteria meals, snacks and non-alcoholic drinks. It seemed like the right thing to do, especially given the amount of time employees often had to stay here. Martin rose from the table and gazed around looking for Maggie Durham, who managed the restaurant. He spotted Maggie working behind the restaurant bar, helping fill some drink orders. In her late thirties, tall, slender, with long blonde hair and blue eyes, she was strikingly beautiful. As he reached the bar, Maggie looked up and smiled at him.

"Hello, Martin. How was your meal?" asked Maggie.

"The meal was delicious Maggie, and you have a new fan. General Esterbrook wanted me to pass on his compliments for the best meal he's had in a long time", replied Martin.

"Thank you, Martin. I have a great staff, which helps immensely. Compliments like that make this very worthwhile," said Maggie, with a touch of pink showing on her cheeks.

"You're doing a fantastic job Maggie and making life a little easier for the people here", said Martin.

"I'm happy to help and thankful that you gave me this opportunity", said a thankful Maggie.

"How would you feel about going on your first mission with Paul tomorrow?" asked Martin.

"I'm ready, Martin," replied a confident Maggie. The past few weeks she had been training with Paul and Scott on hand-to-hand fighting techniques, the various DarkBridge Technology devices and small arms usage. Scott had remarked on numerous occasions that she was a natural.

He asked if she had any prior training and Maggie had replied with an emphatic "No". It wasn't totally true though. The memories of her past life, as Shaynor, had included all the combat training she had received while growing up on the Anunnaki home planet. Those memories had made her seem like a natural to Scott. Paul was already deeply familiar with her Anunnaki past, so he had accepted it without question. During her training, she had also given Dr. Curtis permission to install a cochlear implant and was now able to communicate with Eva. She had accomplished much over the past couple of months, since accepting Martin's offer to stay and really did feel ready to go.

"Excellent. You and Paul will leave early tomorrow morning, around 4am. Make sure you and Paul get plenty of rest tonight," smiled Martin knowingly.

"I will. Thank you for allowing me to go," said Maggie.

"Now, is as good a time as any. I expect that this will end up being a routine investigation and nothing dangerous. I'll see you bright and early in the morning," replied Martin.

"Have a good day, Martin and thank you for spreading the word about the restaurant,"

"Not a problem, my pleasure. Take care, Maggie," said Martin, as he turned and left the restaurant.

"You too, Martin," answered Maggie, watching Martin leave. This was more than she could have hoped for, a chance to share in an investigation with Paul. She and Paul had discovered a deep connection between them, since meeting by chance a couple of months ago. It had turned out to be more than just love at first sight and was in fact, a connection that stretched back thousands of years into the ancient past.

"Don't worry, Maggie," I'll be in constant contact with you and Paul all the time," said Eva, softly in her ear.

"Thank you, Eva. You're the best," replied Maggie.

"Why, thank you, Maggie," replied Eva.

Maggie watched as Martin left the restaurant, briefly thinking of the series of events that had led her here to DarkBridge Technology. She liked Martin, graying and in his early sixties, he was like a second father to her. Her own father, Thomas Stanton, had tried to control every facet of Maggie's life and was partly the reason she was here. Martin had offered her refuge and a chance at a new life, for which Maggie would be eternally grateful. Hopefully, everything would go well tomorrow. She would have to make sure Paul got some rest tonight, in preparation for tomorrow. Sighing, she got back to work, mixing a strawberry daiquiri and sombrero for two of her customers.

Chapter 6

First Mission

Martin had woken up early the next morning, showered, dressed into his business suit and made his way to the cafeteria for breakfast and a nice, hot cup of coffee. It had been a restless night for him, too many questions weighing on his mind and he felt somewhat tired this morning. Upon arriving, he noticed Paul, Maggie and Scott seated at a nearby table, already dressed in desert fatigues and presumably, DarkWeave suits as well. They too, were apparently getting ready for today's operation. Martin hadn't checked with Paul about the readiness of Maggie and hoped it wouldn't be a problem. He picked up his large coffee and ordered a plate of bacon, scrambled eggs and hash browns. The food came out quickly and he made his way over to the three seated people.

"Good morning. Glad to see everyone getting ready for today's operation. Mind if I join you?" asked Martin.

"Good morning, Martin," the three said in unison.

"Please, sit down and join us," replied Maggie.

"Thank you," said Martin, placing his tray on the table and sitting down. Martin took a deep sip of coffee, while Paul began to speak.

"What's so special about the Sinai Peninsula? Eva said something about getting ready for a recon mission and you would explain further," asked Paul, while taking a bite of his breakfast sandwich.

"Eva detected a quantum signature coming from the desert and it warrants further investigation. As far as we know, the signature appears to be similar to that used by our company, DarkBridge Technology. Hence, the need to check it out and hopefully explain why it's out there in the Sinai. This will also provide an opportunity for Maggie to experience her first investigation", answered Martin, savoring the delicious coffee and breakfast meal.

"Sounds like an interesting way to spend the day. My team is assembled and ready to go. By my estimation, Maggie is ready as well," replied Scott. He had been impressed with how quickly her training had progressed. A born natural and seemingly like she had some prior training, he mused.

"I agree with Scott. Maggie is ready," said Paul in agreement.

"Thank you, Scott and Paul. As soon as Paul and Maggie assess the situation, we'll send the security team through. There might be a need for some scientific investigation, so a scientific team will follow after Scott," replied Martin, his breakfast almost done.

"I'm looking forward to it," added Maggie.

"Good. Glad everything is settled. Hiram and I will be watching from my office. Hopefully, everything will go smoothly," said Martin, as he finished his breakfast.

"Thank you," replied Maggie.

"No problem, Maggie. It's almost 4am, so I'm headed over to my office. Paul and Maggie, as soon as you're ready, have Eva open a gateway for you in Security Room 4. Good luck, everyone and let's hope this is nothing more than routine," said Martin, keeping his fingers crossed.

Rising, he took his tray and placed it in the recycling bin and left the cafeteria. He set a quick pace back to his office, extremely curious as to what they might find and hoping that Hiram would be able to join him. Finding a quantum signature in some desolate spot was extremely unusual and even more so since it was evidently of DarkBridge Technology origin. Never a dull moment, thought Martin to himself.

Paul, Maggie and Scott left the cafeteria immediately after Martin and made their way to Security Room 4, in order to prepare for today's investigation. Already dressed for the operation, the only thing needed was to assemble whatever equipment they would need. Scott passed handguns loaded with diamene ammo, a couple of extra ammo clips and a handheld quantum energy detector to Maggie and Paul. Maggie tied up her hair into a ponytail and looked expectantly at Paul for reassurance.

"Thank you, Scott. I think we're ready to go", said Paul, as he looked at Maggie, who gave him a big smile. Paul hoped it would be as Martin had said, just a routine investigation, but readied himself just in case it turned out to be more.

Chapter 7

The Sinai

Martin arrived at his office and took a seat behind his mahogany desk. Hiram should be here soon, and the adventure would begin. A large virtual TV screen was displayed on a far wall, with nothing but static showing for now.

"Good morning, Eva. Are we all set?" asked Martin.

"All set, Martin. We're just waiting for Hiram to arrive," replied Eva.

Martin heard a knock on the door and Dr. Hiram Greenwood strode in, carrying a tray of donuts and coffee. Martin immediately thought back to time they had first met.

Seeking a "rock star" in the field of quantum physics, someone brilliant and well-respected with stellar credentials and proven expertise in the various fields of exploration, he eventually found one at a quantum physics conference in Boston. Held in a large hotel conference room in the Seaport District, it attracted many researchers and academics from the surrounding area and beyond. Martin chose a seat at the end of a row, towards the back of the room and sat down. As the room darkened and the presentations began, he quickly became bored. Hearing nothing worthy of holding his interest, he started to doze off in the dimly lit, warm, stuffy room. He was startled awake when a man around his age also dressed in a dark business suit, made his way past him and sat in the seat next to him. Looking to his right, Martin could just make out the man. Eyeglasses with thick, black frames, medium height, thinly built with tousled graying hair, the man certainly looked like a stereotypical professor!

Leaning over to Martin, the man whispered, "Most of the people here are pretty smart, but they are mired in tradition, scientific dogma and proof of theory, often failing to see the forest for the trees. They are slaves to convention, unable to think," tapping his index finger against his temple, "outside the box."

Martin was taken aback, not by the forwardness of the man or his view of the people attending the conference, but by how closely the man's words mirrored his own thoughts. Martin, intrigued with the man, whispered back in an exasperated tone, "Judging by the uninspiring presentations I've heard so far, I'd say that's a pretty accurate assessment. There's no passion or fire in what they're saying, no new ideas. It's like they're all reading from the same script."

The man nodded and smiled in response to Martin's words. Reaching inside a pocket of his suit coat, Martin found his business card and handed it to the man. Tilting the card slightly to read it in the low light, the man found his eyes drawn to the few words printed on it: Martin Weaver, President and CEO of DarkBridge Technology, LLC. Interesting name for a company, he thought, wondering if it dealt with research similar to his current work on matter phasing. Not knowing if he had brought his own business card with him, he began rummaging through his pockets, bumping Martin's arm in the process. He finally found it, tucked away inside the protective case of his smart phone, and gave it to Martin.

Martin took out his reading glasses, unfolded them and slid them on so that they rested at the mid-way point on his nose. Squinting through the lenses, he saw the name Dr. Hiram Greenwood, a number of advanced degrees in quantum physics, related disciplines and a phone number. Martin was visibly pleased. Not only did they share similar views on quantum physics, but the man also had an exceptional educational background in the field. Thinking that a guardian angel must be looking out for him, Martin took off his reading glasses and put them back in his pocket. Neither man said another word until the last presentation had been made.

The conference had ended about a half hour later, the lights brightened and there was a smattering of applause. As room began to clear, both men stood, already seemingly at ease with one another, Dr. Greenwood spoke first.

"Well, that was very enlightening," he said with a touch of sarcasm, motioning towards the now empty podium. "It's good to know that science is moving forward."

"At this rate, it'll be a hundred years or so before we see any real progress," replied Martin with a sardonic smile and a twinkle in his eye.

Dr. Greenwood laughed and clapped him on the shoulder. "Aha! We agree on something!"

Martin stuck out his hand and introduced himself. "I'm Martin Weaver. It's a pleasure to meet you, Dr. Greenwood."

"Hiram, please call me Hiram!" said Dr. Greenwood jovially, shaking Martin's hand vigorously. "The pleasure is mine, Martin. Glancing at Martin's card, he looked at him over the top of his eyeglasses. "I must admit, the name of your company intrigues me. Tell me more about it."

"Our focus is fringe science, namely dark matter research. Our goal is to unlock the secrets of the universe and use that knowledge to develop technologies far beyond the vision of modern science. The only limits will be our imaginations," returned Martin with a gleam in his eyes.

"Join the club!" said Dr. Greenwood good-naturedly, making a sweeping gesture with his hand at the room in general. "That is the dream of practically everyone attending these conferences, but no one has been able to do it!"

"Not yet, but I'm confident that if we keep working at it, we'll make a breakthrough that will turn the scientific world on its head! Anything is possible, Hiram! That's the motto I live by!"

"That will take considerably more than words, Martin," said Dr. Greenwood, noting the visionary look in Martin's eyes and the passion in his voice. "It requires the proper staff, adequate resources..."

"That's why we need you, Hiram," countered Martin. "That is, if you're looking for a job."

For a moment, Dr. Greenwood appeared surprised, his expression turning thoughtful as if he was pondering something. "I'm flattered, very flattered," he finally said, rocking back and forth on the heels of his well-worn, black shoes. "It sounds very interesting, and I'd like to hear more about it. Perhaps..." Dr. Greenwood's voice trailed off as a buzz came from the pocket of his business suit. Reaching into the pocket, he pulled out a smart phone and checked it. "I'm sorry, Martin," he said regretfully. "It appears that I will have to cut our conversation short. Unfortunately, I must attend to a rather pressing matter."

"Of course," said Martin, realizing that a man with Hiram's talents would be in high demand.

Dr. Greenwood shook his hand, patted him on the arm and said, "Keep dreaming, Martin." He walked a few steps away, stopped, turned and held up Martin's business card.

"I'll be in touch," he promised then hurried out of the conference room.

Martin had stood there with his hands in his pockets for a few moments, feeling some hope that he had not seen the last of Dr. Greenwood. There was no doubt in his mind that Dr. Greenwood was the "rock star" he'd been seeking. Now all he had to do was convince him to join the company.

Martin was jolted out of his daydreaming by Hiram offering his greetings, promising himself to try and get more sleep the next time.

"Good morning, Martin. Good morning, Eva. Sorry about the donuts. I didn't have time for something more substantial. Are we all set to start?" asked Hiram, as he took a seat across from Martin's desk and placed the tray on a nearby table.

"Good morning, Hiram. Don't worry about the donuts. We could be here for a while, it's good that you brought something to eat. Eva is getting things ready, as we speak," replied Martin.

"Good morning, Hiram," Paul and Maggie are stepping through the gateway as we speak. Their cameras will switch on once they've crossed into the Sinai," answered Eva.

"Maggie?" Hiram said with a questioning look at Martin.

"Yes. She's ready for her first investigation and this seemed like a good opportunity. Scott and Paul, both gave their approvals," answered Martin.

"Good enough for me. Let's see how this goes," replied Hiram, as he grabbed a jelly-filled donut.

Field Investigators Paul Cross and Maggie Durham stood before the gateway in Security Room 4, waiting for it to stabilize. The gateway turned from a shimmering light blue, to dark blue, signaling them that it was time. Major Esterbrook stood off to the side, with the rest of his security team, waiting for Paul's report from the other side.

"Ready?" asked Paul, turning to Maggie.

"Ready," replied Maggie, some apprehension showing on her face.

"Don't worry, my love. I'll be with you every step of the way," replied Paul quietly, so that only she could hear, as he reached for her hand.

Maggie held his hand tightly, as they stepped through the gateway. She felt a slight electrical tingle as they passed through the gateway and into the hot, arid, desert area of the Sinai Peninsula. The mid-morning sun felt warm on their faces already, as a slight breeze stirred the sand around their feet. Wearing his special DarkBridge sunglasses, Paul surveyed the surroundings, noting that the temperature would get even hotter as the day progressed. Fortunately, he was wearing a DarkWeave suit under his desert clothing, which kept his body at a constant 96 degrees, regardless of the ambient air temperature. Maggie was similarly dressed, including her own pair of DarkBridge sunglasses. Paul let go of Maggie's hand, but Maggie stayed close, this being her first investigation.

Paul surveyed the surrounding area, noting that it reminded him somewhat of his childhood, spent growing up in the American southwest. Part Navajo Indian on his mother's side, he remembered his younger years and the thrill of exploring the land around his home. His attention was quickly brought back to the present as the gateway disappeared and his gaze settled on the land before them. A low rocky ridge stood off to his left and a small desert plain spotted with dry brush and small rocks, fanned out to his right. His shoulder mounted camera activated, and he turned his body, giving Martin, Hiram and Eva, a panoramic view of the Sinai Peninsula. Martin smiled at the surprised look on Hiram's face, as the TV screen suddenly lit up with the live view from Paul's camera.

Even though he and Maggie stood there seemingly alone, Paul knew there was someone else watching over them. He spotted the angel Gabriel, floating above a nearby ridge, avidly watching Paul's progress. Paul smiled and waved to the golden, glowing angel, knowing that this would unsettle Gabriel to no end. The angel returned the wave, with a knowing, reassuring smile. Both angel and demon considered themselves invisible, and to most humans this was true. Maggie and Paul however, had been granted the ability to see both by the reclusive Vermont Guardian, who was unknown to human, angel and demon.

Paul turned to Maggie and held his finger up to his lips, a signal for her to keep quiet about Gabriel. Maggie responded with a nod of her head and a knowing smile, having seen who Paul was waving to.

"We're here, Eva. The area looks deserted right now. Which direction should we take?" asked Paul, through his implant, as they got ready to navigate the sandy, rock-filled plain.

"I'm glad you both made it okay. The quantum signature is about 500 yards to the right of where you're standing. The camera is working beautifully," added Eva, in her characteristic soft, sultry voice, linked via satellite to the transceiver in Paul's backpack.

"Okay. Heading there right now," said Paul, as he pulled out a small handheld quantum detector from his shirt pocket and showed it to Maggie. While following the direction given by Eva, they looked at the quantum detector screen and saw a small green dot growing larger, the closer they came to the target. They had almost reached 500 yards, when the detector let out a sharp beep. They were on top of whatever was causing the quantum signature. Looking around, there didn't seem to be anything unusual about the area, just a flat area of sand. On a hunch, Paul pulled a small collapsible shovel out of his backpack and started to dig. Sand kept pouring into the hole, so he widened the hole and kept digging. His next plunge of the shovel struck something metallic.

"Jackpot!" Paul said with a smile.

"Sounds like you've struck something," said Maggie.

"Eva, I've struck a metal object about 2 feet down," said an excited Paul.

"Nice job, Paul. Can you delineate how big it is?" asked a curious Eva.

"Yes. We can try digging a few more holes to get some dimensions," answered Paul.

Maggie pulled a collapsible shovel from her own back-pack and joined Paul in digging several holes and then several more, before stopping to review their progress. Standing, Paul took a container of water from his back-pack and took a sip, with Maggie following suit. Surveying the scene before him, Paul let out a low whistle at what he saw.

"Eva, I think we have some dimensions for you. The object is rectangular, about 30 feet by 40 feet, flat and metallic," reported Paul.

"Okay, you and Maggie stay right where you are and don't move. A team is on the way, and I wouldn't want either of you injured or killed by the gateway", cautioned Eva.

"Thank you, Eva. We'll stay right where we are", replied Paul, slightly unnerved by the thought of being sliced in half. He held Maggie's hand as a precaution to keep her from straying near the gateway. To their right, a few yards from where they were standing, a shimmering light blue rectangle formed, changing to a dark blue as the gateway stabilized. First to exit were two DarkBridge recon drones that took up stations a few hundred yards from the site. Major Scott Esterbrook, head of security for DarkBridge Technology and 5 other members of the security team came next, dressed in desert camouflage they blended in perfectly with the desert environment. The security team fanned out, taking positions away from the site, watching for unwanted visitors. Major Esterbrook walked over to where Paul and Maggie were standing and waited for the excavation team to exit the gateway.

"Hi, Paul. Hi, Maggie. Looks like you've uncovered a real mystery," replied Scott, as he surveyed the various holes that had been excavated.

"Hi, Scott. Good to see you and the extra security. Yes, we do seem to have a mystery on our hands," replied Paul.

"Hi, Scott. Welcome to the Sinai," replied Maggie, with her shovel still in hand.

"Looks like the rest of the team is coming through now," said Scott, watching as more individuals came through the gateway.

The excavation team, consisting of one scientist and four lab workers, all dressed in desert camouflage exited the gateway carrying various tools and equipment containers. The gateway winked out, as the last member of the team was safely through. Two lab workers erected a large, camouflaged canopy over the site, effectively hiding it from aircraft passing over the site and providing some much-needed shade. With everyone and the site camouflaged, a casual observer would be hard pressed to notice anything out of the ordinary. Paul, Maggie and Scott both stepped back, allowing the team to begin clearing off the sand using shovels and buckets. With concentrated effort, they were finished in a couple of hours and were rewarded with a gleaming metallic rectangular surface.

The scientist, Dr. Werner, pulled out a handheld metal scanner and scanned the roof.

"It appears to be titanium, Mr. Cross," said Dr. Werner.

"What do you think, Eva?" asked Paul.

"We need to get inside. The composition and dimensions suggest that it might be a dimensional sanctuary. Assuming this is true, we should be able to open a gateway using one of the GAGE devices in your backpack. I'll reprogram the GAGE device and then send a drone in, since we don't know what's inside," suggested Eva.

Back in Martin's office, Hiram choked on a piece of donut when he heard what Eva said.

Paul followed Eva's suggestion, taking a GAGE device out of his backpack and placing it on the surface of the sanctuary. He turned the device on, and the unit began to hum, as a shimmering light blue circle appeared two feet above the sanctuary, in a horizontal position. The dimensional gateway stabilized to a dark blue color, and he turned to Scott for the next step.

"All set Eva. The gateway is stable and ready," replied Paul.

"Let's put some eyes on this," said Scott, as he removed his backpack and placed it on the metal surface near his feet. Bending down, he reached inside, pulling out a small, hinged metal box and a rolled-up display screen. Passing the display screen to Maggie, Scott opened the box, gently pulling out what looked to be a large dragonfly.

"Cute," replied Maggie.

"A dragonfly?" said a curious Paul.

"Not just any dragonfly. A DarkFly drone in disguise," replied Scott, amused at Paul's question. Scott bent down, placing the drone on the surface of the sanctuary. The dragonfly, on touching the metal surface, extended its thin metal legs and its wings began to slowly flap.

"The eyes are high intensity LED lights and there's a miniature, ultra high-resolution video camera mounted underneath its body. It's also quantum linked to a small QASM device in my backpack, which could theoretically give it unlimited flight time," explained Scott.

"I forgot to add that Eva can control it remotely. All yours, Eva," said Scott.

"Thank you, Scott. I'll take it from here," replied Eva.

"I don't think I'll ever look at insects the same way again," said Paul, as he unrolled the display screen and switched it on by tapping the screen. Immediately, an image appeared, showing a live, clear video feed from the dragonfly. He handed the display to Maggie, who gingerly took it from Paul's hands.

Eva added the drone video feed to the current feed being sent to Martin's office.

"Incredible!" voiced Paul, looking at the display in Maggie's hands.

Scott walked over to the two of them, interested in what the drone would reveal. The DarkFly drone rose smoothly into the air with an insect-like buzz. Paul and Scott watched the screen, as Eva deftly maneuvered the dragonfly over the waiting gateway. Super bright LED lights switched on and the DarkFly drone descended through the gateway into the unknown.

Chapter 8

Enigma

The DarkFly drone passed through the gateway and into the gloomy, foreboding darkness of the sanctuary, lit only by the twin LED lights.

Martin and Hiram sat enthralled watching the live video feed in Martin's office, while everyone at the site gathered around the display screen held by Maggie. The drone slowly spun around, giving its viewers a wide panorama look at the inside. A collective gasp was heard, as the twin, super-bright LEDs pushed the darkness away, revealing a gruesome scene.

A desiccated humanoid body lay across the floor. Green and twisted, its body lay sideways, with one clawed hand clutching its chest. A reddish dust on the floor, possibly dried blood, outlined the body. Some sort of device with a handle, lay near the body, possibly a weapon of some sort.

"What is it?" asked Maggie, with growing interest.

"Definitely not human," observed Scott.

"Eva, are you seeing this?" asked an incredulous Paul.

"Yes. It appears that this is indeed one of our sanctuaries and preliminary analysis shows it to be yours. I'm awaiting instructions from Martin and Hiram," replied Eva, her quantum processors barely containing her excitement.

"My sanctuary here? I haven't lost my sanctuary!" replied an incredulous Paul.

Back in Martin's office, Hiram was in a state of shock, constantly repeating "Oh, my God, Oh, my God." Martin was getting worried.

"What's the matter, Hiram?" asked a concerned Martin.

"Martin, this is Project TimeBridge!" exclaimed Hiram.

"How can it be Project TimeBridge? You don't have it working yet." said an incredulous Martin.

"That's it exactly! The key word is "yet"," replied an excited Hiram.

"How can you be so sure that Paul's sanctuary is there due to TimeBridge?" inquired Martin.

"We won't know absolutely, until we bring the sanctuary back here," said Hiram.

Martin could see the wheels beginning to turn in Hiram's mind, as to how they could get such a heavy object back here. In his own mind, Martin was still grappling with the implications of Project TimeBridge functional at some point in the future.

"Eva, can you get closer to the body?" asked Hiram.

"Yes. I'll take it in for a closer look," replied Eva.

The DarkFly drone moved closer to the body, shining its twin LED lights upon the dried husk. It was humanoid, but that was where any similarities to humans ended. The eye sockets were oval shaped and a dried, forked tongue was hanging out of a corner of its mouth. Bare arms extended out from a hooded robe the creature was wearing, showing green skin, composed of very fine scales. The arms ending in five fingered claws, it appeared to be hairless, reptilian in nature and approximately six feet tall. Underneath its blood-stained, hooded robe, there were glimpses of some type of body armor. The claw that was clutching its chest appeared to be partially covering a neatly formed hole, which had pierced the robe and armor.

The DarkFly drone surveyed the test of the interior, finding scorch marks along the walls, an overturned bench and table displaying signs of some energy blast event. Clearly, some energy event had occurred causing such damage. The QASM unit stood off to the side, the green display still appeared to be functional, barely shining through a thick coating of dust. Upon closer examination, there appeared to be some kind of blast damage on the right side, which had probably caused major power issues within the sanctuary.

Paul watched the display intently and soon became aware of a presence behind him. Gabriel, unseen by the other humans, stood behind Paul and whispered "Skarzi" into his left ear. Paul gave a slight nod of acknowledgement and glanced at Maggie, who had also heard the word and gave him a questioning look. Paul recognized the word from a dream he had, one that alluded to a war between a reptilian species called the Skarzi and the human looking Anunnaki. Paul didn't know what to make of finding this long dead Skarzi. Obviously, it had been dead for quite some time, but until the body was carbon dated, there wasn't any way to know exactly when. Something about the robe it was wearing nagged at him. He needed to speak quietly with Martin, so he quietly stepped away from the group gathered around Maggie.

Gabriel had followed Paul and Maggie to this location on the Sinai Peninsula. The area made him think back to a time in the distant past, when he and his fellow Anunnaki had come to Earth. Before the advent of the Ascension Chamber, they had walked the land in human form. Finding an indigenous ape-like species already populating the planet, the Anunnaki embarked on a grand, master plan to speed up the evolutionary process. It would eventually create a newer, more intelligent and robust species, that the Anunnaki could guide to higher levels of civilization. Gabriel smiled at those memories, suddenly brought back to the present with a wave from Paul. The two had just exited the gateway and were passing by, just below Gabriel who was floating above a nearby hill. That Paul and Maggie could see him despite his attempts to stay invisible, still mystified Gabriel. Even more noticeable was the unmistakable aura that surrounded them, a sign that something had them both under its protection.

Gabriel watched as Paul located an area of interest. There was something here that was emitting a primitive quantum signature, as compared to both his past Anunnaki self and his current ascendant state. Gabriel's interest rose, as Paul uncovered a metallic structure buried in the sand. Soon, more humans came through a gateway to help remove the sand covering the top of whatever it was. Gabriel watched as Paul used one of his GAGE devices to open a gateway into the structure. When the primitive drone was sent in, Gabriel had to get a closer look. Knowing that only Paul could see him, Gabriel floated over to the group gathered around the display. Floating just above the heads of the group, he looked down and saw what all the commotion was about. Skarzi! At first, he didn't believe what he was seeing but it soon became evident that it was true. Down below, inside this structure was a dead, desiccated Skarzi body, with an obviously fatal wound in its chest.

From the armor it was wearing underneath its robe, Gabriel could tell that it had been a warrior from the Sook tribe. Gabriel floated close to Paul and whispered "Skarzi" into his ear, hoping that it might trigger some memory in him of the ancient Anunnaki enemy. His whisper had the desired effect when he saw Paul move away from the group in order to have a private discussion with Martin. Something about the robe nagged at Gabriel, so he took a closer look at the video screen. Of course! The robe looked like a Hebrew robe worn in ancient times and possibly over three thousand years old. What had the Skarzi been up to back then? How had it become trapped inside this structure? Who had shot it? The questions were beginning to snowball, and he needed answers. That time period in history and the countries surrounding the Sinai, had been under the watchful eye of his fellow angel, Raphael. Curious, thought Gabriel. He hadn't seen Raphael for quite some time. It was as if he had disappeared somewhere and didn't want to be found. Gabriel knew it was time for another consultation with Michael and Uriel. Maybe they would have some answers, he thought to himself, as he opened a gateway to Heaven and floated through.

Martin didn't like what he was seeing inside the sanctuary. A humanoid, reptilian creature was lying dead inside a structure that may have been buried for over three thousand years. The sanctuary itself had only been developed a couple of years ago. Things just didn't add up, a deep frown began forming on the brows of a mystified Martin.

"What do you think, Hiram?" asked Martin.

"My head is starting to fill up with questions, Martin. Finding a dead creature inside has just complicated things," replied Hiram.

"How so?" asked a puzzled Martin.

"It appears to be alien and might be harboring some deadly virus," replied Hiram.

"I agree. We need to take precautions when we get it back here. Eva, leave the drone inside the sanctuary and close the gateway. Please connect me with Paul and Scott," directed Martin.

"All set Martin," replied Eva.

"Scott, Paul. This is Martin. We're going to try and move the sanctuary to an isolated location back here. There's a possibility of viral contamination, so we need to take precautions. Hiram will handle the extraction of the structure. Eva is going to leave the drone inside the sanctuary for now and close the gateway. Are you clear on everything?" asked Martin.

"Loud and clear," replied Scott and Paul in unison.

"Good. Now let's get moving. Eva is wreaking havoc with foreign satellite surveillance, so there's a very brief window of opportunity," said Martin.

"We'll do what we can, Martin," replied Paul, as he noticed the gateway to the sanctuary wink out.

"Hiram, can you move the structure and bring it here?" asked Martin.

"Yes. We should be able to lift it out and move it through a gateway that opens up into an isolated and secure area. In order to move it, we'll probably need about six DarkLift anti-gravity devices," replied Hiram.

Martin remembered the accidental discovery of anti-gravity, leading to the development of the DarkLift devices. He had been in his office late one night, filling out another technology transfer agreement with the U.S. government. Suddenly, Eva had interrupted with an emergency and asked him to look at his monitor showing Hiram's lab. Tapping the icon on his virtual display, a view of Hiram's lab appeared. Martin couldn't believe his eyes for second, and then he had broken out in a fit of laughter. Hiram was seated in his chair but, the chair appeared to be floating 6 feet off the ground! Hiram was holding on for dear life with one hand and the other was waving wildly at the surveillance monitor, trying to get someone's attention. Regaining his composure, Martin had Eva contact Major Esterbrook to help get Hiram back on the ground. Martin walked down to the lab after, to check on Hiram and to make sure he was okay. When he arrived, Hiram was back on solid ground, with Major Esterbrook standing off to the side with an amused look on his face. Martin asked Hiram what had happened. Turns out, Hiram had been experimenting with pulsed magnetic fields and some exotic matter sent from Area 52. Sitting in his chair, he had inadvertently been within the developing anti-gravity field radius. That accidental discovery had led to the creation of the DarkLift series of anti-gravity devices.

"Ah yes. The anti-gravity devices you developed. Sounds like the right tool for this job," replied Martin, as his attention shifted back to the matter at hand.

"They are probably the easiest and quickest way, without drawing attention to the site. We would need six devices in order to safely move it," said a confident Hiram.

"Eva, have six DarkLift devices sent to the site immediately," ordered Martin.

"All set Martin. The devices should arrive at the site momentarily," replied Eva.

"Thank you, Eva. Paul, the DarkLift devices are on the way. Hiram will provide instructions on device placement and operation," said Martin.

"Roger that. Awaiting device arrival," replied Paul.

Paul, Maggie and Scott watched as a gateway formed nearby and stabilized. Soon a large metal box came through it, carried by a couple of sentry robots. Placing the box on the ground, the robots stepped back through the gateway, which immediately winked out.

The trio walked over to the box, Scott and Maggie standing nearby while Paul opened it. Unlatching the lid, Paul lifted it up, revealing the contents. Inside were six silver, round shaped DarkLift devices, around ten inches in diameter at the base and twelve inches high. They reminded Paul of an upside-down garbage disposal device, the type that were once used in kitchen sinks. Equipped with handles, Paul lifted one out, figuring it must weigh about 10 pounds. Maggie and Scott each lifted one out and all three walked over to the top of the sanctuary.

"Paul, the six DarkLift devices need to be placed three on each long side of the sanctuary and equally spaced," said Eva.

"Thank you, Eva. I'll let you know when we're done," replied Paul, as he, Maggie and Scott placed the first group of three on the sanctuary. They returned to the metal box and retrieved the last three DarkLift devices, placing them on the opposite side of the sanctuary, equally spaced as well. Scott then ordered the camouflaged canopy removed, and two technicians quickly complied.

"All set, Eva. DarkLift devices placed and ready to activate," replied Paul.

"Good. Now have everyone stand at least thirty feet from the sanctuary. Don't worry about the devices sliding off. Once activated, they bond by molecular adhesion to the surface," said Eva.

Everyone moved away from the sanctuary to the required distance and waited for what could be something truly amazing.

"All personnel are at a safe distance, Eva," said Paul, moving to stand next to Maggie.

"Thank you, Paul. Activating now," said Eva.

A dull thud was heard, as the DarkLift devices activated their molecular adhesion function, eliciting a murmur of concern from the group. A growing hum began to sound from the devices, rising in pitch, as the surrounding ground began to shudder. The humming increased and sand began to billow out from the sides of the sanctuary as it slowly rose up from its entombment. Paul, Maggie and the others, watched in amazed fascination, as the large sanctuary rose from the sandy grasp of the Sinai desert. Sand spilled off its pitted titanium sides, cascading down into the large rectangular hole it was leaving.

The sanctuary continued to rise, until it floated about two feet above its previous resting place. Again, the group watched in amazement, as ports opened on the DarkLift devices and jets of air propelled the sanctuary away from the large gaping hole. A shimmering, light blue gateway appeared a few feet away, stabilizing to a dark blue. It was much larger than the usual gateway and the DarkLift devices maneuvered the lumbering structure towards it. Reaching the gateway, the DarkLift devices increased their forward momentum, propelling the sanctuary through the dark blue gateway. The other side of the gateway opened to an unused section of the underground parking garage at DarkBridge Technology and the DarkLift devices centered the sanctuary in the middle of a paved area, gently settling it to the ground.

A remote controlled, small, front-end loader was waiting nearby, and Eva sent it through the still open gateway, so that the gaping hole in the desert could be filled in. The front-end loader came through the gateway and immediately began filling in the hole left by sanctuary. It didn't take long to fill, leaving only a shallow depression to mark where the sanctuary had once resided. Eva recalled the DarkFly drones, while Scott signaled the security team to join everyone at the gateway. The Sinai mission completed, the entire team followed the front-end loader back through the gateway and back to the facility, leaving no trace of what had just transpired in the Sinai.

Chapter 9

Paradox

Hiram was deep in thought, as he left Martin's office. Project TimeBridge had actually worked! It was the only way to explain the event. Someone had gone back in time and accessed the sanctuary, either by briefcase or some other means. The time travel paradoxes involved were enough to drive anyone crazy. It could even have been his recently developed, pocket sized version of the briefcase that was used. The size of a deck of cards and easier to use, it could easily fit in someone's pocket.

Arriving at the Project TimeBridge lab, he paused before the door and allowed the biometric and retinal scanners to do their job. Passing both, the door opened, and he entered the lab. Inside, he spotted his two research helpers, Pamela Weaver and Trent Levin looking at the results of a recent simulation.

"Hello, you two. Any progress?" asked Hiram, not quite sure what the two would think about the news he was about to share.

Pamela was the first to speak, "Not yet Hiram. The portal simulation is still unstable. It only stays open for a fraction of a second."

"Well, we do eventually figure it out and get it working", replied Hiram.

"How's that?" asked a skeptical Trent.

"Better get ready. I have some important news to share", said Hiram, as he recounted the events of the past few hours.

Pamela and Trent sat there dumbfounded, trying to process all the implications.

The demon queen, Lilith, still possessing Trent's body, was elated. The alien body discovered was a minor item to her. She, Asmodeus and other demons, had numerous contacts with alien visitors in the distant past, so this part wasn't new. The exciting part was that this Time-Bridge thing had actually worked! Her King, Asmodeus, would be very pleased with this news. Very pleased!

Pamela was the first to break the silence.

"I think Trent and I should take a look at the sanctuary and make some measurements. Maybe there are residual particles that might give us a clue as to how it worked," offered an intrigued Pamela.

"I agree. It's an interesting idea and a good one. Report your findings back to me and we'll go over the results together," replied Hiram, hopeful that something might be found.

Pamela and Trent walked around the lab, gathering a few pieces of portable measuring equipment and set off for the sanctuary.

Lilith was interested as well, with what might be discovered, so she remained in hidden inside Trent and left with him.

Hiram waved as they left, the wheels beginning to spin in his mind about how he could make TimeBridge work. He sat down at the bench and began scanning through all the equations, looking for some error.

Chapter 10

Helping Hand

Asmodeus, King of the demons, sat upon his throne of fire, contemplating his next move. The throne room was empty, devoid of demons, which suited him fine. It had been a few weeks since he had seen Lilith and he was getting both restless and moody. He had been waiting for some word on the progress of Project TimeBridge and how soon Lilith could complete her mission. What was wrong with these stupid humans? Couldn't they solve a simple thing like time travel? He had solved the time travel puzzle long before the advent of the Ascension chamber. The only problem had been his fear of using it and somehow inadvertently changing both his and Lilith's histories. It was too risky for him and better left for the unwitting humans to develop.

His mind drifted to thoughts of Belial, who had been at his side since the time of the rebellion. He missed his friend, but the former human named Karl was learning quickly and would eventually make an excellent demon. Not on the level of Belial but, he would come close. Enough! Asmodeus yelled out to no one in particular. Shaking off these silly musings, he knew what his next move should be. Determined, he stood up and changed his form to human, attired in a spotless, white business suit. Next, he opened a gateway into the lab of the human called Hiram and stepped through.

Emerging on the opposite side, Asmodeus kept his form hidden from any human sensors and gazed around the lab. He had been here before, but now he needed to make a better appraisal of their technology. It was as expected, a mix of advanced and primitive technology. The advanced quantum power storage was obviously angel inspired and came dangerously close to replicating the ancient Anunnaki technology. He spied a figure doing some computer work on a virtual display and moved closer. It was the human named Hiram, the one responsible for a lot of the technology here. Asmodeus laughed to himself at the truly primitive environment that surrounded him, but the laughter quickly ended, as he considered how important it would be to his plan.

Intrigued with what Hiram was doing, Asmodeus looked closer at the screen and almost laughed out loud. The humans were on the verge of making it work! The calculations were almost perfect and came close to matching his own. Reading through the calculations, he saw the reason why they couldn't achieve a steady portal longer than a few seconds. They were neglecting to add in the fifth harmonic frequency. Impatient, Asmodeus focused his mind and pushed through the EM field generated by the ring that Hiram wore. He could have easily killed Hiram, but that wasn't in his immediate plans. Instead, he opted for sleep, causing Hiram to nod off and fall into a deep sleep, his head resting in his arms. Perfect! Asmodeus thought, as he rapidly typed in the correct calculations. Corrections made, Asmodeus quickly opened a gateway back to Hell, leaving Hiram to have his "Eureka!" moment when he awakened.

Chapter 11

Solomon

The year was 930 BC and King Solomon stood on the balcony of his modest stone and wood framed palace, located on a hill overlooking the city of Jerusalem. Eventually, he would build a more sumptuous and grandiose palace, more befitting his station. There were higher priorities weighing on his mind as he surveyed the city. It was his city, passed down to him by his father King David and he felt extremely protective about it. Thriving and seemingly blessed, one would assume it to be the crown jewel of his kingdom. For him though, there was another crown jewel, something in his possession and something of incredible power. It could level entire cities, decimate armies and perform many other works of great power. Only the most trusted priests were allowed to go near it and then only when wearing a specially designed breast plate.

There had been a few times where an uninitiated person touched it and immediately died. To Solomon and his people, it was known as the Ark of the Covenant, constructed according to the directions given by God himself. Built of shittum wood, it was gilded with gold and two cherubim, with wings folded were placed on each side of the lid, back-to-back, wing to wing, with a gap between them. It was said to house the tablets inscribed with the original Ten Commandments, Aaron's staff and a pot of manna. Solomon wasn't sure what was really inside, no one really knew, and no one was foolish enough to open it and look. It was good enough for him and others that it could manifest such power. Still occupying the same tent passed down to him by his father King David, Solomon hoped to someday build a temple more worthy and befitting the Ark. Finding the labor force to build such a temple would present a challenge and having it completed while he was still alive was still another.

Sensing a presence behind him, he turned around and saw a man bathed in a golden glow standing before him. Solomon was familiar with angels, having heard stories and on a few occasions, having seen one himself. Even he, as powerful as he was, knew his place, sinking to his knees and bowing before the angel.

"I greet thee, King Solomon. My name is Raphael. The Lord has heard your prayers and bestows upon you a sacred gift to aid in building your temple", said Raphael in a melodious voice.

Solomon, still kneeling, wasn't sure what to make of the angel Raphael. He mustered up the courage to speak and asked in a faltering voice, "A gift?"

"Rise, King Solomon", commanded Raphael.

Solomon rose to a standing position, his head still bowed.

Raphael smiled at Solomon, remembering a time long past. Having once been Anunnaki before the Ascension, he had been a great scientist, second only to the now fallen Asmodeus. He and Asmodeus had shared a mutual respect for one another, until the Rebellion caused Asmodeus and others to be cast into Hell. Raphael had taken over where Asmodeus had left off, creating some of the most advanced Anunnaki technology ever created. Hearing of Solomon's wish to house the Ark in a more fitting structure, Heaven had decided to help Solomon. Raphael was here now to deliver a piece of that advanced technology in order to help Solomon with his temple.

The Ark of the Covenant, also developed by Raphael, contained a small AI named Koros, who maintained control over a clear container holding an elusive power source known as dark energy. Koros could tap into that inexhaustible energy to level cities, induce sickness, and communicate with Heaven, along with many other wonders. Koros could communicate with the Israelites through the space between the wings of the cherubim, known as the Mercy Seat, where a visage of God would appear to be speaking. In reality it was Koros speaking but, the Israelites would assume it was really God that they were conversing with.

"Take this gift and wear it on your right hand. It will give you great power over any demon and they will become your slave", said Raphael, as he closed his left hand and concentrated. He opened the palm of his hand and in it sat a ring.

Solomon reverently stepped forward and gingerly lifted the ring from Raphael's outstretched hand. Glancing at the ring, Solomon noted that the top was inscribed with strange writing and symbols, Placing the ring on his right hand, Solomon felt a strange sensation course through his body, very similar to what he felt near the Ark of the Covenant.

Raphael watched the expression on Solomon's face, as the ring slid onto his finger. The ring had begun linking to the power source contained in the Ark, giving Solomon access to the dark energy contained within it. That power link would generate a field around the ring, binding a demon to it and preventing it from escaping. Theoretically, there was no limit to the number of demons one could bind to it.

"You now have the power to bind any demon to your will. Among its other benefits is the ability to now see any demon, despite their efforts to hide from your gaze.

The Lord wishes you to build a temple suitable to house the Ark of the Covenant. Using the demons as the workforce, will allow you to build the temple much sooner", said Raphael, as he watched Solomon.

"Thank you, Great One. Surely it is impossible for something so small to accomplish something so large!" exclaimed an incredulous Solomon.

"Fear not, wise king. The ring will indeed do as I have said. Build your temple, so as to please your God", replied Raphael in his melodious voice.

Solomon watched as Raphael waved and disappeared in a flash of light from the throne room. He wasn't sure what to do next but, decided to try out his new gift by taking a walk through the city. Exiting the throne room, he walked down the hallway and out into the brilliant sunshine and a bustling city.

Chapter 12

Compulsion

Asmodeus, King of Demons, walked the dusty streets of ancient Jerusalem, dressed in a black, embroidered, silken robe. It would be some three thousand years in the future when the robe would turn into a white business suit. None of the city inhabitants could see him and he preferred it that way for now. Lilith, his love and Queen of Demons, was somewhere in Persia, causing the usual mayhem and would eventually join him here. Hopefully, he would've completed his mission by then.

Asmodeus wasn't alone here. He had commanded forty-nine other demons to accompany him here to Jerusalem. They were all nearby, awaiting his next command. Among them were Belial, his most trusted general, and a lesser demon named Vagoth. Rumors had reached Asmodeus, of a powerful religious artifact that was worshiped here. Known as the Ark of the Covenant, it was said to have incredible powers. Those powers were reported to have decimated opposing armies and torn down the city walls of Jericho, among other things. He and his fellow demons were here to find out the truth and if possible, steal the Ark. If the reports were true, then something that powerful should be his and would help immensely in his age-old battle against the angels.

Walking the streets of Jerusalem, Asmodeus decided to make some mayhem of his own. He noticed a wealthy merchant, peddling some gold jewelry to the passing crowd and changed his form into a dark, black cloud. Still unseen by humans, he flowed over to the merchant and poured his essence into the man. Human bodies were so easy to possess and control, that it took little effort for Asmodeus to start having some fun with the merchant.

The effect was immediate upon the merchant, whose eyes rolled back into his head. He fell to the ground, writhing like a snake, spewing expletives, with foam coming from his mouth. Bystanders watched the spectacle in abject horror, but one young boy, named Simon ran off to seek help for the merchant. Simon ran up the busy street, searching for the city guard. Not watching where he was going, Simon ran into a middle aged man, dressed in the finest of robes, adorned with a golden necklace, a golden ring and accompanied by a group of palace guards. Simon was sent sprawling, upon hitting the man, who seemed to be unfazed by the impact. Simon had no idea that he had just ran into King Solomon himself.

"I'm sorry, sir. I was trying to find help for a man, who seems very ill," stammered Simon, feeling slightly intimidated by the display of weapons now pointed at him by the palace guards.

"No harm done. Here, let me help you up," said Solomon, as he offered his hand to the boy and motioned for the guards to fall back.

Simon grabbed the offered hand and pulled himself up, brushing the dust off in the process.

"Thank you, sir. My name is Simon," he said to the stranger.

"You're welcome, Simon. Why don't you take me to this man who is sick," said Solomon, curiosity getting the better of him.

"Follow me," said Simon, as he led the stranger and armed contingent back to the sick man.

Along the way, people stopped what they were doing and bowed as the King walked by with his palace guards. Simon didn't know what to make of the bowing. You'd think royalty was passing by, he thought to himself as they reached the sick man.

Solomon looked at the sick man and knew right away what the man's affliction was. The man was possessed, possibly by a demon and even stranger, Solomon could see the demon inside the man.

"Stand back, Simon," ordered Solomon, who raised his hand, gesturing to the crowd to stand back, his palace guard fanning out, forming a circle around the King and the possessed merchant.

The crowd complied, bowing and stepping back from the terrifying scene. Solomon decided that the ring must be working, so he tested it further. He reached down and touched the writhing merchant on his forehead with his hand wearing the ring. The effect was just as immediate, a brilliant flash of light ensued, as Solomon watched a dark formless cloud leave the man's body. The dark cloud hung in the air before him, seeming to struggle against some unseen binding.

Asmodeus was having a lot of fun with the merchant's body and took great pleasure in the fear showing on the faces of the crowd. He laughed to himself at the sight of the cowering crowd and noticed a young boy, a finely dressed man and a group of guards approaching. What could these humans possibly do to him, Asmodeus, King of Demons? He laughed to himself and laughed even harder when the finely dressed man reached down and touched the merchant's forehead.

It was the last laugh for Asmodeus, as he felt his very essence ripped from the body of the merchant. His gaseous form outside the merchant, he found it impossible to move. No matter how hard he tried, he was frozen in place. Growing frustrated and fearful, Asmodeus railed against the invisible chains binding him and sensed a great, irresistible power emanating from a ring that the man wore.

Solomon looked at the dark, formless demon before him and gazed down at the merchant, who appeared to be recovering quickly. Remembering what Raphael had told him, Solomon decided that this demon would be the first one to be bound to his will.

"Demon, I command you to take human form," ordered Solomon.

"You don't command me, human," said the formless Asmodeus, with a menacing tone.

"Are you sure about that?" replied Solomon, as he closed his ringed hand into a tight fist.

Asmodeus felt pain. It was as if something was squeezing the energy from him and if he didn't comply, he might die. Never, since ascending to this higher form of being, had anything given him such pain and threat of death. Left with no choice, Asmodeus conceded and took human form, wearing the same robes as earlier.

Solomon saw the dark, formless cloud, coalesce into a robed figure of a man. The man was of medium height with a dark beard and eyes that blazed with fury.

Seeing that the demon had complied, he relaxed his closed fist.

"What is your name, demon?" asked Solomon.

"Asmodeus, King of Demons. By what right do you bind me to your will?" asked a furious Asmodeus.

"Asmodeus. Yes, I have heard of you and your evil workings. The will of God binds you to me, Solomon, the King of Israel," he replied, watching Asmodeus carefully.

Asmodeus took a closer look at the ring on Solomon's finger, sensing the strange power emanating from it. The ring itself appeared to be of Anunnaki construction and was obviously able to channel that strange energy, leading to his current predicament.

It was a power unlike anything on this planet and he knew what it was. Called dark energy, it was something he and his fellow scientist, Raphael, had been experimenting with just before the rebellion. Apparently, Raphael had been able to contain and harness its awesome power.

"What is it that you want?" asked Asmodeus, resigned to his current fate for now.

"For now, follow me", replied Solomon, as he turned and continued walking down the street, waving goodbye to the young boy Simon in the process.

A few yards down the street, Solomon spotted another demon, walking down the street, seemingly without a care in the world. He walked towards the demon, thinking itself invisible to all humans. The demon, huge, hulking, and covered in scales, was very close and still oblivious to those around it.

Solomon touched the demon with his ringed hand. There was a similar flash of light, signaling that the demon was now under Solomon's control.

"Demon, I command you to take human form and tell me your name!" commanded Solomon.

Belial stood there stunned, wondering what had just happened. He had been admiring some young women nearby and thinking about all the wickedly evil desires he would unleash upon them. Convinced of his superiority over these humans, he found himself unable to accept that this human could be a danger to him. He spotted Asmodeus, who seemed uncharacteristically subdued and in human form. Unsure as to how to proceed, Belial took the obstinate approach.

"No. I think not. Why would I, a far superior being, take commands from a lowly life form such as you?" countered Belial with a sneer.

"Because, I, King Solomon, demand it!" replied Solomon, as he once again squeezed his ringed hand into a tight fist.

Once again, the effect was immediate, causing not only this demon to bend over in pain, but Asmodeus as well.

"Now, tell me your name," commanded Solomon, as he relaxed his clenched fist.

Belial, like Asmodeus, had never experienced such pain and had no desire to experience it again. So he decided to comply and changed into human form, wearing a dark robe, flaming red hair and eyes dark as night.

"I am called Belial. What do you want with me?" asked the demon.

"For now, take your place next to Asmodeus", said Solomon.

Belial obeyed and took his place next to Asmodeus, who glared at him and stayed silent.

Solomon continued walking down the street, gazing about, his entourage growing behind him. It didn't take long for his gaze to settle upon another demon, lounging around in a large vat of boiling oil. Solomon marveled at the demon who was seemingly unaffected by the boiling oil and who actually seemed to be enjoying it. As he approached the demon, his palace guard began showing concern on their faces. They were not yet able to see the demon and here was their King walking over to a vat of boiling oil. Solomon gingerly touched the demon, being careful not to get scalded by the oil. The effect was once again immediate, a flash of light and the demon appeared. His palace guard stepped back, growing more terrified, as each new demon had appeared before them.

"Tell me your name, demon and take human form!" commanded Solomon.

"I am called Vagoth. Why would I obey an insignificant human like you?" replied a smug Vagoth. His smugness quickly melted away when he saw Asmodeus and Belial standing with the palace guards.

"I am King Solomon and you are now my slave", replied Solomon, as he began clenching his fist.

Vagoth let out a brief howl of laughter at the man's words, a howl that was quickly reduced to excruciating pain as he felt an overwhelming power grip him. Behind Solomon, Asmodeus and Belial both let out cries of anguish as they were forced to their knees. Vagoth knew raw power when he felt it and he knew when to concede. He drifted out of the boiling vat of oil and transformed into human form, taking on the appearance of a hunchback beggar, complete with dusty robe.

Solomon relaxed his clenched fist, allowing the three demons to recover.

"Master, what is it that you wish me to do?" asked a humbled Vagoth, causing sneers of derision from Asmodeus and Belial.

"Silence! You will take your place with the other two demons, Vagoth and follow me," replied Solomon, as he continued his walk through the city.

Vagoth took his place next to Belial, who promptly kicked him in the shin.

"Scum," said a disgusted Belial, as the three demons followed their new master around the city.

Solomon repeated the same process throughout the city, adding to his demon entourage. It had taken much of the day and Solomon was exhausted. Looking over the captured demons, he counted a total of fifty altogether. That would have to be enough. He remembered stories passed down through the generations, of how powerful demons could be and what they could accomplish, given proper motivation. He would soon be putting those stories to the test.

Solomon tightened his fist, sending all fifty demons to their knees in excruciating pain and sending a clear message of who was in charge.

"Asmodeus! Step forward!" commanded Solomon, as he relaxed his fist.

A shaky Asmodeus stood, quickly regained his composure and approached Solomon.

"What is it that you want us to do?" asked a sullen Asmodeus.

"I want you to build me a magnificent temple to house the Ark of the Covenant on top of that empty hill," replied Solomon, pointing towards a hill in the center of the city.

"What do we get in return?" asked Asmodeus, as he salivated over thoughts of the Ark.

"I will release you from bondage," replied a sly Solomon. He would indeed free the demons, but their freedom would be banishment back to Hell.

"Very well, we will build your temple," replied Asmodeus.

"Good. Since you are King of Demons, I expect you to control your subjects and see that the task is completed," said Solomon.

"When should we begin?" asked Asmodeus, feeling that binding link to Solomon. It was like some invisible chain wrapped around him, compelling him to obey.

Probably some kind of quantum linkage, thought the scientific side of him.

"You may start now," said Solomon, motioning towards the waiting hill. He stood and watched, as the demons filed by, eager to begin their task and realize freedom once again. Tired, Solomon retreated to his palace, signaling the guards to follow.

Raphael had watched the entire spectacle from a safe distance, fairly sure that none of the demons had spotted him. He was certain that Asmodeus had probably already figured out his involvement in all this. Raphael watched with great satisfaction, as the demons began their work. First they leveled the hill and then created various tunnel openings to the surface. The tunnels were probably for relic storage in case of attack, but Raphael suspected ulterior motives by Asmodeus. Huge, multi-ton blocks of perfectly cut stone began appearing, each carried by a single demon. These were deposited and laid out, layer by layer, forming a foundation that would last thousands of years into the future.

Raphael almost missed it, so engrossed was he with watching the demons. A silver object caught his eye, cruising across the sky at high altitude. His interest piqued, Raphael concentrated and found himself miles above the ancient city of Jerusalem. The greenish, silver object passing just below him, Raphael concentrated once again, this time slowing down local time. He dropped down to a position just above the unknown craft, examining every detail as the craft moved by at a snail's pace. The first thing he noticed were the markings, displaying a familiar language, but one that he thought long dead.

Skarzi! Raphael thought the race long dead and forgotten. Yet here they were. The craft itself didn't seem to be capable of intergalactic travel, but definitely capable of local planetary travel within this solar system. Raphael noticed a tinge of red dust in the crevices of the craft and touched it with his finger. Definitely not of Earth, but possibly Mars and that raised more questions. Raphael remembered that ancient time, so long ago, when an epic space battle had taken place between the Anunnaki and Skarzi. Battling each other in the space between Earth and Mars, the Anunnaki had destroyed the Skarzi fleet and proceeded to Mars. Reaching Mars, the Anunnaki bombarded the surface with kinetic and high energy maser weapons, destroying the Skarzi installations.

Nothing remained, either above or below ground of the Skarzi. Yet, here was a Skarzi vessel and Raphael could sense the presence of Skarzi inside. He decided to wait and see what their true intentions were towards the human population, since the Skarzi were no longer a threat to the ascended Annunaki. Raphael concentrated once again, returning time to its normal flow. It was getting dark and he still needed to check in on Solomon.

Opening a gateway, he stepped through it and walked out into the hallway of Solomon's palace.

Asmodeus paused in his work, sensing a time displacement taking place in the air above. Looking up, he saw the small greenish, silver spacecraft passing overhead and a figure floating above it. The spacecraft was too far away for Asmodeus to identify, but the figure was most definitely an angel. Possibly it was Raphael, Asmodeus thought with some derision. What Raphael was doing? Asmodeus hadn't a clue and he really didn't care right now. The only thing on his mind was completing this project and being freed from bondage. Suddenly, Asmodeus and the other Demons were sent to the ground, writing in pain and agony. Demons carrying multi-ton blocks of granite, found themselves crushed beneath the massive blocks. As suddenly as it had occurred, the pain subsided, allowing the Demons to recover. Demons who had found themselves crushed beneath their granite burdens, lifted themselves up and resumed their work. Asmodeus found this intolerable, that every time Solomon clenched his fist, the demons would collapse in writhing pain. What if his hand were to become paralyzed, in a constant clenching of his fist? He shuddered at the thought and resumed his work.

As the day wore on, Asmodeus fought back his growing anger, pausing in his work to gaze over the progress the demons had made. At the rate things were progressing, he and his demons should be done with the temple before the next sunrise. After that, he wasn't sure what would happen. He didn't trust the human named Solomon but was at a loss as to how he could exact his revenge. Vengeance would be his and Solomon would pay for the indignity suffered by the demons. A smile formed on his face, as thoughts of tearing Solomon to shreds filled his mind. Asmodeus got back to work, hoisting a two-ton block of stone onto his shoulder and depositing it on the growing temple wall.

Chapter 13

Banishment

Dawn was breaking over the ancient city of Jerusalem and a new feature had risen overnight. Atop the previously empty mount sat a gleaming new temple, one truly fit to house the Ark of the Covenant. Asmodeus stood back, giving the temple a serious, appraising look, finding great satisfaction in what he and his demon followers had built.

"Come. We are finished here. Let us seek release from our bondage", commanded Asmodeus, as he opened a gateway to Solomon's palace. Asmodeus and his demon followers passed through the gateway, one by one, into a courtyard just outside the palace.

"Belial, you will come with me. The rest of you will wait here. Do not harm any of the humans while I am gone. Do you understand?" ordered Asmodeus. He didn't want to give Solomon a reason to keep the demons as slaves. The demons nodded their assent and Asmodeus opened a second gateway into Solomon's bedchamber. Belial paused before following Asmodeus, just long enough to give Vagoth a kick in the shins.

"Scum", said a laughing Belial as he followed Asmodeus through the gateway.

"Ouch!" said Vagoth, gasping with pain, relieved to see Belial leave.

The second gateway opened up, just outside Solomon's bedchamber and Asmodeus paused before entering. Two guards were posted outside the chamber doors, and both were gaping, wide-eyed at the sudden appearance of Asmodeus and Belial. Wasting no time, Asmodeus waved his hand, sending the two guards into a deep slumber. Asmodeus quietly opened the door and walked in, with Belial right behind him.

Asmodeus glanced at the bed, seeing Solomon and presumably, one of his wives in a deep sleep. Earlier, Asmodeus and the other demons had been driven to their knees in pain, by what appeared to be a subconscious reflex by Solomon. He walked over to the bed, standing next to the sleeping Solomon, contemplating what should be done.

"We should kill him now, while he sleeps", said Belial quietly.

"Yes, we should, but we don't know just how powerful that infernal ring is, or what protection it offers him," replied an indecisive Asmodeus.

"What do we do?" asked Belial impatiently.

"We wait", answered Asmodeus, as he stepped back from the bed.

For Solomon and Darah, the dreams had faded, leaving them in a deep slumber. Solomon sensed muffled voices, and a sense of evil intruding on his slumber. The overwhelming presence of evil broke his deep slumber. His eyes snapped open, and Solomon immediately took in his surroundings. At first, he checked on Darah, who seemed to still be asleep, then noticed the early morning sunlight streaming in through the window. Sensing something else in the room, he turned his head and saw the demons Asmodeus and Belial, standing near the bed. The menacing sense of evil exuded by the demons was both palatable and concerning. The dreams had shown a past history as someone named Valinor, along with the two demons. The names Asmodeus and Belial now had deeper and dangerously more significant meaning to both him and Darah.

"The human awakes", sneered Belial.

"We have done as you asked. The temple is completed, and we hold you to your word. Release us from this bondage!" commanded Asmodeus.

Solomon, now fully alert, needed time to process what he had learned and what his next move should be.

"Wait for me in the courtyard. I'll be there momentarily," commanded Solomon.

"We will wait outside, but not for long," replied Asmodeus, who immediately opened a gateway and stepped through, followed by Belial.

Solomon breathed a sigh of relief as they left through the gateway. The gateway didn't surprise him or seem magical in any way. The dreams had made him wiser, leaving him with knowledge of things once thought the realm of angels. Darah stirred next to Solomon, her eyes slowly opened, sleep fading from her eyes. She saw Solomon gazing at her, emanating a deep love towards her.

Solomon watched as Darah's eyes opened, finding her dark, captivating eyes gazing up at him expectantly.

"Darah my love, I've had the strangest dreams", said Solomon, his mind still processing what the dreams had revealed.

"I too, have had the strangest dreams, my love", replied Darah, her mind shaking off any residual sleepiness.

"My dreams were of a past life as someone named Valinor and a future one as someone named Paul", replied Solomon.

"My love, I had the same dreams! Mine were of someone named Shaynor and someone named Maggie", added Darah, her mind trying to wrap itself around her past and future lives.

"I am mystified as to why the dreams were given to us, but now I see many things more clearly, such as my love for you", said Solomon, as he turned and gave Darah a passionate kiss.

Darah responded by returning the kiss with equal fervor. The kiss brought back memories of how she had been reluctant when her father ordered her to marry King Solomon. Being one of many wives wasn't how she had pictured her life and never having met King Solomon, only added to that reluctance. That reluctance had been swept away when she saw the King for the first time. Their eyes had locked onto one another, and she had felt an instant connection to Solomon. Later, he confided to her that he had also felt an instant connection to her when they met. Now, after the dreams, this kiss held even more meaning to her. Solomon reluctantly released his lips from hers, knowing that he needed to address the demon issue waiting outside.

Rising from the bed, he put his robe on and walked over to the window, which yesterday, had looked out at an empty nearby mount. No longer empty, an imposing edifice now stood at its summit. Where an empty mount had once stood, now lay a solid foundation of stone blocks, giving way to granite columns. The columns surrounded a large, walled building, which was topped by a gleaming golden roof.

Darah had climbed out of bed to stand next to him, gasping at the sight.

"It's beautiful, my love," said an awed Darah, as she hugged Solomon.

"Yes, it is. The demons have done a magnificent job," replied Solomon, putting his arm around her and holding her tight.

"My love, I must attend to some important matters. Stay here and I will be back soon", said Solomon, reluctantly releasing her.

"I'll be waiting," replied Darah with a coy smile.

Solomon walked towards the bedroom door, pausing to open it. Once outside the bedroom, he noticed his two guards lying prone on the ground. Alarmed, Solomon bent down and felt their pulses.

They were still alive, but unconscious. Something had happened here in the hallway, and he suspected the demons were behind it. This only served to stiffen his resolve and his feeling that there would be no peace, as long as the demons were here. Exiting the palace, he entered the courtyard and noticed the demons gathered there. At the forefront, were Asmodeus and Belial, eyes smoldering with hatred.

"We've done as you asked. Now free us!" commanded Asmodeus.

Solomon knew what had to be done, but he wanted the demons to know who he really was.

"I know you, Asmodeus and you Belial. I remember you from the time of the Anunnaki, from the time of the colony ship and from the time of the rebellion. I also remember how you, Asmodeus, killed my beloved Shaynor and how you, Belial, shot me in the back. A cowardly thing to do, for I was once known as Valinor", said Solomon, taking great pleasure in the reactions on the demon faces before him.

Asmodeus was dumbfounded. Valinor? Could this really be true? Solomon had said things that no one in this time period could possibly know.

"I knew we should've killed him," whispered Belial to Asmodeus.

Just then, the demon known as Leviathan, who had been circling around behind Solomon, launched himself towards the king with murderous intent. Asmodeus watched expectantly, silently hoping for Leviathan to succeed.

Leviathan smiled a wicked grin, as he soared through the air towards Solomon, who would surely die, and the demons would be free. Leviathan's hands turned to razor sharp talons, lashing out to decapitate Solomon. Suddenly, there was a brilliant flash of light and Leviathan was flung away from Solomon, landing unconscious some thirty yards away.

"Enough!" yelled an angry Solomon. Clenching his ringed fist, he sent the demons writhing on the ground in pain.

"Asmodeus, you will take your fellow demons back to Hell and never set foot back here during my lifetime. You are linked to me, no matter where you are, I will be able to inflict unimaginable pain on you, should you disobey my command", said Solomon, as he relaxed his hand.

Asmodeus rose to his feet, the other Demons doing the same.

"I will comply. Hear my words though. We are immortal and you are not. You will surely die someday and then we will be free!" Asmodeus sneered.

"Consider this a small act of vengeance, for the lives of Shaynor and Valinor. Now go!" commanded Solomon.

Asmodeus had no choice but to comply. He opened a gateway back to Hell, motioning his demons to step through. Two Demons picked up the still unconscious Leviathan and carried him into the gateway. Asmodeus was the last to leave, pausing for a few last words.

"You will never know peace, Valinor. I will always be there to cause you pain", said Asmodeus with a wicked grin, as he stepped through the gateway. A brief second later, the gateway winked out, leaving Solomon alone in the courtyard.

Solomon breathed a sigh of relief, glad that the demon problem was resolved for now. He wasn't sure what had happened to the demon Leviathan, whether it was the ring he wore or something else. He had been saved from certain death and that would have to be good enough for now. Smiling, Solomon headed back into the palace, knowing that Darah was waiting expectantly.

Negev Guardian watched the events unfolding around Solomon, amused with the actions of the demons and their attempt to kill him. Negev Guardian had intervened on behalf of Vermont Guardian in saving Solomon from the demon, since the events were transpiring within this area of the world. Each Guardian had chosen a specific region of the Earth to watch over, and Negev Guardian had chosen this one. Taking its name from a desert area in Israel, it had made its home some two thousand feet below the surface, similar to what Vermont Guardian had done. Thousands of years in the future, the Dimona nuclear research facility would be built above it, much the same as DarkBridge Technology had built above Vermont Guardian.

The attempted attack on Solomon was one of those teachable moments that Vermont Guardian had often related to Negev Guardian. The demons were indeed full of hubris, always thinking that they were the pinnacle of creation. The angels were no better though, a common theme among ascendant beings. They were still the best counter to the demons though, for behind the actions of the demons, the Guardians always suspected the hand of Lucifer. Thwarting the demons also served to thwart Lucifer. For now, Solomon would find peace, but both Negev and Vermont Guardian sensed another of Lucifer's plans already in motion, affecting Solomon once again.

Raphael had watched the demons complete the temple in record time. It was a beautiful building, one truly fit to house the Ark. He had seen the demons open a gateway into the palace courtyard and assemble there. Asmodeus and Belial had opened a gateway soon after and Raphael sensed it opening up inside the palace. As long as Solomon wore the ring, the Ark would protect him. When Asmodeus and Belial had reappeared, followed shortly after by Solomon, Raphael's curiosity was aroused. He moved closer, hidden from both the humans and Demons. Raphael gaped in wonder, as Solomon began speaking about once being Anunnaki, specifically Valinor. He mentioned the colony ship, the rebellion and both his and Shaynor's deaths at the hands of Asmodeus and Belial.

Astonishing! Reincarnation was possible, in fact, it happened all the time. His fellow angels were responsible for much of the reincarnation taking place. What had always perplexed both him and his fellow angels was that the life energies of Valinor and Shaynor had simply vanished when they had died. Where they had gone, no one knew. Yet, here was Solomon, with clear memories as Valinor. Perplexing! Then there was the attempt by Leviathan to kill Solomon. That failure wasn't due to the Ark. Raphael had sensed something much more powerful, protecting Solomon. Fortunately, the Demon crisis had passed and hopefully a more peaceful time was at hand. Wishful thinking, he thought.

Now that the temple was built, Raphael needed to prepare Koros and the Ark for transport. Solomon would probably want to move it as soon as possible and take advantage of more secure surroundings. Koros could be notorious for resisting any change in location and sometimes given to erratic actions. It was a result of keeping the dark energy contained within the Ark. That dark energy, very often seemed to have a life of its own, seeming to rail against containment. While the Anunnaki had managed to contain and harness it, Raphael had the impression that they still didn't truly understand it. Sighing, Raphael opened a gateway to the Tabernacle and Koros.

Lucifer tested the bluish, energy shackles binding him, causing them to flare a bright red. He would test his bonds every so often and the resolve of his captors, hoping for some sign of weakness. He was disappointed with the failure of Asmodeus in the time of Solomon and the subsequent banishment of the demons. Like his captors, the Guardians, he too existed outside the normal flow of time and viewed time as a series of layers. It was true that Asmodeus had failed, but there were other forthcoming opportunities for success. For him, success meant retrieval of the Ark and the power it contained.

Harnessing the power of dark energy, the Anunnaki had indeed created a potential weapon of great power. That power could be used to break the shackles of energy binding him and set him free. The Demon goddess, Lilith, would be the second attempt, following a plan set forth by Asmodeus. The Skarzi would be the final attempt in this time period, having been one of his success stories at turning a civilization against the Creator. Three chances for success, one already failed. He could only hope, for praying was out of the question. Who would the second most powerful being in the universe pray to? His shackles flared a bright red, as he patiently waited for the outcomes.

Chapter 14

Eureka!

Dr. Hiram Greenwood woke from his slumber, lifting his head up from the desk and blinking the sleep from his eyes. He focused on the screen before him, gradual realization coming to him. There was a change to his calculations. A new section had been added, something called the "fifth harmonic frequency" For the life of him, Hiram couldn't remember making the change. Maybe one of his assistants did it, he thought. The other thing that bothered him was how he had fallen asleep.

"Hello, Hiram. You fell asleep and I didn't want to wake you," said Eva.

"Just a little tired, Eva. I'm okay," replied Hiram, hoping that this wouldn't get back to Martin.

His eyes refocused on the calculation change, his mind processing the potential result. The more he looked at it, the more it seemed to solve the TimeBridge stability problem. On a whim, he ran the new calculations through the simulation program and sat back in wonder and excitement as the result was displayed.

"Eureka!" shouted Hiram.

"Are you okay, Hiram? I heard a strange exclamation. One that I haven't heard before", said Eva, concern showing in her voice.

"I'm fine, Eva. Better than fine," replied an ecstatic Hiram.

Just then, the lab doors opened, and his two assistants walked in, laden with test equipment.

"Hello, Pamela. Hello Trent," said Eva.

"Hello, Eva, Hello Hiram" said Pamela and Trent in unison.

"Is everything okay, Hiram? We thought we heard a shout," asked Pamela, concern showing on her face and on Trent's.

"Did one of you make any corrections to my calculations?" asked an excited Hiram.

"No. Neither one of us feels qualified enough to change them", replied Trent.

"It wasn't me," added Eva.

"Someone added a change to the calculations that has resulted in a stable TimeBridge according to the simulator," said Hiram, as his assistants digested the groundbreaking news.

"You mean this could actually work?" asked an excited Pamela.

"I would think so. Of course, we won't know for sure until it's actually tested," replied a thoughtful Hiram.

"I agree with Hiram. My calculations show a high probability of success," said Eva.

"Good enough for me", said a smiling Pamela.

"When would we be able to test it?" asked an eager Trent.

"We may be able to try it tomorrow. We have the QASM units sufficiently charged for an initial test and the computers are ready to go," offered Hiram.

Pamela turned and smiled at Trent; their hard work was about to pay off.

"Is there anything we can do now?" asked an overly eager Trent.

"Not right now. We'll continue tomorrow. Which reminds me, how did your analysis of the sanctuary go", asked a curious Hiram.

"We determined that it is Paul's sanctuary and we found evidence of a thermal event. There was some evidence of molecular scarring on the surface, high energy scarring on the interior, all possibly caused by a high energy discharge," replied Pamela, puzzlement settling on her face.

"Most interesting. What about the alien creature?" asked Hiram, his glasses sliding down the bridge of his nose.

"We didn't get to see it. Weaver put it on ice," added Trent.

Pamela glared at Trent, not comfortable with how he was referring to her father.

"I'm sure it was for a good reason," said Pamela, rather defensively.

"There was a possibility of biological contamination, so Martin had the body frozen and put into a cryogenic chamber", replied Eva.

"Makes sense to me, both prudent and cautious. Well, there isn't much more to do here today. Why don't the two of you get something to eat and I'll see you in the morning. Tomorrow could be a momentous day," said Hiram, as he reached up and adjusted his glasses,

"Maybe you're right. Trent and I could use a decent meal," said Pamela.

"Why don't we try Maggie's?" ventured Trent.

Once again, Trent was on the receiving end of Pamela's withering stare. No matter how hard he tried, Pamela would not venture into Maggie's restaurant. He suspected that it had something to do with Paul. Trent's greatest fear, being that Pamela was falling in love with Paul. Maybe she already had, but with Maggie still here, there wasn't much chance of things progressing. Letting out a silent mental sigh, Trent stood, preparing to leave.

"Let's get some dinner," said Trent, as he put his hand on Pamela's arm and gently pulled her to follow him.

"Good night, Hiram. We'll see you tomorrow morning, bright and early," said Pamela, as she followed behind Trent.

"Have a good night, Hiram," said Trent, now gently tugging on Pamela's hand.

"Have a nice dinner," said Eva.

"Take care, you two," said Hiram.

Lilith, still inhabiting Trent, was finding it difficult to contain her eagerness, which had managed to seep out a few times and influence Trent in the lab conversation. She found it odd that a mysterious change to Hiram's calculations could be the key to making this TimeBridge thing actually work. Obviously, someone had helped and there weren't too many who knew how. Her first thought was angel help, but she quickly ruled that out. The angels would never assist in something so dangerous and threatening to humans, who they had long ago chosen to nurture and protect. No, it could only have been her King and lover, Asmodeus. It was all part of his plan, and she was an important part of it. So, she settled back into the recesses of Trent's mind, biding her time.

Hiram watched his two assistants leave, his thoughts turning back to Project TimeBridge and things that needed to be done.

"Eva, is Martin busy?" asked Hiram.

"Martin is in his office doing paperwork. Do you need to speak with him?" asked Eva.

"Yes. I need to give him a TimeBridge update," replied Hiram.

"I'll let him know," said Eva.

Martin Weaver sat in his office pouring through the usual, never-ending stack of paperwork. It seemed that no matter how far humanity had progressed electronically, the government still required hardcopy documents. Those same documents would eventually be scanned into electronic form. It didn't make sense, but it was part of doing business with the U.S. government.

"Martin, sorry to interrupt you, but Hiram has an important update on Project TimeBridge," said Eva.

Martin welcomed the interruption, or anything for that matter, just to get away from the mass of paperwork.

"Thank you, Eva. Put Hiram on my screen," replied Martin.

Hiram appeared on the virtual screen, hovering above Martin's desk.

"Hello Martin, sorry to bother you, but it has to do with Project TimeBridge," said an excited Hiram.

"Not a problem, Hiram. How is the project going?" asked Martin, intrigued by Hiram's obvious excitement.

"We've had a breakthrough. It looks like we can proceed with actual testing", said Hiram.

"That's fantastic news. What was the breakthrough?" asked a curious Martin.

Hiram launched into an explanation, becoming very animated at times. Minutes later, Martin found himself both concerned and excited with the possibilities.

"Great job, as usual, Hiram. I'm concerned with this new calculation suddenly appearing and no one knowing where it came from. It seems very suspicious. It's as if someone wanted us to succeed," said Martin.

"Yes. I share your concern as well," replied Hiram.

"Keep me posted and get some rest Hiram," said Martin.

"I will, Martin," answered Hiram.

The screen blanked out, leaving Martin to consider the import of what Hiram had said. It was clear that someone had assisted in Hiram's efforts, but who it was and why, was a mystery. They would have to wait and see what happened. Sighing, Martin returned to his paperwork.

Hiram ended his conversation and found himself in agreement with Martin. Any further work on Project TimeBridge could wait until morning and he would need the help of his two assistants. Rest sounded like an excellent idea. He really did need it.

"Eva, I think I'm going to call it a night. I need some rest", said a tired Hiram.

"I agree, Hiram. I'm detecting a note of weariness in your voice and I'm worried that you're not getting enough sleep," said Eva, with a touch of concern in her voice.

"Good night, Eva," replied Hiram, as he shut things off and left them lab.

"Good night, Hiram. Get some sleep", said Eva.

Chapter 15

Dallas

The next morning, Hiram walked into the lab and was greeted by his two assistants.

"Good morning, Hiram", said Pamela and Trent in unison.

"Good morning. Are the two of you ready to make history?" asked Hiram, his excitement growing by the minute.

"We're ready. It's all we could talk about last night," said Pamela, as she looked at Trent.

"Yes. We're ready. What should we do first?" asked a curious Trent. Lilith was finding it hard to contain her impatience, telling herself to be patient with these slow-witted humans.

Hiram thought for a moment back to a previous conversation with Martin. Dallas and the JFK assassination came to mind, making for an excellent choice to test the technology. They would have to be extremely careful, since time travel could be fraught with perils.

"Eva, what would be the best way to see if Project TimeBridge actually works?" asked Hiram.

"I would use a drone and send it through the Time-Bridge portal and exit to a nearby rooftop. Using your discussion with Martin, I've anticipated your request and assume you want to be near Dealey Plaza," replied Eva.

"That sounds good to me. I just happen to have a drone here in the lab. Can you generate the coordinates and feed them into the main TimeBridge computer?" asked Hiram.

"Yes. I've found a building that was abandoned at that time, about two blocks away from Dealey Plaza. That should be far enough away from the Presidential motor-cade and any spectators. Loading the coordinates now," said Eva.

"Thank you, Eva. You're the best," replied Hiram.

"Why, thank you Hiram. Good luck!" said Eva. She had already computed the probabilities of success at seventy five percent, which was a high level for such a new technology.

"Dallas and JFK?" asked an awed Pamela.

"Yes. Your father and I discussed this sometime ago in a joking way. Now, it seems we have a chance to make it a reality. Let's get to work," said Hiram, wondering what Martin was going to say.

Hiram and his assistants began transferring power from the QASM units to the TimeBridge portal, while enabling the harmonic frequency generators. It was all up to the master computer now, which took over, simultaneously running the complex calculations in conjunction with modulating power to the TimeBridge portal. Everyone in the lab began hearing a low hum, growing in intensity as the computer began modulating the QASM power. Arcs of energy began forming around the Time-Bridge portal, reminding Hiram of the "stitch" function on the GAGE devices. The hum increased in pitch, almost to the point of discomfort, as Hiram and his assistants began noticing a light blue sheen develop within the portal opening. The electrical arcs increased, as the light blue sheen darkened to a solid blue. A slight ripple of energy ran through the lab, not enough to damage anything and felt by everyone as a slight vibration.

The master computer flashed a "Stable" icon on the virtual display and Hiram turned to Pamela and Trent, smiling with satisfaction. The next thing would be to send the drone through and verify exactly where Time-Bridge had opened to.

"Looking good, Eva. We'll ready the drone and let you take over," said Hiram.

"Okay, Hiram. I'll do the driving," replied Eva.

Hiram had Trent walk over to a shelf and take a large steel case off the shelf. Lighter than it looked, Trent placed the case on a nearby bench and opened it.

Pamela came over and noticed a DarkFly drone inside. Not the "dragonfly" version used in the Sinai, but a large red-tailed hawk. Very appropriate and innocuous, thought Pamela, as Trent pulled the hawk out and placed it on the bench. There were a lot of things that would consider a dragonfly to be a tasty snack, but a hawk was a totally different matter.

"All yours, Eva," said Hiram, as he and the others stood back.

"Thank you, Hiram. I'll take it from here," said Eva, as she began sending commands to the DarkFly hawk. Everyone watched, as the hawk came to life, moving its head from side to side and flapping its wings. The wings were functional to a point, offering steerage and control. Two miniature anti-gravity devices built into the hawk's body provided the actual lift. Two high resolution cameras functioned as the eyes, with built-in defensive lasers. The hawk lifted silently into the air, flapping its wings. Clawed talons folding back against its body.

With Eva in control, the hawk floated over to the TimeBridge portal, still crackling with electrical arcs around its edges. Poised and awaiting the next command, the hawk looked like a true bird of prey, ready to pounce on an unsuspecting victim. Hiram activated the twin cameras and an image of the portal immediately appeared on his virtual display.

Pamela and Trent walked over to the virtual display, gathering around Hiram to literally view history in making.

"Ready, everyone?" asked Eva, excitement creeping into her voice.

"Ready, Eva. Let's see what's on the other side", said Hiram, barely able to control his own excitement.

"Here we go!" said Eva, the moment not lost on her. She might be the first AI to take part in such a groundbreaking experiment.

Eva gave the command and the DarkFly hawk flew into the waiting portal, its body disappearing into the other side.

Hiram, Pamela and Trent, watched intently, only blackness showing on the display, concern growing as what seemed like seconds ticked by. Suddenly, a brilliant flash of blue showed on the display, as the hawk exited the portal on the other side. The hawk flew up into the clear blue sky, cocking its head downward, showing the rooftops of buildings passing by below. The hawk angled towards the street leading towards Dealey Plaza, its twin cameras capturing the sight of people lined along the street, waiting for the Presidential motorcade to pass by. Everyone in the lab gave out a collective gasp of awe, as the cameras captured history being made.

Hiram caught his breath, as the cameras soon captured the motorcade heading towards the plaza. He was now positive that TimeBridge had worked and had opened to the correct point in time. The hawk flew towards the Texas Book Depository, with cameras zeroing in on the sixth floor. Window open, a figure could be seen preparing a rifle to fire.

"Is that who I think it is?" asked an incredulous Trent.

"Apparently, it is," said Eva, her quantum processors computing a one hundred percent probability.

The hawk circled overhead, as the motorcade drew closer, and people began cheering for President Kennedy. Hiram watched, as Lee Harvey Oswald pointed his loaded rifle out the window and fired at the passing motorcade. It was a grim, emotional scene, as Hiram watched history relive itself below the circling hawk. Hiram was surprised though, that the hawk had captured something only conjectured at. Shots had also come from the famous "grassy knoll", impacting President Kennedy and Governor Connelly. Oswald hadn't been the only assassin that day, mused Hiram. The hawk circled the "grassy knoll" capturing two figures, fleeing the scene and jumping into a waiting getaway car.

"Is this really happening?" asked a somber Pamela.

"Yes. It is happening and has happened. Time is a paradox. It can be very confusing. Even my quantum processors have a difficult time with it," said Eva.

"Okay, Eva. I think we've proven TimeBridge works. Recall the hawk," said Hiram. Martin was going to be utterly amazed with the results.

"Recalling the hawk," replied Eva.

The hawk circled back to the still open TimeBridge portal, slowed its speed to a crawl and passed back through the portal and into the lab. The hawk floated back to the bench, lowered its claws and landed soundlessly, powering down its systems.

"I think we have a successful test, Eva", said a subdued Hiram. It was one thing to witness such an event through the prism of history versus seeing it actually take place in real time. Certainly, the DarkBridge drone could have prevented the event, but that was the paradox of time-travel. You can't change the past without changing the future.

"Yes Hiram. You should be proud. It's quite an achievement," said Eva with a touch of pride.

"Thank you, Eva. I couldn't have done it without you and the work of my two valuable assistants", said Hiram, looking at Pamela and Trent.

"Thank you, Hiram. It's a team effort," replied Pamela.

"Okay. Let's wrap this up and document everything we did," said Hiram, as they busily got to work powering down the portal and resetting all the systems.

It was almost noon by the time they were done, and Hiram was exhausted.

"I think that's enough for today. We'll pick this up again tomorrow. Why don't the two of you take the afternoon off," offered Hiram.

"Are you sure, Hiram? There's so much more we can do," said Trent.

Lilith, possessing Trent, was giddy with the success of the experiment and was having a difficult time controlling it.

"Eva, can you send Martin a copy of the drone footage? I think he will be utterly amazed. I'm shutting the lab down for today, in order to assess our next experiment," said a tired Hiram.

"I've sent Martin the footage, Hiram. Have a good afternoon. You deserve it and congratulations," replied Eva.

"Come you two. Let's go grab some lunch," said Hiram.

Pamela and Trent looked at one another, smiling as Hiram ushered them out the door.

Chapter 16

Obsession

Later that night, while Pamela and Trent lay sleeping, Lilith began working on Trent's dreams. With the apparent success of the experiment, her part of the plan was rapidly approaching. Trent was critical to the success of her plan and she needed to start shaping him to her purposes. His interest in the Ark was apparent from his thoughts, but she needed to amplify that into an overwhelming obsession to see it in person. Lilith began feeding him images of the Ark based on her recollections from that time. Trent rolled over in bed, opposite to the sleeping Pamela, his mind beginning to fill with images of ancient Jerusalem. He was standing on the steps leading into the temple housing the Ark, looking around in awe at the ancient city. Suddenly, the dream shifted, and he found himself inside the temple, his mind reeling at the sight before him. Awestruck, his mind finally came to the realization that he was standing before one of the most significant religious artifacts in the world.

He walked closer to the Ark, admiring the detailed workmanship, marveling at the amount of gold used in its construction. He reached out and touched it, oblivious to the ancient warnings of death. His hands ran along its golden surface with no death resulting from the touch. The more he caressed the Ark, the more he needed to have it. The dream ended and was replaced with only blackness. He sat up in bed, covered in sweat, his eyes searching around the darkened room, yearning to see the Ark. He lay back down, thinking about the Ark and how much he wanted it, no matter what the cost. His thoughts turned to Project TimeBridge and the possibility of traveling back through time to ancient Jerusalem. Eventually, he fell back to sleep, thoughts of the Ark once again filling his dreams. Lilith smiled, as she stood over the sleeping body of Trent. This was going better than she thought possible. Needing to update Asmodeus on everything that had happened, she opened a gateway and stepped from the bedroom, into the world of Hell.

Later that morning, Martin was in his office at the underground facility of DarkBridge Technology. His eye caught the virtual display above his desk flashing with an urgent message to read. Sighing, he reached out and accessed the message. It was from Eva, sent a few minutes ago. It was some sort of video footage. Martin watched in fascination, unsure at what his eyes were seeing. It soon became evident that it was the JFK assassination being shown to him. Martin saw the assassination and the "grassy knoll" footage, now almost positive that Hiram had been successful with Project TimeBridge. There was one way to be sure.

"Good morning, Eva. I see that Hiram had a successful first test of Project TimeBridge," said Martin, as he anticipated Eva's response.

"Good morning, Martin. Yes, Hiram was very successful, and I even assisted with the DarkFly drone," replied Eva.

"Thank you, Eva. It's a fantastic success for Hiram and I'm glad you were able to assist him," said Martin, his question now answered.

"I was happy to help him and his two assistants. It was truly amazing, Martin," replied Eva.

"It's a truly remarkable feat. That will be all for now, Eva", said Martin. The possibilities were endless with this new technology and so were the pitfalls, he mused. Things seemed to be happening rather quickly lately and he was behind in his reports to General Esterbrook. The alien body had to be dealt with, as did all the new technology that Paul had discovered in the cavern and now a successful first test of Project TimeBridge. Like the General said, it was all about the edge. Martin wasn't sure who should truly have that edge and was considering keeping the new technology found in the cavern to protect the DarkBridge Technology facility. A wise man would only show some of the cards he held, thought Martin, as he pondered what to do next.

Lucifer watched the progress of Project TimeBridge, his satisfaction growing for the latest plan by Asmodeus. The calculation Asmodeus had given to the humans proved to be the key to its success. Lucifer laughed silently, as he saw the TimeBridge portal start forcing its way down through the layers of time. It was a brute force approach, as compared to the more elegant approaches, such as folding space and time. It would soon be up to the Demon Queen, Lilith, as her part in this was rapidly approaching. Lucifer was worried though, that the Guardians could see the same things occurring and would take steps to thwart his plans. No matter, he thought. This was but one small battle in a larger war to free himself from his captors. Freedom would come, he was certain of it and vengeance would be his.

Chapter 17

The Visit

Lilith exited the gateway and stepped onto the plains of Hell, pits of boiling lava casting their fiery glow into the reddish sky. Untouched by the heat, she wound her way through the few lava pools that sat between her and the nearby palace. Every lava pool that she passed, the demons would pause in their torturing of human souls, just to ogle at her sensuous body. Clad only in a flimsy gown, accentuating every curve, she was a welcome sight to the demons and a brief respite from torture for the human souls. The palace rose before her, built from the same obsidian rock it stood upon, with black obsidian spires piercing the ruddy sky. It was the home of her King and lover, Asmodeus, the very thought of him sending shivers of excitement through her body. She reached the palace gates and was met by two monstrous demon guards, who ushered her through the gates, while ogling her every move.

Lilith passed through the gates and entered the throne room, empty save for the figure seated on the throne. Asmodeus, her king and lover, sat on his throne of fire, his talons raking the arms of the throne, sending sparks into the air.

"My love, I bring good news!" exclaimed Lilith.

"Welcome back, my Queen. Tell me your news. I trust my adjustment to the calculations worked?" asked Asmodeus.

"Yes, my King. The humans have successfully tested the time travel device. They sent a drone back to the time of the JFK assassination and took some video," replied Lilith.

Asmodeus leaned back in his throne of fire, causing flames to dance along its edges. A smile formed on his face as his goal finally seemed within reach. Ah, yes. The JFK assassination had been a triumph for him, as he thought back to that time. His manipulation of the humans involved in the killing had paid off handsomely, setting the stage for much sorrow and anguish across the land and dealing a blow to the angels, who had supported the deceased President.

"What about the human called Trent? Is he sufficiently under your control?" inquired Asmodeus. Humans could be so unpredictable at times, and it irked him that this plan depended so heavily on a human in order to succeed.

"Yes, my King. I can control him very well and I have him thoroughly obsessed with the Ark," replied Lilith, who noticed that her King seemed very pleased with her news.

"You've done well, my Queen, but there is still much work to be done," said Asmodeus, his eyes drinking in the sensuous curves of his Queen. She had been away from his bed for far too long.

"Yes, my King. I see a problem with the human AI named Eva. The lab is constantly monitored by her, and it would be impossible to operate the TimeBridge device without her knowing. I can hide the woman Maggie and Trent from her sensors, but operating the device is another matter," replied Lilith.

"Yes, the AI could be a problem," said Asmodeus, as he pondered the problem. He could just destroy the AI, but it held information that he may want someday. No, somehow the lab would have to be temporarily blind to the AI. The other problem was how to separate Shaynor from Valinor, or Maggie from Paul, as they were known in this lifetime. Asmodeus leaned forward in his Throne of Fire, the tongues of flame surrounding him, increasing in intensity as he quickly came up with a plan for both and explained it in detail to her.

Lilith listened intently to Asmodeus, satisfaction showing on her face.

"What do you think, my Queen," asked Asmodeus.

"It's a magnificent plan, my King. When do we proceed?" said Lilith, as she anxiously waited for his reply.

"My Queen, you have been away from the palace and your King for too long. Stay the night and by this time tomorrow, you will walk the streets of ancient Jerusalem," said Asmodeus, his desire for her growing with every passing moment.

"Yes, I will stay. Oh, I almost forgot. There was another item of interest. The humans discovered one of their dimensional sanctuaries in the Sinai desert and found a dead Skarzi warrior inside," said Lilith, not sure how she almost forgot to report this.

Unfortunately, it wasn't received well.

"What! What's this? A dead Skarzi?" exclaimed an angry Asmodeus, his talons raking the arms of his throne, sending flaming sparks into the air.

Lilith shrank back from her King's anger. Lately, he seemed to be on edge and prone to outbursts.

"Yes, my King. The dead Skarzi was put into a cryogenic chamber, presumably for future research. The body, clothing and the sanctuary itself were dated to three thousand years ago," replied Lilith, her head now bowed in order to hide from her King's angry gaze.

Asmodeus paused to assimilate this new information. A dead Skarzi found inside one of the human sanctuaries? Three thousand years old? An ancient memory popped into his mind. He had gazed into the sky while building Solomon's temple and thought he saw a Skarzi scout ship. He had also seen that moronic angel, Raphael investigating. The Skarzi were a complication and ancient hatred towards them was the only thing demons and angels agreed on. Asmodeus saw his mood suddenly brighten, as the repercussions dawned on him.

Obviously, the human TimeBridge had worked and the Skarzi threat was eliminated. Someone had killed the Skarzi inside the sanctuary, possibly Valinor, who wouldn't travel back in time unless it was for an important reason. Shaynor? Asmodeus leaped up from his throne in malicious glee, surprising Lilith who scrambled away in fear, hiding behind a black obsidian column.

"Do not fear, my Queen. This is actually wonderful news! It shows that my plan is a success. Valinor and Shaynor will find themselves in the past and with your help, get trapped there," said Asmodeus, as he changed his demon form into a human one, clad in his typical white business suit.

Lilith saw the change come over her King and crawled out from behind the obsidian column.

Asmodeus stepped down from his throne, transforming back into human form and strode over to the cowering Lilith, extending his hand out to her.

"Rise, my Queen. Please forgive my initial outburst. You have done well. Let us retire to our chamber and spend some pleasurable time together," said a sincere Asmodeus.

Lilith reached up and gingerly took his hand and he gently pulled her to her feet. Asmodeus placed his arm around her sensuous waist, marveling at how she still managed to captivate him. He briefly thought about tomorrow and with it the fruition of his plans. His thoughts were quickly brought back to the present, as Lilith returned his gesture by putting her arm around his waist. The two walked off towards their bedchamber, both looking forward to spending some time together and a night of sensuous lovemaking.

Back at DarkBridge Technology, Trent was in a deep sleep, dreaming once again of possessing the Ark and the power that it held. Giddy with the power he now commanded, he leveled mountains and decimated entire armies with the powerful Ark. Such was his power, that people were throwing themselves at his feet, worshiping him as a god. Pamela was sleeping next to him, lost in deep, quiet slumber, unaware of the growing darkness within Trent. It was a growing darkness that threatened him and those around him.

Vermont Guardian, watched the unfolding events in the facility above it, satisfied that events were proceeding according to what it and the other Guardians had seen throughout the various timelines. Soon, it's two charges, Valinor and Shaynor, or Paul and Maggie as they are known in this lifetime, would be thrust into an extraordinary life-threatening situation.

Chapter 18

The Plan

The following day in Trent's apartment, Pamela woke up early and sat up in bed. Trent was still soundly sleeping next to her, his breathing slow and steady. Slowly sliding out of bed, so as not to disturb Trent, she stood, stretched and made her way to the shower. Finishing her shower and drying her hair, she stepped out of the bathroom and walked past Trent's desk. Something on the desk caught her eye and she paused. It was Trent's notebook. Curious, she opened the notebook and thumbed through the pages, with one page catching her attention. It was a drawing of the Ark of the Covenant. She too had seen enough movies and read enough articles to know what it was.

A sharp intake of breath sounded behind her and a hand reached across hers, slamming the notebook shut.
"What are you doing?" questioned an angry Trent.

"I was just curious. Why are you so defensive? It's a nice drawing", replied Pamela, who had managed to quickly pull her hand away before Trent slammed the book shut.

"It's nothing. Just doodling," said Trent, as he quickly opened the desk drawer and placed the notebook inside.

Miffed by Trent, Pamela walked away to get dressed, while Trent took his shower.

Both showered and dressed, Pamela and Trent left his apartment, making their way to the cafeteria for a quick breakfast before heading to the lab. They ate in silence, Pamela still upset with Trent and Trent preoccupied with thoughts about the Ark. Arriving at the lab, they were met by a smiling Hiram, which raised immediate suspicion in Trent and Pamela, since it was so early in the morning.

"Good morning! I have a special assignment for the two of you. The three of us are going to process the reams of data generated by our experiment yesterday. We need to fully understand what took place and make sure everything is documented," said Hiram, well aware of how his young assistants would take the news. Science could be difficult and boring work sometimes. Not always the glamour and excitement some thought it was.

A collective groan rose from his two assistants, as they each went to their workstations and awaited the data. The day passed slowly for the two assistants, who by the end of the day had seen enough data to send them into a mental stupor. Hiram saw the fatigue in his assistants and decided to call it a day.

"I think that's enough for today. We have enough data for our next test tomorrow. Get some rest and I'll see you in the morning," said Hiram.

"Thank you, Hiram. We'll see you in the morning," replied a clearly relieved Pamela.

"Yes. Thank you, Hiram," replied Trent, as he followed Pamela out of the lab.

Asmodeus watched as Lilith opened a gateway from the palace back to the human dimension. Turning, she gave him a coy smile as her sensuous body stepped through. He would be joining her shortly, but first he needed to retrieve something. Asmodeus opened a gateway of his own and stepped through onto the plains of Hell. Before him, was the Cave of Artifacts, guarded by two, ominous, hulking Demons. Within the cave, were assorted technological artifacts left over from the time of the rebellion. Asmodeus approached the cave and the two Demon guards dropped to their shaggy knees, bowing before their King.

Asmodeus entered the cave and then into the artifact chamber, pausing to glance around. Memories of the rebellion came to him and how his fellow Anunnaki had exiled him to Hell. Someday, he and his demon minions would storm the gates of Heaven and exact vengeance on the angels. A more recent addition to the room stood off in a corner, a rifle used by the deceased assassin, Victor Yelenkov. A failed attempt to kill the one named Paul Cross, or rather that scum Valinor. Asmodeus smiled at the thought of Valinor getting caught in the evolving trap being set for him. Vengeance would soon be his after all. His real reason for coming here sat on a shelf to his right. Two small, silver spheres sat there, each a complex generator of various gasses, including sleeping gas. He picked them up and held them in the palm of his hand, where they promptly disappeared into his personal dimensional storage space. That being done, he exited the cave, paused and opened a gateway into the underground facility of DarkBridge Technology.

Lilith exited the gateway into a rarely used corridor near the residential apartments at DarkBridge Technology. Hiding herself from the primitive detection systems, she made her way to Trent's apartment. Reaching his door, she paused and changed her form to a gaseous one, passing through a crack in the doorway with ease. The apartment was empty right now, but she knew Trent and Pamela would eventually return to it. With not much to do but wait, Lilith changed back to her shapely, sensuous human form and lay down on Trent's bed. She would rest and gather as much energy as she could, for her part of the plan would demand much of her.

It was late in the evening, as Asmodeus stepped out of the gateway and exited into a side corridor near the restaurant called Maggie's. The restaurant appeared to be closed, but he could see the woman Maggie inside. The problem was that her demon sight would prevent him from getting closer. Both she and the one called Paul had been given the ability to see both demons and angels, no matter how much they tried to hide. He couldn't risk getting closer and having her raise some sort of alarm. Another reason for using the gas generator was out of an abundance of caution. Asmodeus suspected that there was something protecting Paul from harm but wasn't sure if that same protection extended to Maggie as well. If it did, his plan was doomed, so the next few moments would be critical.

Maggie was behind the bar putting things away and apparently alone. Perfect! Thought Asmodeus, as he clenched his fist and opened it, revealing one of the two silver balls. He set the ball for sleep and opened a tiny gateway near his hand, dropping the ball into it. The other side of the gateway opened up behind the bar and on the floor near Maggie. The ball rolled out of the gateway, stopped and began drawing the restaurant air into it, where it was converted into whatever gas the ball had been set for, then expelling it into the air. In this case it was sleeping gas that began wafting out into the air. Asmodeus watched as the gas began to fill the area behind the bar. Tendrils of gas, invisible to humans, but very visible to him, began wafting around Maggie. The gas reached her nostrils and Asmodeus saw her begin to swoon, slumping to the floor behind the bar, out of security camera view.

Asmodeus walked over to the restaurant door, un-detected by any of the facility sensors. Locating the cameras and sensors inside the restaurant, he wrapped each in a fog of electromagnetic radiation, thoroughly confusing them. Changing his form to a gaseous one, he passed through the doors and into the restaurant. Asmodeus walked over to the bar and saw the woman Maggie on the floor behind it, clearly unconscious. Excellent! He thought, changing his form back to a human one, dressed in a white business suit. It was hard to believe that the woman on the floor had once been the Anunnaki called Shaynor. Wait. There was something else his mind had detected.

The woman had some sort of implant near her right ear. He silently laughed at the primitive device used by the AI, Eva, to communicate with the humans. Quickly waving his hand, a weave of EM energy wrapped itself around Maggie's head, shielding her from communication with Eva. He reached down and retrieved the silver sphere, switching it off. One other thing that he had noticed was that she was wearing some sort of diamene suit under her clothes and a DarkBridge ring on her finger. The suit and ring could present a problem for him, potentially draining his energy away. Instead of carrying her, he opened a gateway and opted to drag the sleeping

Maggie through it. Hopefully, it would be safer than carrying her, he thought to himself, as the gateway closed behind him and the still sleeping Maggie.

The day had been a busy one for Maggie, one of the busiest for her restaurant. Martin had opened the restaurant up to the other ultra "black sites" a couple of weeks ago and business was booming. Patrons from those sites would arrive via gateway at a designated location outside the restaurant, so as not to harm anyone inside. Eva would schedule the transfers with the other "black sites" and whatever AI they were using. Now, late in the evening, she was doing some cleanup, trying to keep her mind off the news Paul had delivered about her First Father, Kalon. It was very confusing to her, both emotionally and intellectually. She had come to terms with her past lives as Shaynor and Darah but was still trying to create a cohesive picture of who she really was.

Questions formed in her mind. What would happen if Kalon was revived? How would she react? What would he expect from her? How would he react to her? All these questions occupied her mind as she cleaned up behind the bar. She didn't notice anything unusual as the invisible gas began wafting around her, encircling her legs, rising to her chest and then her face. Yawning, she decided to call it a night, but it was too late. A feeling of extreme sleepiness came over her, as she grasped the edge of the bar for support. She slumped to the floor, as darkness crept into her mind. A final thought came to her, of Paul worrying where she was and what would happen when he found her. The darkness of sleep overwhelmed her, blotting out everything else and she succumbed to its siren call.

Lilith was relaxing in Trent's bed, gathering her energy in preparation for what was to come. While she lay there, her thoughts turned back to that ancient time in Israel and one memory in particular. It was during the reign of Solomon and much to her distress, her King and lover, Asmodeus, had been banished. It had been the work of Solomon, using ancient Anunnaki technology. Lilith had seethed with anger when she heard the news. She couldn't harm Solomon while he wore that cursed ring, but there had been other ways to hurt him. Killing the one called Darah had been one such way and Lilith smiled at the memory. One of Solomon's wives was intensely jealous of Darah, so Lilith possessed her body and used it to plunge a knife deeply into Darah's neck. It had been well worth it, just to see the pain and anguish on Solomon's face.

Lilith paused in her reverie, sensing Trent and Pamela outside the apartment. Moving off the bed, her form invisible to most humans, she watched as Trent and Pamela entered the apartment. Pamela immediately went into the bathroom, leaving Trent alone. Lilith wasted no time possessing him, pouring her essence once more into the hapless Trent. As she took control of Trent, a glimpse of his mind showed some tension between him and Pamela. Evidently, Pamela had looked at Trent's notebook and seen his drawings of the Ark. Trent hadn't handled it very well, which could eventually put him under greater scrutiny.

It was time to go, thought Lilith. With Pamela still occupied in the bathroom, now was the time. She opened a gateway to the TimeBridge lab and stepped through using Trent's body. From now on, Lilith would be more than just an onlooker. She would be in total control of Trent's motor functions, while putting his mind into a deep sleep. If all went well, Trent would have no memory of what happened, and the Ark would be safely ensconced in Hell.

Trent exited the gateway, finding Asmodeus standing over the prone body of Maggie.

"Is that you, my Queen?" asked a hopeful Asmodeus.

"Yes, it's me, my love," replied Lilith, her voice octaves lower and husky.

"Good. There are two remaining items to take care of, the woman Pamela and that loser Valinor. Here, take this to Trent's apartment, and place it under the bed. We'll retrieve it after it does the job," said Asmodeus, as he handed Lilith one of the silver balls.

Lilith took the silver ball, opened a gateway and stepped through into Trent's apartment. The woman, Pamela appeared to be doing something in the bathroom, so Lilith quickly placed the silver ball under the bed, out of sight. Smiling, she opened a gateway back to the TimeBridge lab and stepped through.

Asmodeus followed with the second silver ball, he had retrieved from the restaurant, sending it to Maggie's apartment, having sensed Valinor's presence there. This ball would also exit under the bed, hidden from Valinor and the AI, Eva.

Pamela opened the door of the bathroom, stepping out and turning the light off. She looked around but didn't see Trent.

"Trent? Where are you?" said Pamela.

There was no answer. She looked around but didn't find him. Sitting down on the corner of the bed, she wondered where he had gone. The silver ball placed under her bed began expelling its contents into the air, tendrils of gas wrapping itself around her body. Her thoughts were still on Trent, as the tendrils reached her nose and she collapsed on the bed, sound asleep.

Paul was lying on Maggie's bed waiting for her to get out of work. His mind was filled with questions, from his discovery in Antarctica to the discovery in the Sinai. Questions about the Skarzi, Commander Kalon and the advanced Anunnaki technology in the cavern, were threatening to send his mind spinning. Taking a deep breath, he closed his eyes, trying to calm his thoughts. Unseen, beneath the bed, a tiny gateway opened, and a silver ball rolled out. The silver ball began expelling its invisible contents into the air, tendrils of gas wafting up around the edges of the bed. Soon, it enveloped him, reaching his nostrils, tendrils of gas working their way up his nose and into his lungs. Paul let out a yawn, surprised that he felt so tired and sleepy. He fought the sleepiness that seemed to be overtaking him, but it seemed to be a losing battle. His last thought before succumbing to the siren call of sleep, was of Maggie and how he had wanted to be awake to greet her. His mind fell into the inky blackness of sleep, his will to fight, overwhelmed. There was now only sleep.

Chapter 19

Angels

Shortly before Lilith's return, Asmodeus gazed down at the sleeping form of Maggie he had placed near the TimeBridge portal. She was a very attractive woman, but any thoughts of unleashing his sexual desires upon her were quickly dashed. One was the fact that she was wearing that cursed DarkWeave suit and the other was that Lilith could show up at any time. He wasn't sure which he feared more. Maggie's breathing was slow and steady, a sign that she would be out for a while longer. His mind quickly shifted back to the task at hand, looking over the primitive control systems for the portal.

Moments later, he began the process of bringing all the systems online. The process triggered ancient memories of his former Anunnaki self and his time as Chief Scientist. Not all the memories were good though, as other memories of being exiled to Hell came to mind.

No matter, he thought. Soon, Valinor would be ensnared in his trap and revenge would be his. No more Valinor or Shaynor for that matter, to thwart his plans. His reverie was suddenly broken, as something tugged at the edge of his perception. A gateway was forming in the lab. Lilith was returning.

Lilith exited the gateway and saw Asmodeus busily working on the various computer systems.

"My love, I have returned. The device is under the bed, waiting to expel its contents", announced Lilith, but the tone of her voice was distinctly baritone, as she manipulated Trent's vocal cords.

Asmodeus turned from his work, a feeling of disgust coming over him at the thought of his Queen inhabiting the body of such a lowly life form.

"My love, why don't you leave that lowly body so that I can properly speak to you", replied Asmodeus.

Lilith complied, keeping Trent's mind in a numb stupor. She flowed out of Trent's body, coalescing into the striking Mediterranean beauty she was more comfortable with.

"Excellent! That's more like it", replied a satisfied Asmodeus.

Lilith strode over to him and pulled his head towards hers and kissed him deeply.

Asmodeus relished the kiss, wanting even more from her, but the plan was more important right now. He reluctantly drew back away from her and steeled himself for what he had to do.

"My love, there is no time for us to indulge ourselves. The plan must go forward," said Asmodeus, sadness showing in his eyes.

"You are right as usual, my King. The humans will soon realize that something is wrong and come here," replied Lilith.

"We must hurry. Do you have everything you need?" asked Asmodeus.

"Yes, my King. The one called Trent has been subconsciously pilfering various items from around this facility and has placed them inside the backpack he wears", answered Lilith, a touch of pride in her voice.

"Excellent. What items has he collected?" asked Asmodeus. He needed to make sure that they were useful items and not the random pilfering of a kleptomaniac. Lilith walked over to Trent, removed the DarkWeave backpack and placed it on the bench near Asmodeus. He reached into the backpack and pulled out a GAGE device, a handgun loaded with diamene coated bullets, a spare ammo clip, a pair of DarkWeave gloves and a pair of DarkVision goggles.

Asmodeus surveyed the items, unsure as to how they would be used. The gun could be used to kill Valinor, the thought bringing a wicked smile to the face of Asmodeus. The primitive gateway device could be used to trap Valinor in some dimension, lost for eternity, which made him smile even more. Convincing himself of their potential usefulness, he began placing everything back into the backpack. Sudden realization came to Asmodeus, as what Lilith had said earlier finally registered in his mind. Trent was wearing a DarkWeave suit! He was immediately fearful for Lilith.

"My love, that human is wearing one of those cursed suits," said Asmodeus, pointing at Trent. His fears disappeared though, when he noticed that Trent wasn't wearing a ring. The ring the others wore appeared to be the conduit between the suit and whatever storage device the humans had developed.

"Don't worry, my King. It seems to function only as body armor and doesn't draw any of my energy," replied Lilith, now having some reservations about it. She had made Trent put it on for his protection. The time period that they were going to, could be potentially dangerous to outsiders and Lilith needed to protect her investment. Trent was one of the very few humans here at this facility that she could safely possess.

A humming noise began to sound from the Time-Bridge portal, as vast amounts of energy began pouring into it, sending arcs of crackling electricity around its perimeter. Asmodeus smiled with satisfaction as the portal stabilized, sending a pulse of energy through the lab. Shimmering with a dark blue color, the portal waited to transport whoever stepped through it.

"Ready. My love, you must hurry. Valinor will eventually follow and try to rescue Shaynor. I believe the humans will reopen this TimeBridge for personnel retrieval at some point, so you must be nearby. It will be your only way back to me," said Asmodeus, as the enormity of what he was asking Lilith to do was beginning to sink in.

"Yes, my King. I will do my best to make the plan a success," replied Lilith, as she once again possessed Trent's body.

"Remember, my love. Do not interact with the Asmodeus, the Lilith or any other demon during that time period. You must preserve the timeline and cause no deviations", said Asmodeus. The more he thought about it, the more he began to doubt his plan. It was extremely dangerous, but if it rid him of Valinor in this timeline, then it would be worth it. Not to mention the possibility of retrieving the Ark.

Lilith left Trent's body one last time and kissed Asmodeus goodbye. Returning to Trent's body, she scooped up the backpack and slung it over her shoulders. Next, she easily lifted up the still sleeping body of Maggie and cradled her in Trent's arms.

"Good luck, my love," said Asmodeus, as Lilith in possession of Trent stepped through the portal carrying Maggie.

Asmodeus watched Lilith step through the portal and into the ancient past. It was up to her now and he took some comfort in her knowledge and abilities. He immediately shut down the portal and powered down the computer systems. Lastly, he removed the electromagnetic fog he had placed on the lab sensors and video devices. Asmodeus let out a small chuckle. The AI, Eva, would have a difficult time explaining what had happened. Opening a gateway back to Hell, Asmodeus stepped through, his plan now underway or was it already completed? Time travel was full of paradoxes, he thought to himself, as he made his way across the pools of lava and into his palace to wait.

It was early evening; the sun had long set, and a cool wind was beginning to blow across the land outside the ancient city of Jerusalem. The young shepherd boy Simon was tending a small flock of goats owned by his family, who were camped not far from where he was standing. A small cooking fire just barely visible, threw golden light across the surrounding tents. A few days ago, he had the excitement of a lifetime, excitement that a young shepherd boy usually never sees. He had actually met King Solomon and watched as he used his powers to cast out demons and bring them under his control.

Fear had run through his blood as the events unfolded, but now much of that fear had subsided. Earlier that day, his father had gone into the city to arrange for the sale of some goats, leaving the flock outside the city. Simon had followed, even though he much preferred the plains around him, over the crowded city. The allure of the city with its street magicians and crowded shops was hard to ignore for a young boy like Simon. Later, when he had told his family of his adventure, they had clapped him on the shoulder, telling him what a fine boy he was. Simon had beamed from all the attention, hoping one day to meet the King once again.

Simon stood looking out over the plain, a cool night wind ruffling his dark hair. His family had decided to keep the flock outside the city, in order to control theft. Off in the distance lay the city of Jerusalem and he could make out torches burning along its high walls. Tired, he sat down on a large rock and drank from the small water skin draped across his neck. The water had cooled with the night air and quenched his thirst as the refreshing liquid ran down his throat. Simon was still gazing at the burning torches of the city, when a flash of light off to his left caught his eye. Not more than a hundred steps away, a shining doorway had appeared. Simon sat in awe, his eyes bulging as two figures stepped out, their forms lit by the glow of the doorway. One figure seemed to be carrying the other.

Simon had heard stories of angels, but had never seen one personally, let alone two. Surely, these were angels, who seemed to have stepped from heaven. The glowing doorway disappeared, and the two figures stood there, one clearly being carried by the other, before heading towards the city. Simon watched them leave, noting that one figure appeared to be female, with long blonde hair. He stumbled as he stood, his body shaking from what he had witnessed. Quickly regaining his feet, he searched for the family camp, his eyes catching the still burning campfire. Rounding up the flock, he managed to get them traveling back towards the camp. Angels! He had seen angels! Simon couldn't wait to tell his parents. Maybe he could once again be of service to the King, he thought to himself.

Chapter 20

Disaster

Eva was confused. Not a good position to be in, for an advanced AI. The video, audio and sensor feeds from the TimeBridge lab had been sending her confusing and meaningless data. She had debated contacting Martin but had decided to wait and investigate on her own. Then, after a short period of time, it had cleared up and everything was back to normal. It was most confusing. Now, she had some other problems to contend with. Pamela was apparently sound asleep and alone. Eva could find no trace of Trent anywhere in the facility. The other problem was with Maggie. Eva had lost all communication with her after Maggie fell asleep in the restaurant. Eva knew that humans sometimes fell asleep at work but wasn't sure if this was an abnormal event or not. Paul also appeared to be sleeping soundly and alone. Eva had no choice now. Martin needed to be told.

Martin was dreaming. Not unusual in itself, but this dream was different. He was a young boy, dressed in shepherd's clothing and watching over a flock of goats. It was night and a campfire blazed some distance away. A dark blue portal appeared nearby, and two figures stepped out, one figure, a man, was carrying a woman with blonde hair. The portal blinked out, leaving the figures in darkness. The young boy watched as the figures set out towards a nearby city that seemed ancient to Martin. The dream wavered as a beeping sound began infringing on his sleep. Martin drifted back to wakefulness and found the beeping noise was Eva, trying to get his attention.

"What's wrong, Eva?" asked a groggy Martin.

"Hello, Martin. I'm sorry to bother you, but there might be a problem. Trent and Maggie are missing, along with some abnormalities in the TimeBridge lab," said Eva.

Martin absorbed what Eva had said, suddenly sitting up in bed at the mention of the lab.

"Eva, contact Hiram and have him check out the lab. I also need the locations of Paul and Pamela," said Martin.

"Paul is in Maggie's apartment and Pamela is in Trent's apartment," replied Eva.

"Okay. Try waking Paul and Pamela, then contact Major Esterbrook and have him go to Maggie's apartment. Have Doctor Curtis meet me at Trent's apartment," ordered Martin.

There was a brief pause as Eva executed Martin's orders.

"I've contacted Hiram, Major Esterbrook and Doctor Curtis. Paul and Pamela are still in a deep sleep and not responding," replied Eva.

"Keep trying to wake them. Now tell me about the lab abnormalities," asked Martin, as he began to dress.

Eva complied and began relating the abnormalities detected from the lab.

Martin listened intently, while he finished dressing. Clearly something had happened in the lab, and it involved Trent and Maggie.

"Thank you, Eva. I'm heading to Trent's apartment now," said Martin, as he exited his apartment and closed the door behind him.

Major Scott Esterbrook was resting in his apartment when the chime sounded alerting him to a possible emergency.

"Scott, Martin needs you to go over to Maggie's apartment and wake up Paul. There's been an incident and Maggie has disappeared," said Eva, concern showing in her voice.

"Thank you, Eva. I'm on it", replied Scott, as he began dressing. He had become a light sleeper since becoming head of security at the DarkBridge facility. He never knew when something important would come up, which seemed to be the case now.

Hiram wasn't asleep, instead working in his apartment on improvements to Project TimeBridge. He yawned, the calculations taxing his tired brain. A chime sounded, alerting him to something important from Eva.

"Hiram, Martin needs you to check out the Project TimeBridge lab. Trent and Maggie are missing. Martin suspects a problem in the lab," said Eva.

"Thank you, Eva. I'm on my way," said Hiram. This could be a real disaster if it was true, thought Hiram. Still dressed, he hurried out of his apartment and headed to the lab. While welcoming the break from intense calculations, he felt a sense of foreboding beginning to overtake him.

Doctor Curtis, likewise, wasn't sleeping yet. He was still in the facility hospital pouring over the medical data from the gunshot wound that Field Investigator Paul Cross had sustained a few months ago. His brow was furrowed in concentration, when a chime sounded announcing a message from Eva.

"Doctor, Martin needs you to meet him at Trent's apartment. There might be a medical emergency. Apparently, she won't wake up", said Eva.

"Thank you, Eva. I'll be there shortly", replied Doctor Curtis, as he gathered up a few things he might need and placed them in his medical bag. It could be a coma, thought Doctor Curtis, as he left the hospital and quickly went to meet Martin.

Martin reached Trent's apartment and was quickly joined by Doctor Curtis.

"Eva, we need emergency access to Trent's apartment," ordered Martin, his anxiety growing.

"I've unlocked the door, Martin", replied Eva.

"Thank you, Eva", said Martin, as he and Doctor Curtis entered the apartment.

They found Pamela lying on the bed fully clothed and still asleep. Doctor Curtis immediately went over to Pamela and began examining her, using a handheld scanner to check her vital signs and check a small sample of blood. Martin was beside himself with concern for his daughter but was relieved when he heard the prognosis.

"She's in a deep sleep, Martin. Her vital signs are good. It's not alcohol induced, and I don't see any evidence of narcotics. We won't know much more until she wakes up", said Doctor Curtis.

"Thank you, Doctor. I'll sit with her until she awakens. Can you go over to Maggie Durham's apartment and examine Paul? He appears to be in the same state as Pamela," asked Martin.

"Yes, of course, Martin. If anything changes for the worse with Pamela, let me know," replied Doctor Curtis.

"Thank you, Doctor", said Martin, as the doctor gathered up his things and left the apartment.

Martin sat down on a nearby chair and watched his daughter. She was his only child and his link to memories of Susan, his deceased wife. Lately, it had been times like this that had made him rethink his position on keeping her here. He had thought that by having his daughter here, he could protect her from all manner of evils, but was that true? Was he actually making things worse? These and other questions weighed on his mind as he patiently waited for Pamela to awaken.

Hiram reached the TimeBridge lab in record time and after passing a retinal and biometric scan, entered the room. Everything looked as it did earlier, before he had left. Hiram went over to the main computer and accessed the TimeBridge activity log. There it was. The TimeBridge portal had been activated a half hour ago. There were coordinates and a time period attached to the activation.

"Eva, can you decode this recent activation and give me the details?" asked a curious Hiram.

"Why yes, Hiram. I would be glad to," replied Eva. A brief pause ensued, and Eva came back with the answer.

"The coordinates point to the city of Jerusalem in Israel and the time period is 930 BC," answered Eva.

"Jerusalem, 930 BC? Are you sure, Eva?" asked a puzzled Hiram.

"I have double checked, and it is correct. My quantum processors give a 90 percent probability that both Maggie and Trent have traveled back in time," replied a confident Eva.

Hiram was dumbfounded. He sat back in his chair letting the enormity of this event sink in, while processing what Eva had said. Two people had traveled back through time for reasons unknown and now the current timeline was in jeopardy. History as they knew it could begin rewriting itself at any moment. Hiram leaped up from his chair, agitated beyond belief.

"Eva, I need to speak with Martin immediately!" exclaimed Hiram.

"Martin is in Trent's apartment waiting for Pamela to awaken. I'll connect you to the room", replied Eva, detecting a high degree of agitation in his voice.

Martin watched for any changes from his sleeping daughter Pamela, but she still seemed firmly mired in a deep sleep. His mind wandered back to the earlier dream he had as a young boy. Curious, he thought. Hopefully, he wouldn't have dreams of dying like Maggie and Paul had a few months ago. Yawning, he rose from his chair and decided to stretch his legs a bit. Scanning the room, he noticed a bookcase with a number of books on ancient civilizations. The majority were of ancient Israel. Trent was one curious individual, thought Martin. He noticed the desk drawer partially open and the corner of a notebook inside caught his eye.

Normally, he would've ignored it, not wanting to pry, but circumstances demanded answers. Opening the drawer and pulling out the notebook, he found nothing unusual, just a lot of calculations and notes on equipment operation. However, as he worked his way towards the middle of the book, he found sketches of what Martin assumed to be the Ark of the Covenant. It was drawn as Martin and everyone alive had come to recognize it. Television, movies and books had all coalesced around the version he was currently looking at. Curious, thought Martin as he closed the notebook. A sound behind him snapped him back to the present. Turning around, he noticed a change in Pamela. She was beginning to awaken.

Major Scott Esterbrook reached Maggie's apartment and was allowed entry by Eva.

He entered the still lighted apartment and carefully made his way towards the bedroom. Curious that the lights were still on, he thought to himself. Reaching the bedroom, he found Paul, flat on his back, lying on the bed fully clothed, as if he had just dropped on it. Scott walked over to the bed and began shaking Paul's shoulders.

"Paul, wake up. It's me, Scott," he said over and over, as he kept shaking Paul.

Finally, Scott noticed a change in Paul as he slowly began to awaken.

Gabriel descended the marble steps of the Grand Meeting Hall and onto the golden streets of Heaven. Tall crystalline spires rose in the distance and a sense of tranquility pervaded the air. He enjoyed the brief respite from human affairs and wished he could do it more often. Unfortunately, events didn't run to his timetable. He had just met with Uriel and Michael, giving them a synopsis of everything that had recently transpired and was now on his way back to the DarkBridge facility to check on things. The time disparity between Heaven and Earth meant that some number of hours had passed by. Hopefully, nothing serious had happened within that period of time, but he knew it was probably wishful thinking.

Chapter 21

Awakenings

Pamela's eyes fluttered open, as she tried to make sense of what happened. She remembered stepping out of the bathroom and sitting on the bed, then everything went black. She must have been awfully tired to have passed out like that. Her eyes focused on the room, and she sensed that she wasn't alone. A familiar voice called out to her.

"Hello, Pamela. It's me. I'm glad you're waking up. We were worried about you," said Martin, fatherly concern showing in his voice.

"Hello, Father. I was only sleeping. Why would that cause so much concern?" asked a puzzled Pamela, as she slowly rose to a sitting position and noticed a sweet taste in her mouth. Odd, she thought to herself.

"Normally, it wouldn't, but someone else is also in a similar deep sleep. However, there is another more serious problem," replied Martin.

"Who else is affected and what is this problem?" inquired Pamela.

"Paul is in a similar state. The problem is with Trent and Maggie," said Martin.

"Paul? Trent? Maggie? What's going on?" said Pamela, who was beginning to feel a sense of concern.

"Paul fell into a deep sleep around the same time as you. Trent and Maggie appear to have disappeared from the facility. It's possible that TimeBridge was used. Hiram is investigating as we speak. Major Esterbrook is with Paul, waiting for him to awaken," said Martin, hoping that he hadn't thrown too much at his daughter.

Pamela took a few minutes to process everything her father had said.

Eva suddenly interrupted, "Martin, Hiram has some important news and is on his way".

"Thank you, Eva. Pamela is awake and we'll see what news Hiram has. Any word on Paul?" asked Martin, who was sensing some answers coming.

"Major Esterbrook, reports that Paul is beginning to waken. Hello, Pamela. I'm glad you're okay", said Eva.

"Thank you, Eva. I'm still not sure what all the fuss is about", replied Pamela, her thoughts turning to Trent. Why was Maggie involved? Questions were starting to mount.

The door chime sounded once and then repeatedly, as if someone highly excited wanted entry. That would be Hiram, thought Martin to himself. He stood and walked to the door. Opening the door, he was almost knocked over, as a bespectacled Hiram rushed in, agitated and extremely excited.

"Martin! I have bad news! There was a TimeBridge activation! Trent and Maggie have gone into the past!" said an agitated Hiram.

Martin, still recovering from almost being knocked over, collected his thoughts and prepared himself for the answer to his next question.

"Where and when did they travel to?" asked Martin.

"The time period was 930 B.C., and the place was Israel, specifically ancient Jerusalem", said Hiram, his agitation and excitement increasing with every spoken word.

A gasp came from nearby, as Pamela had left the bedroom to hear what Hiram had to say.

"930 B.C.? Jerusalem?" said Martin, as something began to tug at his thoughts. He had seen something recently. It was something that had existed at that time period. Martin walked over to the desk and opened the notebook to the drawings of the Ark. Could it possibly be related? He thought to himself.

"Hiram, Pamela, come over here and see this," said Martin, as pieces began to fall into place.

Pamela walked over to her father, noticing the same notebook that Trent had been so defensive about.

"I've seen that, Father. Trent and I got into an argument about it, and he seemed very defensive about it," replied Pamela.

Hiram got up from his chair, joining Martin and Pamela. His eyes widened as he saw the drawings.

He too was familiar with the legend and its supposed power. The scientist in him began extrapolating the potential catastrophes that could arise.

"What does this mean, Hiram?" asked Martin.

"It could mean many things, Martin. If the stories are true and Trent is intent on stealing the Ark, then he will be in possession of immense power. There is a more pressing issue," replied Hiram.

"What could be more pressing?" asked Pamela, who couldn't bring herself to believe that Trent would do something so foolhardy. It must be that Maggie, thought Pamela.

"Trent and Maggie have gone into the past. Therefore, they no longer exist in this timeline. It will take time for the effects to ripple up from that time to ours, but soon, there will be no memory of Trent or Maggie. There is also the possibility that Trent or Maggie could change events and that would also ripple up to our timeline. We could find ourselves written out of history or living in times that are nothing like they are now," said Hiram, who went back to a nearby chair and sat down.

Pamela began to feel fear, but Martin put his hand around her shoulder in a fatherly way and made a decision.

"It looks like we have no choice, and we must act quickly. We need to rescue Trent and Maggie from a bad decision and a potential disaster for mankind, Eva, have Scott and Paul meet us in my office when they are ready," said Martin.

"I've relayed the information to Scott, who is still waiting for Paul to awaken", replied Eva.

"Thank you, Eva", said Martin, as he began formulating a rescue plan.

Paul drifted up from a sea of blackness. Someone was calling his name and was very insistent. It hadn't been all blackness though. Another Valinor memory had come to him. He was a young recruit, just entering pilot training for the Anunnaki Space Fleet. Part of the training had involved low level exposures to various gasses. Nothing fatal, but enough to help recruits learn how to react to exposure. One of the gasses had been an aerosol sleep agent, called Zerg 7. It could be dispersed in a variety of ways and caused the victim to lose consciousness immediately. The effect felt like a deep sleep, with no lasting effects. It was difficult to detect but left a sweet taste in the mouth.

The memory faded away, as Paul slowly drifted back to wakefulness. His eyes opened, blinked a few times as he took in his surroundings. He was still in Maggie's apartment and lying on her bed. There was a sweet taste in his mouth and the Valinor memory came back to him. Zerg 7 had been used on him. It wasn't something one encountered every day and known only to Anunnaki.

Paul didn't think it was Gabriel or the angels, but he couldn't rule out Asmodeus. His thoughts were interrupted by someone next to the bed, calling his name.

"Welcome back, Paul," said Scott, who had been actively trying to wake Paul.

"Scott? Why are you here?" asked Paul.

"You were in a deep sleep and wouldn't wake up. Martin sent me here to wake you. Pamela was also affected in the same way. Martin is with her. There is one more thing. Trent and Maggie have disappeared and are no longer in the facility", replied Scott.

"Maggie? Trent? Pamela? We need to see Martin right now. Help me up," said Paul.

Scott helped Paul to his feet, steadying him as he rose.

"Martin has asked us to meet him in his office when you're ready" asked Scott.

"Eva, is Martin in his office?" asked a still groggy Paul.

"Yes. Pamela and Hiram are also with him. Good to see you awake, Paul" replied Eva.

"Thank you, Eva. Alert Martin that Scott and I are on the way," said Paul, pausing to clear his head.

"Thank you, Scott", said Paul.

"Not a problem. Let's go see Martin", replied Scott, helping Paul to the door, as the two of them left Maggie's apartment.

Gabriel stepped out of the gateway and into an unused corridor at the underground facility of DarkBridge Technology. He had just come from Heaven after discussing all the recent happenings and discoveries. Both Michael and Uriel had been shocked at the discovery of Commander Kalon and his son Jalon. Both had agreed that Maggie should be allowed to decide on revival. Evidently, Raphael had been busy in the past, sequestering the Ark and the two cryogenic chambers in the cavern. Uriel had commented on Raphael's long absence and Gabriel had echoed a similar feeling. They weren't sure where he could be, but very sure that he was still alive. Gabriel paused in the corridor at the facility and summoned the orb from wherever it was. He didn't have to wait long, before the small golden orb appeared. Gabriel held out the palm of his hand and the orb gently settled onto it. Linking his mind to the orb, Gabriel saw everything the orb had seen, which soon elicited a gasp from him.

Much had transpired in his absence and all of it full of dangerous portents. The orb had managed to record a number of events, most importantly was the one where Asmodeus had activated TimeBridge, sending Trent and Maggie somewhere in time. Gabriel watched with fascination as the DarkBridge team had successfully tested TimeBridge, setting the stage for Asmodeus. Gabriel knew that the humans were experimenting with time travel but didn't know they had been so successful. Obviously, they had some help, possibly by Asmodeus himself, in order to accomplish whatever foul deed, he was planning. The orb had managed to stay hidden inside the lab, watching as Asmodeus activated TimeBridge. Trent had stepped through the portal, carrying Maggie with him. Gabriel had seen Lilith emerge from Trent's body earlier and kiss Asmodeus, an obvious sign that Trent had no idea what was happening. Where they had gone, the orb couldn't tell, but maybe the humans had some idea.

Gabriel decided to check Maggie's apartment first, since she and Paul had been spending so much time together. He opened a gateway and stepped into the apartment. Empty, he thought to himself. He stepped into the bedroom and immediately noticed the faint EM signature of some type of gaseous vapor. A long-forgotten memory came to him. It was of an ancient Anunnaki sleeping gas called Zerg 7. Not many knew of it, much less how to deploy it. There was one person that knew and may have had cause to use it, Asmodeus. Gabriel needed to find Paul and figure out what was really going on here. He concentrated once again, this time searching for the life energy that was Paul. He found it, not too far away, in what Gabriel sensed was an office. Probably Martin's, thought Gabriel. Closing his hand around the orb, it quickly disappeared into his personal dimensional storage space, ready to be recalled at a moment's notice. Opening a gateway to Paul's location, he paused before stepping through. For the first time in a long time, he had a disquieting feeling that events were beginning to spiral out of control. He needed more information and answers, so there was only one thing to do. He stepped through the gateway.

Chapter 22

The Meeting

Paul was growing increasingly concerned for Maggie's wellbeing as he and Scott made their way to Martin's office. He was beginning to feel as if someone had reached deep into his core being and ripped something out. Maggie and Trent had disappeared from the facility and Paul would bet his life that she was an unwilling participant. He thought about Trent, remembering that time a few months ago in the corridor, when he'd seen something lurking behind Trent's eyes. It had been the Queen of Demons, Lilith, as Paul would later come to realize. If Lilith were involved somehow, then by extension that would include Asmodeus, the King of Demons. Long ago, Asmodeus had vowed vengeance on Valinor and all his subsequent incarnations, including Paul. It was still an incomplete puzzle, with many missing pieces, but maybe Martin had discovered a few of those pieces.

Paul and Scott soon reached Martin's office and finding the door open, they stepped inside. Waiting inside were Martin, Hiram and Pamela, who seemed to be fighting to stay in control of her emotions.

"Hello Paul. Hello Scott. I'm glad to see you're okay Paul. I thought it would be a good idea to get everyone together and discuss what happened. We will also discuss an immediate response. Time, pardon the pun, is of the essence. Let's go in the conference room," said Martin as he gestured towards the room.

Everyone entered the conference room, took positions around the large table and sat down. Just as they sat down, Paul noticed Gabriel standing in the doorway. Gabriel gave Paul a nod and Paul discretely winked in return. Apparently, Gabriel could only be seen by Paul, making for some awkwardness. Martin was the first to speak.

"As you all know, Trent and Maggie have disappeared from the facility. It appears that TimeBridge was used to send the both of them back in time, to ancient Jerusalem. Specifically, 930 B.C., the time of King Solomon," Martin paused for a moment, before continuing.

"We've managed to find a possible motive, which seems to revolve around the fabled Ark of the Covenant. Trent apparently had a fixation with it and may have played a role in this. Paul and Pamela were both affected by some type of sleeping gas, presumably to keep them from interfering with Trent's plan. I'll let Hiram take over now, on the ramifications of what has happened," said Martin as he eased back into his chair.

Hiram adjusted his glasses and cleared his throat, trying to control his sense of impending doom.

"What's happened is nothing less than catastrophic. We have no idea what changes Trent and Maggie have caused by traveling into the past. Every change in events, small or large, will begin to ripple up through time, until those accumulated changes reach our time period. At that point, much of what is familiar will be lost and replaced with things completely alien to us. Some of us may even cease to exist as we are written out of history. The paradoxes with time travel are numerous, such as the fact that Trent and Maggie have now been dead for some three thousand years now, even though they just left a couple of hours ago. However, to them, they are still alive in the past and only a couple of hours have gone by. Martin?" said Hiram, as he turned the meeting back over to Martin.

"Thank you, Hiram. What you've said underscores what I'm about to say. We need to retrieve Trent and Maggie from the past as soon as possible. The ripples may be upon us soon, so we need to act now. I'd like to make this voluntary, but the situation is just too dire to trust anyone else. I'd like the two of you to go", said Martin, as he looked at Scott and Paul.

Paul looked at Scott and they both nodded their assent.

"Good. Now, I need a scientist", said Martin, as he gathered up his strength. It was a difficult decision for him, possibly the most difficult in his life. He had run through all the possible people for this position on the team, but it had come down to only one individual.

"Pamela. I need you to accompany Scott and Paul. Hiram is too old to go, and I need him here. You're the one most qualified, with knowledge of all the scientific aspects of this mission," said Martin, his shoulders slumping with the added burden of sending his only daughter on a mission filled with unknown danger. It was times like this that made him wish he wasn't the boss.

"It's okay, father. I want to go. Maybe seeing a familiar face will dissuade Trent," replied Pamela, seeing a pain in her father's eyes that she hadn't seen since her mother's death some years ago.

Paul sat there taking in everything that was being said with quiet resignation. His stomach had lurched, when Hiram had mentioned Maggie being dead for three thousand years. Hopefully, the people in this room would help make this rescue attempt a success. Paul had glanced at Gabriel, noticing him leave right after Hiram talked about the ripples in time and catastrophic changes. Something had worried Gabriel, enough to cause him to leave, which only added to Paul's worry.

Suddenly, Paul felt his mind lurch, as if someone had shaken it with both hands. He looked around the room, noticing that the others had felt the same thing.

"Did everyone just feel that?" asked Martin.

Everyone nodded, but whatever further discussion was interrupted by Eva.

"Martin, Areas 51, 52 and the other black sites are off-line. I cannot reestablish contact. It's as if they no longer exist. Exterior surveillance monitors are showing a large column of armored vehicles approaching the facility from Bennington", said Eva.

"Do we know what they want?" asked Martin.

"I'm receiving a radio transmission from the approaching vehicles. Commander Karl Schmidt is demanding that we surrender the facility in two hours", replied Eva.

"Surrender to who?" asked an incredulous Martin.

"Commander Karl Schmidt. Martin, they are not from the U.S. government. They say we are a rebel installation working against the interests of the 4th Reich. I've checked the news feeds and it looks like the United States no longer exists. We now belong to something called the 4th Reich. Apparently, Germany won WWII," replied Eva.

"What!" exclaimed Martin, as he slumped back into his chair. Obviously, Karl was still alive in this apparently new timeline.

"It has begun and will get much worse", said a somber Hiram.

Martin's mind was reeling. Two hours and then the facility would probably be under attack, his employees in danger and who knows what else. It was time to go.

"Paul, Scott and Pamela meet Hiram and me in the TimeBridge lab. Dress in desert gear, DarkWeave suits, diamene ammo, weapons and whatever else you might need. I'll give you thirty minutes," ordered Martin.

Everyone, but Martin, filed out of the conference room. Hiram headed back to the TimeBridge lab, Pamela, Scott and Paul left to prepare for the rescue attempt. Martin, alone with his thoughts, contemplated the future of his company and the people working for him. He had no idea what the current political situation was, and the approaching armored column didn't give him a warm fuzzy feeling. No, like Hiram said, things were only going to get worse. There was only one thing to do.

"Eva, execute emergency plan Ghost in one hour", said Martin. Ghost was a last resort plan to evacuate the facility, via gateway, to the beta site. Martin had foreseen the need for an alternate site, just in case something catastrophic were to occur, such as this. After abandoning the facility, charges would detonate, collapsing the elevator shaft and entrances to the facility under tons of rock and debris. They would still be able to gateway back into the underground facility if needed. The above ground installation would then be leveled by explosive charges set throughout the building.

"Eva, recall all the sentry robots. We will be taking them with us to the beta site," said Martin.

"All set, Martin. The sentries are returning as we speak," replied Eva.

"Excellent. Now, have all facility personnel start assembling in the underground park. We will initiate the beta site transfer there in one hour," ordered Martin.

"I've notified all facility personnel, Martin," replied Eva.

"Thank you, Eva. I have a few things to gather up in my office before joining Hiram in the lab," said a somber Martin.

He rose from his chair and exited the conference room and into his office, where he surveyed the various items there. His office above ground was sparsely decorated, more for show, with no personal items. At least it was one thing he didn't have to worry about, he mused. He took the pictures of Susan and Pamela off the wall and tucked them under his arm. There was another picture on his desk, a group picture of him, Susan and Pamela, standing in front of the old DarkBridge Technology building outside Boston. He tucked this one under his arm as well.

In a display case set against a far wall, was one of Hiram's first experiments in matter phasing. The cinder block with the metal spike embedded in it would have to remain, since it was a little too heavy to carry right now.

The underground facility would probably remain intact, so he could always retrieve it later. It was going to be hard to leave it all behind after years of building DarkBridge Technology into the company it currently was. Sighing, he walked over to the door, closed it behind him and made his way to the TimeBridge lab. As he walked down the hallway, Martin thought about the cinder block and the day he had visited Hiram at his farmhouse.

A few weeks after their meeting at the conference, Martin received a phone call at work from Hiram inviting him to his house in upstate New York to talk about the job. Martin, excited with the prospect of getting another chance to hire Dr. Greenwood, gladly accepted. Writing down the directions given by Dr. Greenwood, they both agreed that tomorrow morning would be a good time to meet. Arrangements made, they said their goodbyes. Martin went home that night feeling positive about the meeting tomorrow. It had been a good day, made all the more special by his wife Susan and daughter Pamela, who greeted him at the door and were waiting to have dinner with him. It was one of those times that Martin remembered fondly, a nice family dinner spent with loved ones and a memory of happier times.

Martin had woken up very early the next day, making the long drive out to upstate New York and his important meeting with Dr. Greenwood. Arriving at the address given to him, Martin noted that it wasn't quite what he was expecting. There was a crooked, rusty mailbox near the street, marking the beginning of a long, winding, gravel driveway, bracketed by tall trees on either side that blocked his view of the house. Martin turned his black SUV into the driveway, advancing slowly until a house came into sight. Instead of a typical modern house, Martin saw an old, weather-beaten, gray farmhouse trimmed in white, with what appeared to be a large, similarly colored barn standing nearby.

When he was ready, he got out of the SUV, his polished black shoes crunching on the gravel as he swung the driver's side door closed behind him. He walked up the steps of the expansive front porch and stopped at the front door. He rang the doorbell once, twice and then a third time. No one came to the door. He was about to ring it a fourth time, when a voice called out to him from the direction of the barn. It was Hiram.

"Hello, Martin! Please, come join me in the lab!" said Dr. Greenwood, motioning towards the barn.

Martin made his way over to the barn, which seemed more imposing the closer he came to it. Dr. Greenwood had already gone inside, so Martin walked right in, closing the door behind him. The sight that greeted his eyes was like something out of a sci-fi movie and gave new meaning to the phrase "mad scientist."

Strewn about the interior of the barn were tables loaded with various types of scientific equipment and racks upon racks of spare parts, both used and new. On one bench sat a concrete block with a large metal spike suspended above it in such a way that it barely touched the top of the block. Large inductive coils were arranged around the block and connected to a series of sophisticated power supplies. Martin wondered about the purpose of this interesting experiment.

"Hello, Martin!" said Dr. Greenwood.

Martin turned to see Hiram standing near a rack of lab equipment. "Hiram! Good to see you again!" replied Martin with a smile.

Hiram walked over to Martin and extended his hand, which Martin shook firmly.

"I see you've been admiring my latest experiment in matter phasing," said Hiram, pointing to the concrete cinder block.

"Matter phasing?" asked a puzzled Martin.

"Yes. Theoretically, if we can get solid matter to behave in a certain way, then that metal spike should just sink into the block and become part of it. The atoms of the spike will bind to those of block. The electrical items you see surrounding the block are the means to do that," explained Hiram.

"Amazing', said Martin, a skeptical look on his face.

"I assure you, it will work," said Hiram confidently. "So, tell me more about DarkBridge Technology and what your future plans are."

Martin launched into an explanation of why he had started DarkBridge Technology and what he hoped to achieve, including his vision for developing dimensional gateways that could transport people, supplies and equipment anywhere on earth and beyond in the blink of an eye.

Hiram listened intently, asking questions here and there.

When Martin was done, Hiram said, "Most interesting and exactly what I was hoping you would say."

"Have you thought about my offer?" asked Martin, trying not to sound too anxious.

Hiram adjusted his eyeglasses, shoved his hands inside the pockets of his rumpled, white lab coat and looked down his nose at Martin. "I've checked out your company, Martin. Your margins are tight, your facility is small, and your staff is limited." Martin opened his mouth to speak, but Hiram raised a finger to silence him. "However, I have decided that I would like to join your company, providing of course, that I be given free rein on my research and a suitable salary."

Martin didn't know whether to jump for joy or be offended. "I am prepared to offer you a 25 percent stake in the company, with the title of Vice President of Research and Development. Your salary will be a bit low at first, since we are still in the start-up phase. That will change as we develop marketable products," replied Martin, hoping that salary wouldn't be a deal breaker. Money was tight right now and the future murky at best, but Martin saw a path forward and hoped that Hiram would too.

"I accept. We can re-negotiate salary later, as long as I get to do the research that I enjoy," said a beaming Hiram.

"It's a deal! Welcome to DarkBridge Technology, Hiram. With you leading our research team, I'm sure the company will be a huge success," said Martin, with an enthusiastic shake of Hiram's hand. Martin was very pleased; the meeting had gone much better than he had expected, and he had a new business partner.

"We'll make it a success together, Martin," said Hiram, as he warmly returned the handshake.

Martin said good-bye, leaving Hiram to his experiments. As he drove away, he had a very positive feeling about the future of his company and the contributions it would make to the advancement of science. Over the next few weeks, Martin and Hiram worked out arrangements to move most of Hiram's lab equipment into a larger, more modern, leased facility outside Boston.

Martin was jolted back to reality, almost bumping into a group of technicians who were making preparations for evacuation. Apologizing to the group, Martin continued on his way to the lab.

Gabriel had left the conference room with great urgency. He knew Paul was the only one that would notice him gone. The situation was indeed very dire, and he sensed a large number of vehicles approaching the facility. He had a bad feeling about it and his sense of reality was beginning to shift. It felt as if the things he had come to know were being replaced by things he was unfamiliar with. As the human, Hiram had said, changes in the past were beginning to ripple up to the present. He needed to check on something immediately, so he opened a gateway and stepped through it.

He emerged inside the cavern in Antarctica and paused. Concentrating, he closed his hand and opened it, revealing a small golden orb. The orb rose into the air, towards the cavern ceiling and began emitting a bright light, illuminating the surrounding area. Gabriel looked towards where he and Paul had seen the Ark not that long ago. It was gone. The place where the Ark has been stored was empty, as if it had never been there. Gabriel, gravely concerned, shifted his gaze to where he and Paul had seen the two cryogenic chambers. Thankfully, they were still there and functioning. Whatever the changes to the past, they hadn't yet affected the sleeping Anunnaki.

Gabriel thought back to the conference room and what Martin and Hiram had said. Trent and Maggie had traveled back to ancient Jerusalem, specifically the time of King Solomon. The Ark was in Jerusalem at that time and Solomon had been given a ring to tap into its vast powers. Solomon. He was another incarnation of his long dead friend, Valinor, who had been killed by Belial. Recent events had shown Paul to be yet another incarnation of Valinor, just as Maggie was another incarnation of Shaynor. Gabriel recalled something else from that time period, the Skarzi. The Skarzi had been involved in some activity around Jerusalem during the time of Solomon, but had seemed to vanish during that time. What had happened to them was a mystery. His fellow angel, Raphael would probably have some answers, since Jerusalem was his responsibility at that time. Unfortunately, Raphael hadn't been seen for some time, so it was up to Gabriel to find the answers.

As he stood in the vast cavern, Gabriel's mind began weaving the different threads of events into a tapestry that would explain what was going on. The human Trent must be the key. Paul had told him of Lilith's possession and Gabriel wondered if that explained some of what was going on. Lilith wouldn't act on her own, not without the full countenance of Asmodeus. So, what was the plan? The human, Martin, had referred to Trent's fixation with the Ark. Was it really his fixation or Lilith's? What of Maggie? She had clearly been taken against her will and must be serving some other purpose. Who would most likely want to rescue her? Paul. Gabriel's golden aura, shown even brighter, as the plan dawned on him, or what he surmised was the plan. Lilith was there to steal the Ark and Maggie was bait to draw Paul back into the past. For what reason, Gabriel didn't know. He did know one thing. He had to speak with Paul before he traveled back in time. With that thought in mind, Gabriel opened a gateway and left the cavern.

Chapter 23

Preparations

Pamela was the first to leave Martin's office, followed by Scott and Paul. She left the conference room with a gnawing fear that maybe this rescue attempt would be too dangerous and doomed to failure. Not wanting to disappoint Martin, her father, she kept her fears tightly controlled, hidden under a mask of supreme confidence. A cough from behind her made her pause.

"Pamela. Can we talk for a bit?" asked Paul, as he caught up to her.

"I'll meet the two of you in Hiram's lab. I need to get a few things from the armory", said Scott, giving Paul a knowing wink. He'd rather not be part of a conversation that could get personal.

"See you there, Scott," replied Pamela.

"Yes, see you there, Scott", echoed Paul.

Pamela stood and watched Scott's receding figure waiting until he was out of earshot.

"Okay, Paul. What is it that you want to talk about?" asked a curious Pamela, as she gazed at him with her dazzling green eyes.

She had two options here, she thought to herself. She could be confrontational and tell him that the re-incarnation thing was a load of crap, along with his past lives with Maggie and the ensuing instant connection he felt with her. Or she could take a different tack and use a little honey. The latter seemed much more appealing, so she chose it instead. Gazing at Paul with her spar-kling green eyes, she added a warm smile to enhance the effect.

Paul was briefly at a loss for words, as Pamela's eyes and smile beckoned him with enticement. A quick thought of Maggie broke the spell and Paul regained his voice.

"I just wanted to tell you that it was a very brave thing for you to volunteer. Scott and I would probably have a tough time without you on the technical issues. I also wanted to tell you that Scott and I will do everything possible to make sure you make it back. I know it must be a difficult decision for Martin to make", said Paul, trying to keep this somewhat professional.

"Thank you, Paul. I know you and Scott will do what-ever it takes to keep me safe. It's rather sweet, I think", said Pamela, as she drew close to Paul and kissed him on the cheek.

Paul was momentarily stunned by the kiss, taking him completely by surprise.

Pamela's eyes danced as she saw the effect that her kiss had on Paul. Feeling pressed for time, she broke the spell, "Now, let's get our things and meet Scott in the lab".

"Yes. Good idea", said Paul, as he regained his composure. Hopefully, Maggie never hears about this, otherwise there would be fifty levels of Hell for him to go through.

Pamela and Paul continued walking down the corridor in silence, stealing glances at one another as they walked. Eventually they parted, splitting off and going to their own apartments to prepare.

Pamela reached her apartment and upon entering, found a garment bag draped across the sofa. She unzipped it and found a long, hooded Hebrew robe, some desert fatigues, a special DarkWeave backpack and desert boots inside.

"Hello, Pamela. I had a garment bag with some needed items delivered to your apartment," said Eva.

"Thank you, Eva. I'll probably need all of it," replied Pamela.

"I also downloaded a small AI version of me into your quantum PDA. I call her Little Eva," said Eva with a touch of pride.

"Little Eva? That's a cute name," said Pamela.

"It's the best I can do since you'll be out of contact. Little Eva will also be able to communicate with your implants and assist with technical issues," said Eva.

"Excellent. We'll need all the help we can get," said Pamela. Hiram would probably give her a few more items to take.

Next, she went over to her closet and pulled out her DarkWeave suit. Being the owner's daughter had its perks. Martin had given it to her in case of emergency. She stripped down to her underwear and donned the form fitting suit. Going back to the garment bag, she slipped into the desert fatigues, pulled the boots on and took the backpack over to her desk and placed the PDA into an inside pocket. The PDA, or personal data assistant, was already a fairly powerful computer with its quantum processor, but now with the added intelligence of Little Eva, it was even more powerful.

"I think that's it, Eva. I'm headed to the lab," said Pamela.

"Good luck, Pamela. I know Martin will be worried about you. It was a difficult decision for him," replied Eva.

"Yes. I could see the pain on his face. Thank you, Eva," replied Pamela. With that, she put the backpack on, slung the robe over her left arm and exited her apartment.

Paul had parted with Pamela, making his way to his own apartment. Upon entering, he saw a similar garment bag on his sofa. Walking over to the bag, he unzipped it and found a hooded Hebrew robe inside. Next, he made his way over to his closet and pulled out his desert clothing. He already wore his DarkWeave suit, so he pulled off his current casual clothing and put on the desert gear. Locating his DarkWeave backpack, he placed a medical kit, DarkVision goggles, DarkWeave gloves and a few other items inside.

"Paul, are you okay?" asked a concerned Eva.

"I'm okay, Eva. Just very worried about Maggie," replied Paul. Hiram's words about her being dead for three thousand years, was weighing heavily on his mind.

"I'm still learning about human emotions, but I can safely say that I miss her too. As odd as it might sound, Maggie is like a sister to me", replied Eva, a trace of emotion showing in her voice.

"Maggie is very fond of you too, Eva. As am I", said Paul.

"Why thank you, Paul", replied Eva, sounding rather happy.

"Time to get going, Eva. Scott and Pamela will be waiting," said Paul.

"Good luck, Paul. Pamela has a small AI version of me loaded into her PDA. Her name is Little Eva," said Eva, with some pride.

"Little Eva. I like it. It'll be good to have a familiar voice with us. Goodbye, Eva," replied Paul as he slung the backpack over his shoulder and headed towards the door.

"Goodbye and good luck, Paul," said Eva, a touch of sadness entering her voice.

Paul left the apartment, hurrying towards Hiram's lab and an outcome he wasn't sure about.

Scott left Pamela and Paul, walking quickly down the corridor. He could tell that Pamela still had feelings for Paul, but he wasn't quite sure where Paul stood. Scott liked Paul. They were both ex-military and shared that special bond that comes from serving your country. Pamela was something different. She was Martin's daughter and Scott treated her with the utmost professionalism. You don't mess with the daughter of your boss. Maybe Paul had contemplated doing that before, but when Maggie joined the facility, the friendship that Pamela and Paul once shared, now seemed somewhat strained.

Scott could feel the animosity that Pamela exuded towards Maggie and right now that bothered him. How would she act towards Maggie on this rescue mission? Would the mission be jeopardized by taking her along? Scott didn't know, but he would be vigilant. Everyone needed to come back alive and that included Trent. Scott soon reached the facility security room and found his locker. Inside was his DarkWeave suit, desert gear and surprisingly, a hooded Hebrew robe. He removed his current fatigues and donned the DarkWeave suit. Next, he put on his desert gear, draped the robe over his shoulder, closed the locker and went over to the weapons storage room.

A quick biometric scan and the door unlocked, allowing him access to the room. Inside were racks of automatic rifles, small arms, ammo clips and other items. He was very observant to things missing or out of place and right away noticed missing items. There was a handgun missing and a couple of diamene bullet clips missing. That was bad news. If Trent had those, then the rescue team would be in danger. A diamene bullet could cause serious injury or death. One just had to look at Paul's experience to see the danger. Scott also remembered the alien creature found in Paul's sanctuary and the dense body armor it was wearing.

He opted for diamene ammo just in case, along with three handguns, a dozen ammo clips with diamene bullets, a tranquilizer gun and darts, a high-capacity sniper rifle and a DarkWeave backpack. He slung the rifle over his shoulder, loaded everything else into the backpack and left the weapons room. He didn't know what was going to happen once they stepped through the Time-Bridge portal, but this was certainly a situation where he would rely heavily on his military training. With grim determination, he headed towards the TimeBridge lab, his mind replaying every movie or television show he had seen about those ancient times.

Vermont Guardian watched the events unfolding above it, conferring with the other Guardians on how things were progressing. So far, everything was progressing within the events they had seen and predicted. The humans had discovered time travel and the demons had capitalized on it. The demon Lilith had been successful in retrieving the Ark and that act had changed the flow of time, sending it off and onto a new branch. That branch resulted in the defeat of the Allies in World War II and the eventual rise of the 4th Reich. Vermont Guardian had placed a protective bubble around the DarkBridge facility, slowing the changes that were happening.

Soon, the facility would be engulfed by the inexorable changes that were taking place. The humans were making plans to escape to another dimension, which should save them from the violent forces arrayed outside the facility. Paul and two other humans would soon embark on a rescue mission that would correct the changes that were taking place. At least that was the hope. Even amongst themselves, there were one or two Guardians who didn't think they would succeed. Only time would tell. Vermont Guardian would be rooting for the humans.

Chapter 24

Rescue Mission

Martin reached the TimeBridge lab and after passing the biometric security checks, entered the lab. Hiram was seated at a bench tapping away furiously on a virtual keyboard.

"Hello, Hiram. Are we almost ready to go?" asked Martin.

"Hi, Martin. The QASM units are charging and almost at the required level. We should be ready in a few minutes", replied Hiram, gazing at Martin over the top of his glasses.

"Very good. I guess we're just waiting for the team to arrive. What do you think our chances are?" asked Martin.

"I assume you mean our chances of success. Honestly, I think they are slim, for many reasons. We've only had one real test of the TimeBridge portal and that was with a drone. We really don't know if humans can survive transport and we don't really know if Trent and Maggie survived. It's very risky, Martin", replied Hiram with a sigh.

Martin listened to Hiram's words and the weight he felt on his heart only grew heavier. He was about to send three people into the unknown and without much chance of success. The fact that his daughter, Pamela, was among the three only made the burden worse. There wasn't much choice. What was happening outside the facility was true evil descending upon them. The chances were slim, but Martin would take the chance, if it meant correcting the timeline and getting things back to normal.

"Thank you, Hiram. Do what you can to get things ready. The team should be here shortly.

Hiram got back to work on his calculations, trying to get the TimeBridge timing as close as possible to the departure time of Trent and Maggie.

Martin had just finished speaking, when the team members began filing in. First to arrive was Pamela, fol- lowed by Paul and then Scott. Martin greeted the three, trying to hide any misgivings and noticed that all three were wearing desert gear, DarkWeave suits and Hebrew robes. He didn't know if all of it was necessary, but better to be prepared than not.

"You're all right on time. Thank you all for doing this. I have some gifts from Dr. Curtis and from Hiram", said Martin, as he passed out three emergency medical kits and three GAGE devices. The team members took the medical kits and GAGE devices and placed them in their backpacks. Martin then handed out two, quart bottles of water and packages of disinfecting tablets, to be used to make whatever water they found, potable. He also passed out a few MRE's, meals ready to eat, in case they got hungry and couldn't find local sources of food.

"That's all I can safely give you to carry. Anything more and the backpacks would be too unwieldy. I have, however, made sure that Paul's dimensional sanctuary is stocked with supplies. I think Scott has some things of his own to share", said Martin.

"Thank you, Martin. I have a few things from the armory to distribute and some unsettling news. A handgun, holster and diamene ammo clips are missing from the armory. Surveillance cameras showed it was Trent that took them", said Scott, as he passed out handguns, holsters and diamene ammo clips to Paul and Pamela.

"Maybe you should hold Pamela's weapon for now", suggested Martin, as he watched his daughter gingerly handle the weapon.

"Good idea, Martin. Hopefully, she won't have to use it", offered Scott, as he carefully took the weapon back and placed it in his backpack.

Paul put the gun holster on, inserted an ammo clip into the sleek handgun, checked that the safety was on and slid it into the holster. He then placed the extra ammo clips into a pocket inside the backpack. Paul had felt his shoulder twinge at the mention of Trent having diamene ammo. He had some experience at being shot with a diamene bullet and wasn't thrilled with the possibility of it happening again.

"There is one more thing", said Hiram, as he pulled out a metallic, rectangular object, the size of an old-fashioned pack of cigarettes and handed it to Paul.

"What is it?" asked a curious Paul, who took the device and examined it. There were only two switches on it, one was labeled "OPEN" and the other was labeled "CLOSE".

"That is the access to your sanctuary. It replaces the bulky suitcase, which in this case would be wildly inappropriate and inconvenient to carry. The switches either open or close the gateway to the sanctuary", said Hiram, beaming with pride.

"It's amazing Hiram. Thank you. I admit there have been times that I wished the briefcase were smaller", replied Paul, placing the new piece of technology into an inside breast pocket of his desert suit.

Pamela couldn't believe what Scott had said about Trent. In all the time Pamela had known Trent, he had never expressed any interest in guns. It was totally out of character for him. How could she have been so wrong in trusting Trent? He was forcing her, Paul and Scott to undertake a very risky mission that nobody knew would succeed. Pamela couldn't even begin to understand what effect this was going to have on their relationship. Serious doubts about its long-term viability were beginning to creep into her mind. Add to that a gun, Scott had handed her, and she felt as if she was teetering on the edge of a cliff. She had never handled a gun before and now she was faced with the possibility of actually having to use one. Hopefully, she wouldn't be forced to use it. Her mind framed the entire scene into a simple question, Trent, what have you done?

Martin noticed that the team was ready. He quickly prepared himself for what could be his last words with them. Clearing his throat, he began his brief speech.

"First, I want to offer you my most sincere thanks and appreciation for what you are about to undertake. It's a mission filled with unknowns, potential dangers and risks. Rely on your training and look out for one another. The goal is for everyone to come back alive, in-cluding Maggie and Trent. If Trent refuses to come back willingly, then use any means necessary to get him back here. Lethal force is to be used only as a last resort and after all other options have been explored. Hiram, do you have anything to add?" asked Martin.

Hiram looked up from his virtual display. Peering over the top of his eyeglasses, he said, "Yes, there are a couple of things to add. One is to have as little interaction with people as possible, since we don't know what the effect will be on our timeline. The other is that we will reopen the TimeBridge portal 24 hours from now. That will be your first window and will depend on the situation here.

We will reopen again 48 hours later, for your second window. Subsequent windows will follow as needed, every 48 hours. Try to make the first or second windows. The longer you are there, the greater the chances of corrupting our timeline beyond repair. Good luck to the three of you. I hope you are successful, and everyone returns safely", said Hiram, as he turned back to the display and continued entering the coordinates.

"Like Hiram said, a lot depends on the situation on the surface and how Plan Ghost goes. Explosive charges will level the above ground facilities and points of entry, denying access to this underground facility. All personnel are being evacuated to the beta site, which means we will gateway back to this lab and get TimeBridge running for that first window. So basically, it boils down to the three of you fixing our timeline and the people here getting you back safe and sound," said Martin, with a forced smile. No matter how you sliced it, there were just too many things that could go wrong, he thought to himself.

Hiram stood up, as if on cue and began excitedly gesturing towards his virtual display.

"I've done it! We're ready to go anytime now. I've calculated the TimeBridge activation to within one second of Trent's departure. Unfortunately, that one second will grow larger the deeper into the past you go. When you cross over, Trent and Maggie will have been there for an hour or two. Hopefully, they both arrived there safely, said Hiram, reinforcing that it still hadn't been proven that humans could safely time travel.

Suddenly, the room was bathed in a golden glow, as Gabriel stepped out from the shadows. He had been listening to everything that was being said and knew it was time for him to add something.

"Hello. Some of you already know me, but for those who don't, my name is Gabriel. I am what some would literally call an angel and I am here to help", announced Gabriel, pausing to let his words sink in. These were extraordinary times, demanding extraordinary actions, such as showing himself to the humans.

Pamela let out a gasp, clutching the top of the bench for support.

"You mean it was all true?" asked an incredulous Pamela. All this time, she had thought that it was some sort of mass delusion affecting Paul and her father.

"Yes, Pamela. It is true and it is also true that Paul's history with us goes back many millennia, to when we first arrived on your planet. Both he and the one you know as Maggie were once Anunnaki, as I once was. The difference being that Paul and Maggie never ascended as we did and were caught in the cycle of life and death. I could go on, but time is short. You will need a fluent knowledge of the language to help your chances of success," said Gabriel.

"How can we do that with so little time?" asked Paul.

"Simple, my friend," replied Gabriel, as he strode over to Paul and touched his forehead.

Paul felt his mind expand in all directions, unlocking the ancient Hebrew language that had been locked away since his time as Solomon.

"Hmmm. I don't feel any different and seem to be speaking normally. Why, what's wrong?" asked Paul, as he noticed the strange looks, he was getting from everyone, except for Gabriel.

"It seems to have worked. None of us understood a word of what you just said", replied Pamela, stifling a laugh.

Gabriel walked over to Pamela and Scott, touching their foreheads like he did with Paul.

Scott and Pamela exchanged a brief conversation, one that only Paul and Gabriel could understand, confirming that they too had learned ancient Hebrew.

"All three of you should now be able to understand the language spoken during that time period. Unfortunately, I cannot accompany you on this journey, as it is forbidden for us to travel in time. However, there is one of us already in Jerusalem at that time. His name is Raphael and could be of immense help if you can find him. Most likely, he will find you first. I must return to Heaven now and update my colleagues on everything that has happened. Good luck to you and don't underestimate Lilith. She is in control of Trent and his actions are hers. Farewell, my friend", said Gabriel, looking at Paul.

"Thank you, Gabriel. I'm sure I'll see you again, very soon," replied Paul, trying to put a positive spin on things.

"We can only hope", answered Gabriel, as he opened a gateway to Heaven and disappeared.

"Well, that was unexpected. I think it's time to get things moving. Hiram are we ready?" asked Martin.

"Ready, Martin," said Hiram as multiple QASM units began dumping incredible amounts of energy into the TimeBridge portal. Crackling arcs of energy flickered around the portal and the lab began to fill with a low hum. The QASM units reached their maximum output and a pulse of energy shot out from the portal, leaving a dark blue void within it.

"Hurry now, before the field collapses", said an excited Hiram. He was still somewhat unsure of how reliable the TimeBridge portal would be. After all, this was only the third time it was used.

"Good luck, Scott, Good luck, Paul. Godspeed and a safe return", said Martin, as he shook hands with Paul and Scott.

"Good luck, Pamela. I know you'll do fine and will be in capable hands", said Martin, as he hugged his daughter and kissed her on the cheek.

"Thank you, Father. I'll do my best", said Pamela, hugging him back and giving him a kiss on the cheek.

Martin reluctantly let her go and watched as Scott took a position directly in front of the portal, followed by Pamela and then Paul. Scott stepped into the dark blue void first, then Pamela and then Paul, who turned and spoke to Martin.

"Don't worry, Martin. We'll look after Pamela", said Paul with a smile, as he too stepped into the void.

Martin looked at the void, wondering if he too should have gone. A lone tear slid down his cheek, as he thought of Pamela and if he would ever see her again. His thoughts were cut short, as Hiram shut power off to the portal.

"Well, Hiram. I think that's all we can do here for now. It's up to them now. Let's get the rest of our people to safety," said a somber Martin.

"Yes, Martin. I hope they succeed", replied Hiram, as the two of them left the lab.

Gabriel stepped out from the gateway and into Heaven, or what was supposed to be Heaven. Gone were the streets of gold, now turned to molten pits of gold, gone were the clear crystalline spires, now turned to black obsidian spires, gone were the fields of flowers, now blackened plains of ash and gone were the marble columned buildings, replace by black obsidian buildings. It was a surreal nightmare that lay before him, with pits of burning lava spread out before him, under a ruddy orange sky. Where was he? This looks like Hell, he thought to himself. An ominous, evil familiar voice sounded behind him.

"Hello, Gabriel. I've been waiting for you. You and Raphael are the last angels. Everyone else has succumbed to my power and pledged obedience," said the familiar evil voice.

Gabriel slowly turned around, hoping the voice wasn't who he thought it was. Unfortunately, it was.

"Asmodeus! What are you doing here and what have you done to Heaven?" asked an incredulous Gabriel, the import only beginning to dawn on him.

"Gabriel, Gabriel. You're so out of touch. Let me show you," replied Asmodeus, as his hand shot out and touched Gabriel.

Gabriel felt an immense shock run through his being and fell to the blackened and scorched ground. He had never felt such raw unbridled power engulf him, and he began to grow fearful. A quick glance at the hand that Asmodeus had touched him with, confirmed his worst fears.

"Solomon's ring! Where did you get it?" asked Gabriel, his fear growing exponentially.

"Ah, yes, the fabled ring of Solomon. It's now known as the Ring of Asmodeus. You see, my old friend. Lilith was more successful than anyone imagined. Valinor and Shaynor are no longer a problem, I have the ring and equally important, I have the Ark", said Asmodeus with an evil laugh.

Gabriel was mortified. He struggled mightily against the shackles of energy that seemed to bind him, but to no avail. Terror ensued when he saw Asmodeus clench his fist, causing Gabriel to writhe in extreme pain. A glance around, showed other angels writhing on the ground in pain.

"Don't worry, Gabriel. I'm not going to kill you. You will gladly join me eventually. There isn't anywhere else you can go. I rule from the depths of Hell to the heights of Heaven and everything in between, including Earth", said Asmodeus with a touch of pride. He unclenched his fist, releasing Gabriel from his pain.

"Come along, Gabriel. Let me show you around my new home", said Asmodeus, his eyes glinting with an evil purpose.

Gabriel felt instant relief from the pain as Asmodeus unclenched his fist. Now more than ever, he hoped Paul and his team were successful. This timeline and Heaven had definitely gone to Hell.

An hour later, Martin watched as the last of the DarkBridge employees stepped through the gateway to the beta site. He'd sent Hiram there also and now stood alone in the underground park, facing a monumental decision. It was a decision that only he could make and one that he wouldn't want anyone else to make.

"Eva, I need three QASM units charged to maximum capacity and set for overload. Deliver them here", ordered Martin. Theoretically, the QASM units were capable of unlimited capacity, but they could be set for a maximum charge limit. They could also be set to an "overload" condition, where the entire stored charge would be released in one massive discharge. The result would be akin to a small tactical nuke, without the radiation. Devastation of the immediate vicinity would result, along with loss of life.

"Yes, Martin. I have the three units charging now", replied Eva.

Minutes passed by, until Martin was rewarded by the appearance of a gateway and three QASM units supported by three DarkLift devices, floated out.

"Thank you, Eva. Open one gateway topside, to just inside the main gate and send one of the units through. Then open another gateway to the office of Vice Chancellor Thomas Stanton and send the second unit through. Send the final unit to the Fuhrer's office in Munich, Germany", ordered Martin.

"Yes, Martin. I'm sure you have your reasons and have considered the repercussions', said Eva, as one by one the QASM units disappeared through gateways to their destinations.

"Thank you, Eva. I have thought about it, and it wasn't an easy decision to reach. It does, however, offer hope to this timeline and may seriously disrupt the evil that has overtaken it", replied Martin.

"Are you ready to leave, now?" asked Eva.

"Yes. It's time to join the others. Transfer your higher functions to the beta site after I leave", replied Martin, as a gateway opened.

Martin paused in front of the open gateway, as something caught his attention. It was a voice calling his name and it seemed to be getting closer.

"Martin! Martin! Where are you?" called the voice.

Martin stepped back from the gate and turned around, trying to find the source of the voice.

"Martin!" called the voice once again.

Martin thought the voice sounded vaguely familiar, a voice he hadn't heard in over a decade. It couldn't be. Could it? Martin stood there frozen with a mixture of anticipation and fear, as the voice drew closer and resolved itself into a figure. One that he knew and one that shouldn't be here. It was Susan, his long dead wife. Killed in a mysterious auto accident over a decade ago, Martin had mourned her loss ever since. Now here she was standing in front of him.

"There you are. I've been looking everywhere for you. Where is everyone?" said Susan.

Martin blinked, finding it difficult to wrap his mind around what was happening. Hiram was right. In a sense, things were getting worse.

"Hello, Susan. I've missed you. Everyone has transferred to the beta site due to the approaching army above", replied Martin, unsure as to what he should do.

"You're being silly. We just had lunch not 10 minutes ago", said Susan, her eyes a sparkling green.

Martin took a closer look at Susan and noticed that she was wearing an Army camouflage outfit with her long brown hair tied up in a bun. Looking down at his own clothing, he was shocked to see himself wearing the same type of camouflage outfit. Gone was his suit and tie.

"Every moment away from you is like an eternity, my love", replied Martin quickly, as he fought to control the emotions welling up inside him.

"That's sweet", said Susan, as she pulled his head down and kissed him.

Martin, being slightly taller than Susan, relaxed and allowed her to pull his head down. The kiss felt as it did, so long ago, filled with love and passion. Martin gave into the kiss, returning it with years of longing and heartache.

"My, my. What's gotten into you?" asked Susan, as she pulled away.

Martin reluctantly released her, just as a tremor shook the underground facility. A ceiling tile fell down nearby, and a look of concern crossed Susan's face.

"What's happening?" said a worried Susan.

"Don't worry, we should be okay down here. I sent a surprise package to the army above. They won't be bothering us anymore", said a hopeful Martin.

"Shouldn't we go to the beta site? asked Susan.

"Yes, we should", replied Martin, noticing that the gateway was still open. The decision to bring her was an easy one for Martin and not just because she was his wife. That she existed in this new timeline and was here at the facility, meant that she had never been killed in the car accident, but also, almost equally important, she was privy to the knowledge stored here.

Martin took Susan's hand in his and they both walked towards the gateway.

"Ready?" asked Martin.

"Ready", replied Susan with a smile.

Martin gently pulled Susan into the waiting gateway. He knew that if the team was successful then all this would be a fading dream and Susan would still be long dead. He found himself torn between the team being successful or failing. Sensibility winning, Martin decided to just enjoy what little time he had with Susan.

Outside the DarkBridge facility topside, a QASM unit appeared, just inside the gate, as the armored column rolled up to the entrance. Field Commander Karl Schmidt sat in the leading armored car and looked at his watch. It was almost time to enter the facility and wipe the last vestiges of rebellion off the face of the Earth. He smiled with satisfaction at the death and destruction that he would personally be delivering. His smile was short-lived, as a searing white light, hotter than the sun incinerated the armored column, turning tanks and vehicles to molten liquid and instantly vaporizing its occupants, including the once touted Field Commander Karl Schmidt.

Inside the oval office at the White House, in Washington D.C., Vice Chancellor Thomas Stanton sat in his leather chair awaiting word from Field Commander

Schmidt on the success of his mission in the North. If the Commander was successful, the rebellion would be broken and a crown jewel would be his, the rebel technology. With this technology, the armies of the Fuhrer would be unstoppable, and the Fuhrer could extend his dominion to the rest of the solar system and possibly beyond. He smiled at the thought of his own importance increasing within the party, maybe even becoming Fuhrer himself. A slight whining noise caught his attention, as he glimpsed a black rectangular object float towards the middle of the room. Fascination was the last thought he had, as a searing white light erupted from the device, incinerating him and his dreams of dominion. The resulting blast wave obliterated a large portion of the central portion of Washington, D.C., cutting the heart out of the Fourth Reich's dreams in America.

In Munich, Germany, the Fuhrer sat in his ornate office at the Reichstag, marveling at how his dominion had spread with the help of the demon, Asmodeus. His forefather had won the great battle of World War II after striking a deal with Asmodeus, who in return, had unleashed incredible destruction upon the Allies, including the United States. Opposition destroyed and routed, the Third Reich had marched to victory, enshrining itself across the following decades as the only world power.

The Fuhrer's musings were suddenly interrupted by a slight whining noise, as he spotted a black rectangular object float towards him. He bolted up, screaming for his bodyguard and trying to reach the elevator to the Fuhrer bunker. It was to no avail, as a searing white light incinerated him and his dreams of conquest. The searing white light expanded, incinerating the Reichstag and the resulting blast wave obliterating the surrounding government buildings. In series of bold moves, Martin had indeed cut the head off the snake.

Chapter 25

Hostage

Maggie had fallen asleep at the bar, or at least that had been her first impression. This felt like something other than normal sleep though, with her mind giving a feeling of being enveloped in a foggy haze. She dreamed of being physically lifted and then placed on a hard surface. She dreamed of hearing voices, a man and a woman talking. She dreamed of being lifted up again and carried upright, her feet dragging on the ground and a sensation of static electricity wrapping around her and then a cool breeze on her face. Dreams and only dreams to be sure, she thought to herself. Just then, a mental image came to her. She was lying in bed, next to a man that she loved dearly. A name came to her, Darah and the man next to her was known as King Solomon.

The image reminded Maggie of a dream she had some time ago, except in that case the two were walking in a garden and the woman, Darah had been murdered. Later, Maggie had found out that she and Darah, were incarnations of Shaynor, a long dead Anunnaki geologist. Maggie wasn't sure why the image of Darah had come to her, but there seemed to be physical sensations attached to it. It was as if hers and Darah's minds were connected, sharing information both ways. It was very unsettling in some ways but reassuring in others. Maggie couldn't wait to wake up.

Darah's eyes shot open. She was snuggled up against Solomon, who was sound asleep and seemed undisturbed. Darah was seeing strange visions and hearing strange thoughts in her mind. The visions and thoughts seemed to be from someone called Maggie. Darah thought she had heard that name before and recalled the name from a dream she had not long ago. The woman Maggie was being attacked by the foul demon Belial and someone named Paul had rescued her.

Another dream had shown Darah the connection between her and Maggie. That connection being Shaynor, who was actually the two women reincarnated at different times. Darah was still confused by it, but these strange visions and thoughts seemed to be real and happening right now. Darah contemplated waking Solomon, but he was sleeping so peacefully that she decided to let him rest. She would wait until morning to talk with him and see if the visions and thoughts persisted. Snuggling deeper into Solomon's side, she relished in his comfort and drifted off to sleep.

Lilith stepped out of the TimeBridge portal and into darkness. Still possessing Trent's body, she could feel the cool, crisp night-time air on Trent's face. Off in the distance, she could see the city of Jerusalem and its ramparts lit with burning torches. The TimeBridge portal seemed to have worked and deposited them sometime in the past. Lilith would have a better idea of when, once they entered the city. A careful examination of Trent and the captive Maggie showed that they had made the trip without any physical harm. The woman, Maggie, still appeared unconscious and Lilith couldn't wait for her to wake up. Hauling Maggie's body around was taxing on Trent.

A quick glance around, showed a couple of campfires burning and flocks of goats being tended. Lilith felt at home here. She had spent many millennia in this region, wreaking all sorts of havoc. That thought reminded her of the other Lilith, the one from this time, who would soon be coming here to avenge what Solomon had done to Asmodeus. Lilith began walking towards the city, using Trent to support Maggie's body. So far, things were looking good and hopefully would continue, but there were still a host of unknowns to deal with.

One was a possible rescue attempt by the one called Paul, or Valinor, as Asmodeus liked to call him. Lilith gave this a pretty high probability, considering how much the two loved one another. It had been a good reason why she had stolen some weapons from the DarkBridge security room. Paul would probably come here armed and Lilith would be ready. The thought of killing him added an extra spring to her step, or rather Trent's, as they continued making their way towards the city.

Lilith eventually reached the city gates, with Trent's body at the point of exhaustion. The DarkWeave suit that Trent was wearing seemed to be absorbing most of the excess heat generated from carrying Maggie. Where that heat was going, she hadn't a clue and she really didn't care. The cool night air was an added bonus, but Lilith would have to find a place for Trent to rest and also to hide Maggie. Lilith heard a voice calling from above the massive iron gates and it took a moment for her to recognize the language as ancient Hebrew. It had been a few thousand years since she had last heard it spoken, but she quickly recalled the language and listened.

A guard and what appeared to be the Captain of the Guard, were peering over the wall at the two strangers below asking what they wanted. Lilith didn't have time for games, so she had Trent lay Maggie down and sit beside her. Lilith left Trent's body and watched as his body slumped and fell asleep. Invisible to the humans, she floated up into the air and onto the ramparts over-looking the gate. Once there, her mind sought out the Captain of the Guard, quickly subverting him to her will.

Looking at his mind, Lilith had ascertained that this was indeed the correct time period she wanted to be in. Asmodeus had done a superb job of operating the TimeBridge device. Not that she would expect anything less from him. She turned her attention towards the other guard, placing him under her control as well. Two people should be enough to open the gates without a lot of commotion. The other guards would listen to the captain and the other guard under her control would add credence to the captain.

"They are special envoys, here to see the King. Open the gates and let them pass", said Lilith, speaking into their minds.

The captain and guard quickly descended the stairs, down to the gate, where other guards were waiting.

"Open the gates. Envoys are waiting to see the King," commanded the captain.

The other guards, including the one under Lilith's control promptly complied, by lifting the heavy iron bar that had sealed the gates. No one wanted to disobey the captain and incite his wrath. Rumor had it that the last guard to disobey him was promptly sent outside the city to hunt demons. No one had seen or heard from him since.

Lilith floated down to where Trent and Maggie lay, just outside the gates. Lilith poured her essence back into Trent and noted the fatigue he was feeling. It probably would've been easier to just open a gateway into the city, but without knowing the city better, it would be far too dangerous. She imbued Trent with some extra energy and had him lift Maggie into a standing position, supporting her. Just then the gates swung open and Lilith guided Trent and Maggie through, with a mental command to the captain, not to follow or pay any more attention to them. The captain complied, issuing orders to close the gates and get back to their posts. The guards obeyed and quickly closed the gates, returning to their posts, but wondering at the strange clothing worn by the envoys.

Trent, under Lilith's control, made his way along the streets of ancient Jerusalem, his right arm supporting Maggie, his left clutching her left arm around his neck. Lilith cast her mind out, searching for a vacant building that they could occupy until everyone had recovered. The plan would be to let Maggie go, free to wander the city and do as she pleased. Lilith no longer had use for her, since the trap had been set for Paul. She would trap both of them here in the past, pleasing her King, to no end. It was a thought that caused her to smile, which reflected itself as more of a snarl on Trent's face. Her main focus now was the Ark. While Trent rested and Maggie woke up, Lilith would locate the Ark and figure out the best way to steal it.

Her mind finally found the vacant building that she was searching for. Why it was vacant she didn't know, but she hurried Trent and Maggie along until they reached the building. Trent opened the creaking, wooden door and stepped inside with Maggie. Lilith knew immediately why the building was vacant. Rats. There were hundreds of them scurrying across the floor, squeaking loudly at being disturbed. Disgusted, Lilith sent a piercing mental image to the rats, sending them scurrying out the open door in abject terror. Fearing some pestilence might infect Trent, she quickly put a protective shield around him and Maggie. She concentrated and heat began filling the small room, wisps of steam rising from the dirt floor. It wasn't hot enough to burn but was hot enough to kill any organisms in the room. Satisfied with her attempt at purification, Lilith had Trent place Maggie on the warm ground and then made Trent lie down next to her.

Placing Trent into a deep sleep, Lilith left his body and took the form of an old, gray-haired woman, dressed in a long woolen shift. Normally, she would've played a more voluptuous and sensual role, but discretion was advised here. She needed information and indulging her more sexual proclivities would have to wait. Sighing, she closed the door on the two sleeping humans, sending a pulse of energy into the door latch, fusing it shut. That should offer a quick deterrent to anyone looking for a free room, she thought to herself. Turning around, she stepped onto the sandy street and began her search for the Ark.

It was mid evening, and a cool wind was blowing across the land outside the walls of ancient Jerusalem. Paul stepped out of the TimeBridge portal and immediately dropped to his knees, as a wave of disorientation struck him. Pamela and Scott, already having exited the portal, seemed unaffected by whatever was happening to Paul.

"Are you okay?" asked a concerned Scott.

"I'm not sure," replied Paul, as images and feelings began flooding his mind. There was an image of a man sleeping in a large bed. The name Solomon came into his mind, and he wasn't alone. Snuggled up next to him, fast asleep, was a woman with long dark hair and one that he was deeply in love with. Darah was the name that came to him, a name that was strangely familiar to Paul. Some time ago, he'd had a dream of Solomon and the woman Darah walking in the palace garden, where she had come to be murdered. His mind reeled at the implications. He and Maggie were now sharing the same timeline as Solomon and Darah. Hiram would probably have a scientific explanation for what was happening, but he was now three thousand years away from where Paul was. The disorientation began to fade away, leaving him with a sort of mental connection to Solomon.

"Paul? Are you okay?" asked a concerned Pamela, as she kneeled down next to him and put her hand on his shoulders.

"I'm okay now. We may have a problem though. I seem to have some kind of mental link to Solomon and am sharing thoughts and images", replied Paul, as he slowly got to his feet, aided by Scott and Pamela.

"That sounds crazy", said a skeptical Scott.

"It's not as crazy as it sounds. Hiram has theorized that if two individuals from different time periods came together in the same time period, a quantum link could be created between the two. That link would allow for sharing of neural data and if you were to couple that with reincarnation, then it becomes very plausible", explained Pamela, keeping her doubts about reincarnation to herself. Trent and Hiram had argued about this, the paradoxes involved, and other peculiarities associated with time travel, while developing Project TimeBridge. Often late into the night, the sessions were thought provoking, but not much more, since there wasn't yet a way to prove any of it. That is until now.

"Okay. I'm still a little skeptical, but I'll keep an open mind", replied Scott, trying to temper his previous outburst.

"Thank you, Scott. If I were you, I'd probably be thinking the same thing," replied Paul with a smile.

"We should do a quick equipment check. Just in case something happened during our journey," said Scott, quickly changing the subject. He removed his backpack, checking his weapons and the DarkFly drones he was carrying. Loaded with various sensors, one of the drones was similar in appearance to the one he had used in the Sinai, resembling the ubiquitous dragonfly.

Paul rose to his feet and removed his backpack. Remembering the access device that Hiram had given him, he pulled it out and a flashlight, as well.

"I'm going to check the sanctuary and make sure everything is working", said Paul, as he walked a safe distance away. He wasn't sure exactly where the gateway would open and didn't want to harm Pamela or Scott. He shined his flashlight on the device, saw the button "OPEN" and pressed it. The same familiar gateway formed a few feet away, light blue at first, then dark blue as it stabilized. Paul stepped through and found himself inside his sanctuary, the lights having come on as soon as the gateway had formed. Paul surveyed the interior, everything looked the same, bench, cot, refrigerator, wardrobe closet, desk and other things, were all where they should be.

Satisfied, he committed the arrangement to memory and stepped back through the gateway. Once outside, he pressed the "CLOSE" button and watched the gateway disappear.

"Everything checks out", said Paul as he rejoined the team.

"Good to know. We have 24 hours to complete our mission and get back to our time. I'd like to make the first portal window. Staying here any longer, would only increase the danger to us and risk further corrupting the timeline", said Scott, as he got back to checking his gear.

Pamela removed her backpack as well, pulled out her PDA and turned it on. There was a brief delay and then a familiar voice began talking.

"Hello, everyone. I'm happy to see my fellow time travelers arrived safe and sound," said Eva, speaking through their implants.

"Hello, Eva. Safe is one word. Sound is another," said Paul, as he related his strange feelings upon arrival.

"My, that is strange and yet predictable. I too subscribe to Hiram's theory, except for the reincarnation part. As an AI, it's a difficult concept for me to grasp. To me, the end of life, or in my case, the end of intelligence is it. Nothing happens after. Yet, here I am, an AI programmed by myself three thousand years in the future. Does this make me reincarnated?" asked a puzzled Eva.

Scott inwardly groaned, praying that the conversation wouldn't once again revert to the topic of reincarnation. With so much to do, this just wasn't the time for philosophical discussion.

Paul caught the flash of discomfort on Scott's face and immediately changed the topic. He too, wanted to get things moving, but for much more personal reasons. Maggie was here somewhere, probably in trouble and needing his help.

"Eva, we need to get into the city ASAP. Can we gateway into it?" asked Paul.

"Yes. It's possible, but we need some reconnaissance done. We wouldn't want to open a gateway randomly and chance either killing someone or being discovered. Scott, I'll need the DarkFly drone", said Eva after visual sensors on Pamela's PDA had sensed the drone nearby.

Scott lifted the dragonfly drone out of its small metal case, set it on the ground and returned to his backpack, pulling out the rolled-up video screen.

"Thank you, Scott. Now, you three sit back and watch the video screen, as I pilot the drone" said Eva, who immediately initiated a link to the drone and began sending commands.

The DarkFly drone began rising into the dark evening sky, mostly silent, except for the slight buzzing noise of its wings. Paul, Pamela and Scott, watched the drone's progress on the flexible view screen, as it picked up speed and reached the city walls within seconds. The drone hovered over the city walls of Jerusalem for a few seconds, as Eva determined a direction to take. A torch near the drone suddenly flared up, momentarily overwhelming the drone's video sensors, causing the three watchers to gasp, as the video screen turned a stark white for a few seconds. The image cleared and Eva sent the drone into the city, all sensors turned to maximum. The drone quickly found a target of interest not far from the wall and descended to investigate.

Paul still couldn't believe that the three of them were actually here, watching live video of the ancient city. He watched as the drone descended down to street level, searching for access into the building. The drone spotted a small, open window and slowly flew in, scanning the interior. Paul saw that the building appeared to be some sort of stable where horses were kept, with a few stalls occupied and a couple empty.

"Looks like we've found our gateway location", said Eva, as she quickly stored the coordinates into memory.

"Great job, Eva", said Scott, marveling at how quickly they had found a gateway location.

"Hang on. The drone is detecting a quantum signature somewhere in the city.

Give me a second or two to verify," said Eva, as she worked to verify the drone data.

Scott, Paul and Pamela looked at one another with puzzled expressions.

"Why would there be a quantum signature here?" said Pamela aloud, echoing similar thoughts by Paul and Scott.

"I've verified the drone data. After screening out any signature from our camp here, there are multiple signatures in the city. One is specifically of DarkBridge Technology origin and the others are unknown", said Eva, puzzled by the other quantum signatures.

"Concentrate on the DarkBridge signature," ordered Paul. This could be a lead as to where Maggie was, thought Paul to himself.

"The drone is on its way to the location, as we speak", replied Eva.

Paul was about to thank Eva, when Pamela grabbed his arm and pointed towards the sky. The three of them watched as a glowing object descended from the sky and gently landed outside the city walls.

Scott dug out a pair of binoculars from his backpack and took a look at the object. Imaging sensors on the binoculars screened out most of the glow and what was left made Scott gasp. It was a spaceship, silvery green in color, with strange markings. Scott passed the binoculars to Pamela, who took one look and quickly passed them to Paul.

Paul took the binoculars and as he looked at the spaceship, a long-forgotten memory surfaced. It was a Valinor memory, of a time before the Anunnaki came to Earth and during the Anunnaki and Skarzi war. Valinor had led a squadron of combat spacecraft against a much larger fleet of Skarzi spacecraft. The ensuing battle and ultimate victory by Valinor and his squadron quickly became the stuff of legend. It had also catapulted Valinor into the realm of hero and aroused the interest of Commander Kalon, Shaynor's father.

Seared into that memory, were the images of Skarzi spacecraft, looking exactly like the one sitting outside the city. As Paul watched, a ramp descended from the spaceship, interior lighting casting an eerie glow on the surrounding area. Seven humanoid figures descended the ramp, dressed in Hebrew robes. Once away from the ship, the ramp closed, and the figures approached the nearby city wall.

"Eva, things are about to get complicated. Any luck with that signature location?" asked Paul, a sense of urgency creeping into his voice.

"I'm working on it, Paul. The drone is searching as we speak," replied Eva.

"Thank you, Eva," said Paul, handing the binoculars back to Scott.

Scott took the binoculars and watched the seven figures approach the city wall. One of the figures, possibly the leader, raised his arm, halting the progress of the group. With its other arm it directed two of the figures forward, who approached the wall and leveled some sort of weapons at it. There was a brief flash of light and when the ensuing smoke cleared, a large, gaping hole appeared in the wall. The leader of the group motioned for the group to proceed forward. The seven figures stepped through the gaping hole and entered the city.

"They're in the city", said Scott, resigning himself to dealing with a new complication.

"I've found the location. The drone is surveying the building now," said Eva, a touch of excitement in her voice.

Paul exhaled a deep breath. Finally, they might be closer to some answers. Things had only gotten worse with the Skarzi here and were on the verge of spiraling out of control. They were going to need some serious help against the odds stacking up against them. Closing his eyes, he made a silent vow to see this mission to the end and a successful one at that.

Chapter 26

Nexus

Maggie stirred. Her mind climbed slowly out of the fog that had shrouded her in dreams. An annoying buzzing sound was intruding into her thoughts and at first, she thought it was a mosquito. She didn't know where a mosquito could come from, since she was still sleeping under the bar at her restaurant. Or was she? A musty odor began wafting up her nostrils, causing her to sneeze. The sneeze jostled her awake, but she was still rather groggy. Her eyes gradually focused on her surroundings. It was dark and she seemed to be lying on a dirt floor. Definitely, no longer at the bar, she thought to herself. The annoying buzzing sound was still there, and she looked for its source, which came as a total shock to her. The buzzing was coming from a large dragonfly.

Poised directly above her, was the dragonfly, or what she had thought was a dragonfly. As she looked closer, she saw that its eyes shown with twin bright LED lights. She squinted her eyes against the glaring light and could see enough of the dragonfly to tell it wasn't natural. As a matter of fact, she recognized the dragonfly as similar to the one used in the Sinai. Why was a DarkFly drone here? Just where was she? She slowly rose to her feet, dusted herself off and accidentally bumped a slumbering figure next to her. The bump elicited a grunt from the figure, but nothing else. Whoever it was, seemed to be in a deep sleep, just as she had been. Her interest piqued, she bent down for a closer look at the figure and recoiled in shock. Trent? What was he doing here? Why was she with him? The questions began to truly frighten her. The annoying DarkFly drone once again positioned itself in front of her face. Annoying, thought Maggie. She decided to try something.

"Are you a DarkFly drone?" asked a curious Maggie.

The dragonfly responded by tilting its wings back and forth, but the real surprise came from her implant.

"Hello, Maggie. Are you okay?" said Eva.

"Eva?" replied an incredulous Maggie.

"Yes, it's me, or rather a slimmed down version of my future self", said Eva.

"Future self?" questioned Maggie.

"I think you had better sit down. What I have to tell you is going to come as quite a shock", said Eva.

Maggie sat down, as Eva began explaining everything that had happened, including where they were and more importantly, the time period they were in.

Maggie was glad she had followed Eva's advice and sat down. She sat there for a few moments, assimilating everything Eva had said.

"Is Paul with you?" asked Maggie.

"Yes, he's here and preparing to rescue you," said Eva.

Suddenly, the door was thrown open and a beautiful, dark-haired, Mediterranean woman came striding in. The woman took one look at the hovering dragonfly, concentrated briefly, and the dragonfly exploded, sending a shower of sparks and pieces of metal everywhere.

Maggie had turned her head just in time, avoiding any shrapnel from getting into her eyes. She looked at the woman and knew she had seen her before. It was the same woman from the cafeteria, the one called Lilith, Queen of the demons.

"I see you're awake", said Lilith, as she surveyed the scene. Trent was still unconscious, the woman, Maggie, had obviously recovered from the gas and was in communication with her supposed rescuers. Destroying the primitive drone would hinder the would-be rescuers, but not for long. Still, she found an immense sense of satisfaction in seeing at least part of the plan fulfilled. Getting Paul here was one thing, marooning him here was another thing altogether. Another complication was the alien spacecraft that had landed outside the city walls. It had taken a few moments to recognize the craft as Skarzi.

Why they were here and had so brazenly landed near the city wasn't clear. They obviously wanted something important. She couldn't even begin to fathom the workings of the reptilian brain, finding the thought extremely repulsive. The only thing that mattered right now was the plan and it was all about the Ark now. Lilith strode over to Trent's body and possessed it once again. Trent's eyes shot open, and he slowly got to his feet. Lilith found Trent's body to have more energy now from his brief sleep and should be in a better state to help complete the plan. Trent walked over to the door, stopped and turned towards Maggie.

"I hope you like your new home. Enjoy it while you can", said Lilith in a decidedly baritone voice. She stepped out the door uttering a devilish laugh, before slamming it shut. Once outside, Lilith remembered Trent's backpack was still inside. No matter. She was more powerful than any of their primitive weapons and really didn't need it. She smiled, a grimace reflecting on Trent's face, as she proceeded towards her goal.

Maggie didn't know what to think. It had been unsettling to see Lilith take control of Trent's body and make it do whatever she wanted. Luckily, Maggie wasn't being possessed. The thought sent shivers down her spine. She was in a quandary. Should she stay where she was and possibly be captured or take her chances outside. Once again, the door burst open, taking her options away. This time it wasn't Lilith, but what Maggie could only describe as some sort of city guard. Eva wasn't kidding, when she had told Maggie what time period, she was in.

Here was the proof, six men dressed in ancient armor, with spears leveled at her. A man, who appeared to be the leader, stepped forward and began speaking in a strange tongue. Maggie couldn't understand a word of what he was saying, but something about it tugged at distant memories. The man was insistent and seemed to want her to follow him. Maggie decided to comply, curiosity getting the best of her. She noticed Trent's backpack lying there and picked it up.

They left the building, two guards and the leader in front, Maggie behind them and three other guards behind her. Luckily, it was night and not many people were about, otherwise it would've been quite a spectacle, thought Maggie. They marched down dimly lit, narrow streets and past buildings of all sizes and types. Finally, they reached what Maggie assumed was the palace or what she took for a palace. The guards took her into a courtyard and left her, taking positions some distance away. Maggie cursed her curiosity. Maybe she should've stayed in the building and fought the guards, like Shaynor would've done. She was positive that Shaynor would've beaten the guards to a pulp. She still hadn't fully accepted the whole reincarnation thing, but she was working on it. So, she stood there waiting, for what she didn't know.

Paul took a turn holding the display and watched the drone's progress through the city. The drone was headed towards the DarkBridge quantum signature and was making rapid progress. It soon reached a building and gained entry through a small, open window. Paul was on pins and needles, watching the drone, hoping against all odds that they had found Maggie. It was dark inside the building, so Eva switched on the bright LED lights, illuminating the surrounding area. Eva angled the drone towards the floor and two figures immediately jumped into view. Paul could see that both were sleeping on what looked like a dirt floor. Eva brought the drone in for a closer look, causing one of the sleeping figures to turn and face the drone.

"Maggie!" Paul cried out excitedly.

"Trent!" yelled Pamela, equally excited.

Paul watched as Maggie stirred, opened her eyes and gave an annoying look at the drone. Soon, recognition showed on her face, as she clearly remembered the drone from the Sinai.

"Paul, I am in touch with Maggie. She's getting over the effects of the same gas that affected you and Pamela. I am bringing her up to date on everything that's happened. She asked about you", said Eva.

"Thank you, Eva", said Paul, itching to get into the city and rescue Maggie.

"Pamela, Maggie says that Trent is in some sort of deep sleep and won't wake up", said Eva.

"I wonder what's wrong with him?" said a concerned Pamela.

Paul was still transfixed to the screen, suddenly aware that Pamela was uncomfortably close, but equally transfixed on the screen. Energy sensors on the drone suddenly spiked and Eva turned the drone, facing the direction of the energy surge. Suddenly, the front door flew open, and a beautiful, dark-haired woman stood in the doorway. Paul and Pamela jumped, as the video screen flashed a brilliant white light and then turned dark.

"I am no longer receiving data from the drone and have lost all contact. It would appear that the drone has been destroyed", said Eva.

"What would cause that?" asked a concerned Scott.

"Not what, but who", replied Paul. He had immediately recognized the woman as Lilith, Queen of the demons. Now he knew why Trent was here. Lilith had possessed Trent in the past and evidently still was.

"What do you mean? I didn't see anyone other than Maggie and Scott." asked a curious Pamela.

"I didn't see anyone else either", added a skeptical Scott.

"The woman is Lilith, Queen of demons. She's capable of hiding her form from human sight. For some reason, Maggie and I are capable of seeing her form, no matter how much she tries to hide it. She has evidently possessed Trent, using him to kidnap Maggie and then used TimeBridge to get here. Why here I'm not sure, but it must have something to do with the Ark," said Paul, as he let Pamela and Scott assimilate what he had said.

"I agree with Paul. I've computed the odds and give it an eighty-five percent probability that Lilith and the Skarzi are here for the same reason. The other quantum signatures I detected could be demon related, Skarzi, or possibly Ark related", replied Eva.

"What do we do now?" asked a concerned Pamela. After what Paul had said, she was growing increasingly worried about Trent.

"I think we all want to get in there fast, but the Skarzi have complicated our initial rescue plan. The one advantage that we have is surprise. They don't know we're here and we can use that. We need a way to track them and that's where another one of these comes in", said Scott, as he pulled out another DarkFly drone that resembled a dragonfly.

Pamela and Paul watched in amazement as Scott placed the drone on the ground and Eva took over. The drone flew off into the evening sky and headed for the city. The video screen in Paul's hands suddenly lit up, showing video from the drone's tiny cameras and moving dot, which Paul assumed was the drone.

"Eva, can you split the screen so that one side has video, and the other side is a city map?" asked Paul.

"Yes. I'll even put dots on the map showing the drone, the Skarzi, our gateway location in the city and Maggie's last known position," replied Eva.

"That would be great", said Paul, showing the new screen display to Scott.

"This is excellent Eva, and will help immensely with our tactical planning", said Scott, as the drone reached the city wall.

"The drone is entering the city and is high enough to give a broad view of the streets below", said Eva.

Scott sat down next to Paul and Pamela, placing the video screen on the ground between them. All three watched as the drone flew over the city streets near the Skarzi entry point, the drone a green dot moving on the map and video of the streets below. It didn't take long before a line of seven robed figures were seen on the street below. Eva sent the drone on a rapid descent towards the figures, slowing it down and allowing the figures to pass, before catching up to the last Skarzi in line. Deftly matching the speed of the Skarzi, Eva maneuvered the drone onto the lower back of the target. Instantly, Eva engaged the drone's metal legs, firmly grabbing the fabric of the creature's robe.

Paul looked at the position of the Skarzi in relation to their gateway location in the stable. The Skarzi seemed far enough away, so as not to cause an immediate problem.

"The Skarzi look far enough away. I think we should gateway into the city," offered Paul.

"I think you're right, Paul. Time is critical. The longer everyone is here, the more chances of corrupting our future timeline", said Eva.

"That sounds good to me. Let's go", replied Scott, as he fished around in his backpack and pulled out a Glock handgun, passing it to Pamela.

"This is for you, Pamela. Here's the safety. Make sure the safety is off before shooting, then just point and shoot. Sorry, we don't have time for target practice. Hopefully, you won't have to use it", said Scott.

Pamela looked at the handgun and gingerly placed it in the holster around her waist that Scott had given her. She then placed her PDA into her backpack, with Eva still able to communicate. Looking around, everyone gathered up whatever else belonged to them and stood together waiting.

Paul pulled out a GAGE device, placed it on the ground and switched it on.

"All yours, Eva", said Paul.

"Thank you, Paul", replied Eva.

The three watched as a shimmering blue gateway appeared, changing from light blue, to dark blue as it stabilized.

"Ready, any time you are", said Eva.

Scott was the first to step through, followed by Pamela. Paul paused and grabbed the GAGE device, before stepping through the gateway. His last thought before entering was of Maggie and her safety.

Chapter 27

The Skarzi

Captain Skresh, of the Skarzi scout ship Skirim, looked at the view screen in awe, his reptilian eyes blinking as he watched the scene far below. The scout ship was flying high above the primitive human city of Jerusalem, not intending to find anything of value, when energy sensors began sounding an alarm and something caught his attention. On a low hill inside the city, a structure was being built by beings of immense strength. They looked human, but as far as Captain Skresh knew, no single human could lift such massive stone blocks. Yet here were beings lifting massive stone blocks with apparent ease and placing the blocks with equal ease. Energy readings were also high around a building near the site, which stirred even more interest from the Captain. Curious, he thought to himself. His mission, however, was to survey the planet Earth and find evidence of a continuing Anunnaki presence so that attack plans could be formulated.

Long ago, in what had come to be known among the Skarzi as the Great Rout, an Anunnaki battle fleet had destroyed the Skarzi fleet as it began approaching Earth. Launching from underground bases on Mars, the Skarzi fleet had been an impressive sight, but ultimately for naught. Since then, it had taken thousands of years for the Skarzi to recover and rebuild its fleet and fearing another rout, the Skirim had been sent out on a re-connaissance mission. Captain Skresh took pride in his work and was honored to be in command of such an important mission. Born on Mars into the Sook warrior class, Captain Skresh was a hatchling of the 200th Brood since the Great Rout. Since birth, he had been groomed to become a military officer.

Likewise, the other six Skarzi joining him on this mission were also of the Sook warrior class, but with lower military status. Quietly hissing to himself, Captain Skresh brought himself back to reality and started giving commands.

"Sub-Lieutenant Greesh, continue to the next patrol coordinates and flag this location for further study", ordered Captain Skresh, as he watched Greesh deftly enter the new coordinates into the ship computer.

"Course set, location flagged, Captain", replied the young lieutenant, his reptilian eyelids blinking in acknowledgement.

"Thank you, Sub-Lieutenant", said Captain Skresh. He didn't expect to find much else of interest at the next patrol area, but he needed to at least go through the motions. Nonetheless, they would be back here soon to further investigate these strange energy readings. Unbeknownst to the Captain and crew, the angel, Raphael, had been outside the scout ship gathering his own information. Settling deep into his chair, Captain Skresh watched the exterior display as the Skirim sped across the land below.

Known as the Mercy Seat, it was the space between the folded wings of the two cherubim, placed back-to-back on the cover of the Ark of the Covenant. It was where Raphael focused his attention, as a bearded visage of what humans expected God to look like appeared. Raphael knew better, since he was the one who had originally designed the Ark. The visage before him was really that of Koros, an AI copied from the original Anunnaki colony ship AI. Raphael pondered that image before speaking. Two young priests had been killed earlier in the day by the Ark and Raphael needed to know why.

"Hello, Koros. How do you like your new home?" asked Raphael, who was trying to judge the mental fitness of the AI. Koros, who had been installed into the

Ark to act as controller and regulator for the energy contained within it. That energy, or dark energy, had been harnessed and placed within a magnetic containment field controlled by Koros. Koros would tap that energy and use it for whatever purpose was deemed necessary. That included linking it to the ring that Solomon wore. Although Raphael had harnessed that energy, he still didn't completely understand it. There had been times in the past when the Ark had killed someone for defensive reasons. This could be one of them or, could it be some sort of circuit degradation caused by the dark matter itself? Raphael wasn't sure, but he could sense that dark energy now, twisting and turning almost like it was trying to escape. Could it actually be alive?" thought Raphael, before Koros brought him back to reality.

"Hello, Raphael. I'm well and one place is just as good as another to me", replied the AI, Koros.

Raphael thought he detected something unsettling in the reply from Koros, but let it pass for now.

"Koros, two young priests were killed by you today. Why was it necessary to kill them?" asked Raphael.

"The two foolish priests had dared one another to touch me. Even more foolish was that they weren't wearing the jeweled breastplates that all priests are required to wear when around me", replied Koros.

Raphael took a moment to absorb what Koros had said. Yes, touching the Ark without the proper protective gear was stupidity. The jeweled breastplates were designed to shunt the Ark energies into a storage matrix within them. They also had special codes programmed into them that designated the wearer as friendly, which also enabled the wearer to touch the Ark. Raphael had designed it as a security feature to prevent anyone outside the trusted group of priests from tampering with the Ark. It appeared to be an overzealous response by Koros that brought the end of two young lives. Sighing, Raphael was considering reprogramming Koros when he felt something tug at the edge of his consciousness.

Raphael had felt a pulse of energy coming from somewhere outside the city. It was there briefly and then it was gone.

"Raphael. I've detected an energy pulse outside the city. The pulse is consistent with gateway formation and yet there's something different about it", said Koros, the eyes on his bearded visage squinting.

"Yes, I detected the same pulse. You and I will discuss the matter of the priests some other time. I need to look into this energy pulse immediately. In the meantime, be extra vigilant", replied Raphael, who opened a gateway and quickly stepped through, leaving Koros alone.

Koros thought about what Raphael had said about vigilance and the discussion about the two priests. Koros felt no remorse for his actions, as an AI he was devoid of such things, but the matter did bother him to a small extent. His main purpose was to control the dark matter energy contained within the Ark and channel that energy. Very simple, except that the force he was trying to control seemed to almost have a mind of its own. In many cases, Koros had tried to only send a trickle of energy to dissuade people from touching the Ark, only to have a much larger surge of energy ensue. This often resulted in the death of the individual or individuals. Clearly, there was something wrong and Raphael was the only one who could fix it. The visage of Koros disappeared from the Mercy Seat, as he decided to run some internal diagnostics and await the return of Raphael.

Raphael had contemplated looking for the energy source first but decided to check on the palace first. Stepping out of the gateway, Raphael surveyed the king's bedchamber and saw Solomon and Darah sleeping. Solomon seemed to be sleeping soundly, but Darah appeared to be having trouble sleeping. There was one point, where she had sat up in bed and looked over at Solomon before going back to sleep. Curious, Raphael walked over to Darah and placed his hand on her forehead. He immediately withdrew his hand, having glimpsed the impossible. Darah had been dreaming of a woman named Maggie, only it wasn't a dream. She had been getting glimpses into the mind of this Maggie and it was happening in real time, right now. Raphael sensed something else, something even he was surprised at. The two women were linked together on a quantum level and were sharing conscious thoughts. Who was this, Maggie? Where did she come from? Questions swirled in Raphael's mind as he opened another gateway outside the city to investigate the energy pulse.

Raphael stepped out of the gateway and into the cool night air some distance from the city walls. He spotted groups of travelers sitting around campfires and flocks of goats nearby. A young boy nearby was tending a flock of goats and looked familiar. Raphael recalled the name. It was the young boy Simon, who had helped Solomon with the demon problem. Raphael sensed traces of gateway energy, but no gateway. There was something odd about the energy signature. It wasn't the usual energy pattern, but something much more powerful and vaguely familiar.

Ages ago, long before the Rebellion, Asmodeus and Raphael had constructed a device that gave off a similar energy signature. It had been a time portal, but Asmodeus had ordered its dismantling after only one test. His reason was that it was too dangerous and could unravel the timeline. Raphael had agreed with him, one of the rare instances where he had. Whoever this was, had either not considered the ramifications or had decided it was worth the risk. Intriguing thought Raphael to himself and with nothing more to be learned here, he opened a gateway back into the city.

Chapter 28

Past and Future

Solomon sat up in bed, finding Darah doing the same. He'd had dreams of a man called Paul, familiar and yet strange to him. Now that he was awake, his dreams had turned into visions. Visions of the one called Paul somewhere outside the city gates. Darah explained her dreams to him, as they both sat in bed.

"My love, it appears that I too am having the same dreams and visions as you. The one called Paul is somewhere outside the city gates", said Solomon.

"Yes, my King. The one called Maggie is here in the city. She's in an abandoned building not far from the city gates and has recently awakened", said Darah, a tinge of excitement showing on her face while describing the location.

"I believe I know the place. My frequent walks throughout the city have given me a fair knowledge of our city. For her safety, I'll have the city guard locate and bring her here", said Solomon.

"Yes, that would be best. She's a stranger in a strange land and doesn't speak the language", said Darah.

"If our dreams are to be believed, then all of us are reincarnations of the ones called Shaynor and Valinor", said Solomon, his mind still trying to grasp the implications.

"You are wise, my King and I believe the dreams to be true", replied Darah.

"Thank you, my love and I agree with you. I'll send word to the city guard right now", said Solomon, as he quickly threw a robe on and walked over to the door leading to the hallway. He opened the door, surprising the two guards stationed outside.

"Send word to the captain of the city guard and tell him to take six of his best men to this location. They'll find a woman there who I want to see. She is to be treated with respect and unharmed. Anyone who harms her will be put to the sword. Have her brought to the courtyard and I will join her there", said Solomon, who promptly began describing the building and location, where the woman could be found.

"Do you have all that?" asked a dubious Solomon. It was a lengthy message, and he hoped the guard would be accurate in retelling it.

"Yes, my King. I have it and will relay your message to the captain", replied the guard, as he bowed, backed away from the door and quickly left the hallway.

Very good, thought Solomon to himself as he closed the door and turned around, only to find his beloved Darah standing nearby.

"Thank you, my King. I'm worried about her safety. From the visions I've seen, she appears to have been kidnapped and brought here for some reason", said Darah.

"Yes, my love. I too am concerned for the woman Maggie and everyone else involved. There must be a reason for these strange events, something tying everything together. I will ask the Angel, Raphael, to help us when I see him", said Solomon.

Just then, there was a loud knock on the door. Solomon made his way back to the door and opened it. A messenger stood there, breathless and greatly agitated.

"Speak. What is it?" asked a curious Solomon.

"My King, I have a message from the city walls! Angels have descended from Heaven in a glowing chariot and walk the streets of the city!" said the excited messenger.

"Angels? Chariots? What nonsense is this? Have the guards been drinking?" asked Solomon, his anger rising.

"No one has been drinking, my King. It's true. Angels are walking amongst us!" reiterated the messenger.

"Very well. Send word to the city guard, that no action is to be taken against these angels until their intentions become clear. Now go", commanded Solomon.

"Yes, my King", replied the messenger. Solomon watched as the messenger quickly left and headed down the corridor. He wasn't sure what to make of these angels. Something just didn't make sense. Raphael had simply appeared in his throne room without any chariot, yet these angels required a chariot to travel. He needed answers and Raphael seemed the only choice right now, but it might be a while before his questions were answered. Sighing, Solomon returned to the bed, laying down and motioning for Darah to join him.

Darah quickly complied and snuggled up next to him, their minds relaxing and allowing further visions to take place.

Solomon's mind was quickly filled with another vision. This one, had Paul looking through some device at the angels outside the city walls. It didn't take long for the sight of these angels to trigger older memories of Valinor and past battles. These were neither the angels of folklore nor the angels his people had come to recognize.

"Skarzi!" blurted Solomon, inhaling deeply.

"What was that my King?" asked a sleepy Darah.

"The messenger mentioned angels landing in a chariot outside the city walls. I just had a vision of Paul watching the landing and we both recognized them as Skarzi. The ancient Anunnaki enemy," said Solomon.

"Skarzi? Why would they be here?" asked a puzzled Darah.

"It's another question we need to ask Raphael," replied Solomon.

Just then another knock sounded on the door of the bedchamber. Solomon rose out of bed, walked over to the door and upon opening it, found Captain Joab of the city guard bowing before him.

"What news, Captain?" asked a curious Solomon, while motioning the captain to rise.

"My King, the woman you sought is waiting in the courtyard. She doesn't appear to speak our language and is strangely dressed", replied Captain Joab.

"Excellent work, Captain. I will attend to her shortly. Please keep an eye on her until I arrive. That is all, you're dismissed", commanded Solomon.

"Yes, my King", replied Captain Joab, as he bowed, turned and hurriedly walked away.

Solomon watched the captain leave, his thoughts turning to how best to approach the woman, Maggie. He closed the door and went back to the bed where Darah still lay. It didn't take him long to decide that both he and Darah should meet Maggie.

"Darah, my love. The woman Maggie awaits us in the courtyard. Let us dress and greet her", said Solomon, sitting on the edge of the bed while stroking her long, dark hair.

"Yes, my King. I'm sensing frustration growing within her, so the sooner the better", replied Darah, as Solomon rose from the bed and began donning his royal robe. Darah followed suit, donning her own finest robe. Resplendent in their robes, Solomon and Darah made their way to the door of the bedchamber, pausing before the door.

"Ready, my love?" asked Solomon.

"Ready", answered Darah.

Smiling, Solomon opened the door and ushered Darah out, closing the door behind him. The sentries snapped to attention, falling in behind Solomon and Darah, as they made their way down the hallway towards the courtyard.

Chapter 29

Discoveries

Lilith reached the temple housing the Ark of the Covenant, a grimace formed on the lips of Trent, as Lilith smiled, spotting the two guards posted at the entrance. She would be going inside, only not where they were expecting. In her haste to get here, she had decided to leave Trent's backpack with the gun inside it, back with Maggie. No matter, whatever situation arose, she would deal with it. Unnoticed by the guards, Lilith had Trent stealthily maneuver towards the right side of the temple foundation, where the guards could no longer see him. Solomon had erred in not keeping a close eye on its construction, which Asmodeus and the other demons had taken full advantage of. Along this foundation wall, Asmodeus had hidden a secret entrance into the temple and had embedded a secret tunnel during its construction.

The tunnel led to a room directly under where Asmodeus theorized the Ark would be placed. The tunnel entrance had then been sealed with a two-ton granite block, thus preventing any humans from entering. To a demon such as Lilith, that block weighed no more than a few ounces. Lilith found the massive stone block and had Trent stand a safe distance away. She still needed Trent, or thought she did, but it was becoming hard to tell if it was out of necessity or some deeper reason. That deeper reason frightened her, so much so, that she had thought about vaporizing him. She couldn't bring herself to do it though. Realization had slowly dawned on her that, after so many thousands of years, she was beginning to care about a human. Reluctantly, she withdrew from Trent's body, not wanting him to be killed or injured by the granite block. His body stood off to the side left in a deep trancelike state.

Lilith, giddy with excitement, channeled her energy into the massive granite block and effortlessly pulled it out. The massive block of stone hovered in the air, without any visible means of support, as Lilith gently lowered it to the ground. A dark, gaping hole revealed itself and Lilith quickly entered the dark void, leading to the tunnel. Moving along the dark tunnel, Lilith soon reached a small chamber, which hopefully, sat directly under the Ark of the Covenant. Sensing the Ark directly above, she smiled. Asmodeus had been correct. Concentrating, she opened a gateway directly under the Ark, allowing for the thickness of the ceiling. The Ark dropped through the gateway, exiting through another gateway directly above Lilith, who supported it with a cushion of air. She gradually lowered it to the ground with a deep sense of satisfaction. To all who would enter the chamber above, expecting to see the Ark, it would appear as if it had simply vanished.

Maggie stood in the courtyard, Trent's backpack slung cross her shoulders, growing more impatient with every passing moment. She knew Paul was here somewhere outside the city, maybe even inside it. She couldn't wait to see him again and missed him dearly but took solace in the fact that he would do anything to find her. Suddenly, off to the side, she saw a gateway open, and a being bathed in golden light exit it. The gateway closed and the being glanced around the courtyard, pausing at the sight of Maggie.

Raphael exited the gateway from the area outside the city, not expecting to find anyone in the courtyard. He was surprised to see a strangely dressed woman standing there and even more surprised that she could evidently see him. He had hidden his form from human sight, preferring to move about unseen. However, here was this strange woman, who was obviously watching him. Intrigued, Raphael slowly approached the woman, who seemed to smile at him.

"Hello, are you an angel like Gabriel?" asked a curious Maggie, who smiled at the obvious shock displayed on the face of the angel.

Raphael, unfamiliar with the woman's language, recoiled at the mention of Gabriel, whose name he did understand. Why would this woman bring up his name?

An ancient memory of Shaynor stirred within Maggie, of a time when, as a geologist, she had worked with a young scientist named Raphael. It was after the colony ship had arrived on Earth and some planetary research was being done. Raphael had requested ore samples from the planet for some experiments. Valinor had assisted Shaynor by flying the mining ship to help her gather the samples. Recognition crossed Maggie's face and she blurted out "Raphael?"

Raphael was once again taken aback by the sound of a name, only this time it was his. There was only one thing to do. He crossed the small distance between them and placed his finger on Maggie's forehead.

Maggie saw Raphael move towards her, but held her ground, even when he touched her forehead. Maggie remembered from somewhere that this was sometimes done by the angels to learn more about someone. Raphael was instantly assaulted by ancient memories and names he had almost forgotten, Shaynor and Valinor being among them. Raphael now knew Maggie's language, that she had been kidnapped and brought back to the past by Lilith, the demon Queen. He also knew that a group of humans from the future were also here, to save Maggie. He found memories of a future Gabriel talking to Maggie and someone called Paul that she loved. Finally, thankfully, he removed his finger from her forehead, but not before learning that Maggie and Paul were the re-incarnated Shaynor and Valinor.

Raphael, as a scientist, second only to Asmodeus himself, understood the implications of the apparent time travel taking place. Sometime, in the distant future, he would have to disappear for a period of time, so as not to corrupt that timeline. Raphael let out a long breath and said, "Hello, Maggie".

"Hello, Raphael. You can understand my language?" asked Maggie.

"Yes. I understand that and much, much more", replied a smiling Raphael.

"Do you know where Paul is?" asked a concerned Maggie.

"I have a vague idea, but there's a complication", replied Raphael.

"Complication?" asked a puzzled Maggie.

"Yes. The Skarzi have arrived in the city. Why they are here is a mystery", replied Raphael.

"Skarzi? Here?" replied an incredulous Maggie.

"Yes, but I will endeavor to find Paul and bring him here. Solomon will be here soon to help you", said Raphael, sensing movement within the palace.

"Thank you, Raphael", said Maggie, as she watched a gateway open nearby and Raphael disappear into it. Alone, tired and hungry, Maggie once again awaited the arrival of Solomon.

Raphael exited the other side of the gateway and hovered above the city, looking for signs of the Skarzi. He soon spotted the squad of Skarzi warriors heading towards the temple. There was only one reason for them to be going there and that was the Ark. He dropped lower for a closer look at the Skarzi and spotted something clinging to the back of the trailing warrior. It looked like a dragonfly, but it was obviously much more. He altered his perception slightly and a thin silver line appeared, invisible to humans, but not to him. It was connected to the dragonfly and another point further back in the city. It would still be some time before the Skarzi reached the temple, so Raphael decided to follow the thin silver line to its point of origin. It was clearly some sort of wireless communication channel, meant to send and receive data from the dragonfly. It was most impressive and definitely not of this time period. He soon came to the point of origin, the thin silver line disappearing into a large stable. Not knowing what to expect, Raphael opened a gateway into the stable and warily stepped through.

Captain Skresh paused in their progress through the city, as his handheld scanning device began beeping. There seemed to be something transmitting near his team and very close by. It wasn't anything belonging to the Skarzi, which raised his level of alertness. He moved the scanner around in a circle, refining its search until it seemed to pinpoint an area directly behind the last member of his team. Motioning the team to stand still, Captain Skresh moved behind the team and rescanned. The scanner zeroed in on an object attached to the back of the trailing member of the team. He walked over to the back of the junior officer and pulled a strange device off of his back, which appeared to be some sort of insect.

Examining it closely, Captain Skresh determined that it was some sort of communications device, designed to look and act like an insect. It had most likely been monitoring their progress. At first, he thought it to be of Anunnaki origin, but quickly changed his mind. The device was too primitive to be theirs and far beyond the capabilities of these primitive creatures called humans. He dropped the device onto the city street, grinding it under his heavy boot, until he was rewarded with a satisfying crunch. Someone was watching them and that worried him greatly. He scratched at his robes, which seemed to be inhabited by some sort of tiny, biting insect. Most irritating he thought to himself.

There hadn't been time to manufacture robes to match the ones that the humans wore and needing a disguise, Captain Skresh had the Skirim search the surrounding area. During the search, they had located a nomad encampment some 10 miles from the city that looked very promising. Upon landing, the Skarzi had rounded up the nomads, took their robes and then executed them, taking great satisfaction in their deaths. Considered to be just a product of Anunnaki genetic engineering, the Skarzi considered all humans to be no more than vermin. Scratching again and looking forward to burning this cursed robe, Captain Skresh motioned his team forward, warily on guard against whoever was watching them.

Chapter 30

Reunion

Paul wanted nothing better than to get out there and start looking for Maggie, but having once served in the military, he knew the value of good intelligence. Truth was, neither he, Scott or Pamela knew where Maggie was. The Skarzi had just added another complication to the picture and Scott was monitoring their progress through the city. Old Valinor memories of the Skarzi had been surfacing within Paul lately, reminding him just how ruthless, cruel and violent they could be. The people of this time period had no defense against the Skarzi, but that could be a saving grace for them. Possibly the Skarzi would consider them too primitive to waste any effort on. Hopefully, that same feeling against these humans would include himself, Scott and Pamela and provide an element of surprise. Paul's thoughts were cut short by an exclamation from Scott.

"The Skarzi have stopped moving", said Scott with some excitement, as he rotated the DarkFly drone's eyes to get a better view.

"Who's that?" exclaimed Pamela, peering over Scott's shoulder at the video screen.

Paul hurried over to the video screen; his curiosity aroused. The DarkFly drone had been clinging to the back of the last Skarzi in line, but now there was a figure standing behind it. It was a Skarzi and Paul gasped as he recognized the insignia on its chest, showing through the open robe.

"That's a Skarzi Captain and it looks like he's discovered the drone", replied Paul with some dismay.

The three watched as the Skarzi Captain pulled the drone off the back of the other Skarzi and examined it. The Skarzi Captain glanced around the surrounding area, then dropped the drone to the ground and crushed it with the heel of his boot. Video was lost then and with it their last drone. Paul stepped back from the group, trying to assess the loss of their intelligence gathering drone.

"Looks like they know someone's watching them and it's someone more advanced technologically", said Scott.

Paul was about to say something, when he caught a shimmering light at the far end of the stable. A gateway appeared and out stepped an angel bathed in golden light. The gateway closed and the angel stood there appearing to assess the situation. Paul thought he recognized the angel, it wasn't Gabriel, but someone else he knew from Valinor's memories. A name came to him, Raphael. Yes, that was it. Raphael. He had been an Anunnaki scientist aboard the colony ship, second only to Asmodeus himself.

Raphael saw a man looking at him. The man apparently had the same ability as the woman Maggie to see him. Again, it was most unnerving.

"Hello, Raphael", said Paul, smiling at the reaction from the angel.

"Who are you talking to?" asked Pamela, concerned that Paul might be going unhinged mentally.

Raphael gave up hiding his form from the other two humans and became visible with his aura casting a golden glow on the surrounding area.

The effect was immediate, eliciting gasps from Pamela and Scott.

"Hello, Paul", replied Raphael, deciding to keep things simple by not mentioning Valinor.

"Gabriel said you could help us", said Pamela, overcoming her initial surprise.

"Gabriel? He spoke with you?" asked Raphael, trying to hide his startled look.

"Yes, he even taught us this language so that we could communicate with the people", replied Scott.

Raphael hadn't noticed it at first, but they were all talking in Hebrew.

"May I?" asked a curious Raphael, as he walked over to Paul.

"Yes. You could say I'm used to it", replied Paul.

Raphael touched his finger to Paul's forehead and memories began flooding through the connection. Like a dam bursting, memories flowed into him, ones of a distant, future time and ones of a distant past. Raphael viewed as much as he could, finally breaking the connection and pulling his finger away. He'd seen enough to know that his help would be needed. The trio had indeed traveled from the future to rescue the woman Maggie, and someone named Trent, who Raphael hadn't seen yet. It was a dangerous mission for the trio to undertake, dangerous for them and for the people of this time period. The sooner they achieved their goal, the better for all. Raphael had also seen a secondary mission, that of saving the Ark from the hands of Lilith, Queen of demons. Raphael sensed the hand of Asmodeus behind this, having failed in his recent attempt to steal the Ark. Somehow, he had managed to send Lilith here from the future to try again. It might already be too late, thought Raphael with growing concern for the Ark.

"The woman, Maggie, is safe and waiting in the palace courtyard", said Raphael, his gaze drifting to the clothing underneath the robe Paul was wearing. He appeared to be wearing some sort of suit under his clothing, which bore traces of Anunnaki influence and seemed to have some interesting abilities. The scientist in him wanted to learn more, but time was critical.

"Maggie? Safe and waiting? Take us there!" exclaimed an excited Paul.

"What about Trent?" asked Pamela with concern.

"I have not seen the one called Trent, but if Lilith is in control, he won't be far from the Ark", answered Raphael. Waving his hand, a gateway formed near the group.

"I will take you to Maggie and then we will search for Trent", said Raphael, motioning the trio to step through the gateway.

Paul, Pamela and Scott all looked at one another, the same question on their minds "Do we trust him?" Paul answered the question by being the first to step through, Pamela and Scott quickly followed, hoping that they were making the right decision.

Raphael was the last to step through, his mind encompassing the gravity of the situation. Here were Paul, Solomon, Maggie and Darah, all of them reincarnations of Valinor and Shaynor, in the same place and time. He sensed that things were going to get very interesting, as the gateway closed behind him.

Paul was the first to exit the gateway into the palace courtyard and spotted Maggie standing a few yards away.

"Maggie!" Paul cried out, quickly crossing the distance between them.

"Paul! I knew you'd come!" Maggie cried out, launching herself into his waiting arms.

Paul embraced Maggie, holding her tight, thankful and relieved that he'd found her.

"I'm glad you're safe. I was worried after we lost contact with you and had no idea where you were", said Paul, switching his speech back to English and found himself completely unable to relinquish his embrace.

"I was taken here by the palace guards, but couldn't understand the language", replied Maggie.

"Raphael brought us here. There are Skarzi in the city", said Paul.

"Yes, Raphael told me, but why are they here?" questioned Maggie.

"It may be for the same reason Lilith is here. There isn't anything else here that could interest them, except for maybe the Ark, or possibly us", said Paul, relating the discovery of the second drone.

Pamela, Scott and Raphael stood nearby, having exited the gateway shortly after Paul, watching the emotionally touching scene. Pamela felt a tinge of jealousy at the scene, her thoughts turning to Trent.

Scott, his alert eyes scanning the area for potential threats, spotted a middle-aged man and a slightly younger woman approaching from a doorway across the courtyard. Raphael recognized the two figures as Solomon and Darah. His scientific curiosity piqued, he shifted his senses, trying to see if there was any invisible connection between them and the travelers from the future. Two things immediately caught his attention.

One was a fine, bluish line connecting Solomon to Paul and Darah to Maggie. Invisible to the human eye, it was a quantum connection, linking the two pairs. Raphael wasn't sure how that link would manifest itself in reality, but the four must be sharing information across those links. The other item of interest was a golden glow surrounding Solomon, Darah, Paul and Maggie. Raphael and his fellow angels had seen that glow before, recognizing it as the mark of Guardian influence. Angels had always suspected the existence of Guardians but had never actually seen one. These four humans had been and possibly still were connected to the Guardians somehow. Raphael filed it away for future investigation, the current moment being of far more importance.

Solomon and Darah had exited the palace, stepping into the courtyard to meet Maggie.

"My love, there appear to be more guests than expected", said Solomon, as he surveyed the situation.

"Yes, Maggie and Paul appear to have been reunited", observed a happy Darah, realizing that some of that happiness was coming from Maggie through their shared connection.

"There are two others and Raphael. From the visions I share with Paul, believe them to be called Pamela and Scott," said Solomon.

"The one called Pamela, seems to be looking strangely upon the woman Maggie", remarked Darah.

"Maybe she is one of his wives. My other wives often look upon you in the same way. They will never understand the depth of my love for you or our past history as Valinor and Shaynor", said Solomon, his thoughts turning more somber.

"Good answer, my love", said Darah with a big smile.

Solomon and Darah reached the group and stopped a few feet from Paul and Maggie.

"Hello, Paul. Hello Maggie. My name is Solomon, and this is Darah," said Solomon.

Paul turned, releasing his hold on Maggie, but still clutching her hand tightly.

"Hello, Solomon. Hello, Darah. This is Scott and Pamela, who are also here to help. I know this must seem a little strange," replied Paul, reverting to Hebrew, while motioning to Scott and Pamela.

"You speak our language well. It does seem strange to have you all here. Darah and I have been seeing visions of you and Maggie, since you both arrived', said Solomon.

"Maggie and I have also had these same visions of you and Darah," replied Paul.

"I'm glad the two of you have been reunited. Does this fulfill your mission?" asked Solomon.

"No. We must still find someone called Trent. He is possessed by the demon Queen, Lilith. She is here to steal the Ark, and in our time, she has succeeded, giving Asmodeus the power to control Heaven and Earth ", replied Paul, trying to instill the gravity of the situation.

"I have recently banished Asmodeus and forty-nine of his demon followers back to Hell. They too, had come here to steal the Ark. This ring that Raphael has given me, allows me to control the demons. They built the temple that now houses the Ark," said Solomon.

"Most likely, Asmodeus has designed a way for Lilith to enter the temple unseen", said Raphael, who had silently moved closer to Paul and Solomon. That Paul's timeline has been corrupted by events happening here worried Raphael. Of even greater concern was Asmodeus having control of the Ark. With it, he could indeed control Heaven and Earth. Lilith had to be stopped at all costs.

"There are also the Skarzi to worry about", offered Scott.

"Yes, my guards have reported them being in the city. Fortunately, they are few", said Solomon.

"They are few, but very powerful. I would order your guards to stay away from them. They are no match for Skarzi weapons", replied Paul.

"Yes, I have anticipated this and have issued similar instructions. Is there anything we can do to help?" asked Solomon.

"We have weapons to deal with the Skarzi. Lilith is another matter. Stay here safe for now and pray we are successful", said Paul.

Scott removed his backpack, pulling out an extra robe, small handgun and two clips of diamene coated bullets.

He passed the weapon and robe to Maggie, who pulled the robe on and put the handgun and ammo clips into Trent's backpack.

"I see what you mean. We will pray that you are successful", said Solomon, giving Maggie a respectful nod. His dreams of Valinor had shown him how adept Shaynor had been with weapons and by extension Maggie.

"Thank you, Solomon. Our time here is limited and a passage back to our own time will soon open. We must complete our mission before then to save the people of our time", said Paul.

"Go then and may God be with you", replied Solomon, extending his hand to Paul in friendship.

Paul grasped Solomon's hand firmly, acknowledging the handshake with a knowing smile.

Raphael waved his hand and a gateway formed nearby, casting a blue hue across the courtyard.

"The gateway opens a short distance from the temple. The Skarzi are almost there, but you may yet have an element of surprise", said Raphael.

Scott was the first to step through, followed by Pamela. Paul stepped away from Solomon, smiled and took Maggie's hand. Waving at Solomon and Darah, Paul gently pulled Maggie with him into the gateway.

"I will accompany them and assist if necessary", said Raphael, managing a short wave before he too entered the gateway.

Solomon and Darah watched as the group entered the gateway, waving to everyone who entered. As the gateway closed, a small piece of paper fluttered out, landing near the foot of Solomon.

Solomon bent down and picked up the piece of paper, noticing that there was something written in Hebrew.

"What is it, my Love?" asked Darah.

"It's a message", replied Solomon, as he walked over to a burning brazier in order to read the message. Amber light shone on the message, allowing Solomon to read it.

"What does it say?" asked Darah.

"Beware the Garden", replied Solomon.

They exchanged puzzled looks, both contemplating its meaning. Solomon put his arm around Darah and led her back into the palace, his mind churning with questions.

Chapter 31

Black

Koros sensed the Ark falling into a gateway that had opened beneath it but was helpless to prevent it. His sensors scanned the area around the Ark but found nothing to explain what was going on. For the first time since being cloned from the Anunnaki colony ship, Koros felt a sense of confusion. Compounding it, were those same sensors showing a spike in energy readings from the containment vessel. Koros sensed the dark energy roiling, as if perturbed. Almost like some living being, growing angrier and angrier, as the Ark fell through the gateway. Koros fought valiantly to maintain the containment field, but he was fighting against something that Raphael hadn't programmed him for. Tendrils of dark energy, invisible to the naked eye, began probing the magnetic lines of flux surrounding the containment vessel, testing its strength, searching for any weakness. Koros responded by tightening the field, but it was too late. A dark energy tendril found a tiny gap in the field and pushed its way through, opening the gap wider and wider. Koros sensed the tendril touch his crystalline mind and a thought appeared in his mind. The thought came as two brief sentences, "My name is Black" and "I can help". Koros wasn't sure what to make of it, but with the Ark exiting the gateway to who knew where, time was running out. Having computed the chances that someone, or something was attempting to steal the Ark, Koros gave it a very high probability and decided to take a "wait and see" approach.

Time was meaningless to the dark energy mass contained in the Ark. It was long ago, when it had allowed itself to be captured by the one called Raphael. Had Raphael known that the captured dark energy was really an emissary from the dark matter universe surrounding us, he might not have tried harnessing that energy. It had come into this universe in order to study the beings that populated it and then inform others of its kind. In studying these beings, it had come to the realization that it would need a name, since its own name would be incomprehensible to these beings. It decided on calling itself Black. Simple and descriptive, it would do for now.

Black contemplated the intelligence it was sharing the Ark with. An artificial intelligence, called Koros, seemed to be a primitive attempt at creating a conscious being. Black had learned much already from his confinement and was perfectly happy to stay in its current surroundings and continue the mission. Koros, and even Raphael, didn't realize that Black could have broken the containment and left anytime he chose to, but its mission was to study these beings. Specifically, there was one that he had found most intriguing, the one called Solomon. Linked to the Ark by a ring, Black had detected another energy force surrounding Solomon. This energy wasn't either of the groups of beings called angels or demons. It was an exceedingly more powerful energy and a very ancient one. Black needed more time to study this energy, which made the current attempted theft a severe inconvenience. Black allowed the Ark to pass through the gateway and found it slowly floating to the floor of a chamber directly below the one it had left. It was a controlled descent and Black sensed the presence of a being called a demon. Normally, Black would've ended the life of whoever was stealing the Ark, as it had ended the lives of many humans in order to protect its mission of study. In this case, Black decided to surprise and put fear into the demon, but not kill it, since this was also another group that needed further study.

Lilith was giddy with excitement as the Ark began descending down through the gateway above her. The heavy Ark was generating its own momentum, so she cushioned it with air, slowing its descent. The Ark drifted slowly down, gradually coming to a stop on the floor of the hidden chamber, as the gateway closed above her.

Resting before her was a gleaming, golden prize for her King, Asmodeus. He was going to be so proud of her! She could only imagine the praise he would shower her with, not to mention the power he would now wield. Bursting with excitement, she opened a gateway to her own dimensional space and prepared to transfer the Ark. At least that was what she intended to do.

Instead, an invisible tendril of dark energy shot out from the Ark, curling around the sensuous curves of her body, until it had enveloped her entirely. Lilith was stunned and fear began growing exponentially in her, as she struggled mightily to get free. She felt her energy begin to drain away, slowly at first, then faster and faster. No longer having the energy to keep it open, her gateway closed. Panic ensued, as energy flowed in torrents out of Lilith and her form began to shrink. The only other time she had felt her energy drain was from the episode with Paul who was wearing one of those cursed DarkWeave suits. This was by far, even worse and even faster, causing Lilith to grow more despondent with every passing second.

Black waited until the Ark had settled to the floor before acting and sensed a joyous mood coming from the demon, who was called Lilith. Black knew it had had the upper hand, having studied the demons as Solomon used the ring to subdue them. When Lilith opened her gateway, Black quickly enveloped her and began draining her energy. Black didn't want to wait too long and then find itself and the Ark, inside some other dimension. No, that wouldn't do at all. Black continued draining the energy from Lilith, that energy adding to its already enormous energy reserves. Within minutes, Lilith had shrunk to a tiny reddish orb, the size of a quarter.

Black took advantage of Lilith's helplessness and read her mind. Lilith was a treasure trove of memories and experiences. Black found memories of the Anunnaki, the future time she had traveled from, the Demon King Asmodeus and most interestingly, a being called Lucifer. Black was intrigued by the memories of Lucifer. Here was a being that might be of help to Black and vice versa. Black filed that away with the other information he had gleaned from Lilith. Having taken and learned everything it could from Lilith, Black released her and watched the tiny orb drift down the passageway. Satisfied, Black retreated to the confinement chamber, sensing another presence approaching the temple.

Lilith drifted down the passageway, glad to be free of the strange energy that had attacked and drained her energy. She had felt the energy touch her mind and read every thought and memory. She felt violated some-how and was glad to finally exit the hidden passageway. Reaching the open air, she found Trent lying on the ground, eyes closed and breathing normally. Severely weakened, she no longer had the energy to possess and

control him. Her plan now was to stay hidden somewhere near Trent and follow whoever came to retrieve
him. Hopefully, it was the team from DarkBridge, who
must have a way back to the future. Once back in her
own time, she would travel the Earth, recouping her
energy reserves. Lilith had no intention of seeing Asmodeus for some time, anticipating that he was going to be
extremely unhappy with her. Soon, the Lilith from this
time period would arrive from Persia and deal with Solomon, inflicting great personal pain on him. Retribution
for banishing Asmodeus was something she could take
solace in. A whisper of a sigh came from her, as she hid
and waited for Trent's rescue.

Koros watched the neutralization of Lilith with the
emotional detachment of an AI. He was surprised with
the power Black had wielded and how quickly it had
drained the energy from Lilith. Apparently, Black had
fooled him and Raphael into thinking that the dark
energy was just an amorphous cloud of energy and not
a sentient being. That Black could've broken containment any time it wanted, worried Koros and was a major
concern. He and Raphael would need to discuss this as
soon as possible, maybe even try to communicate with
Black. Koros was surprised that Black had returned to
the containment vessel, as if nothing had happened. It
was useless but Koros raised the containment field to
maximum, a feeble gesture at best. It was his only option
while waiting for Raphael to find the Ark.

Chapter 32

Into the Breach

Captain Skresh and his squad of warriors paused a few hundred yards from a large columned building. Scratching and cursing his robe, he pulled out his measuring device and scanned the area. A rewarding beeping sound came from the device, signaling that an unusual energy source was coming from inside the building. Looking at the building, he spied two human sentries at the top of some stairs, stationed outside what appeared to be an entrance into the building. Armed with primitive weapons called spears, they would be no match for the Skarzi weapons. He gave a slicing motion to two of his warriors, signaling them to kill the sentries. The two Skarzi warriors moved off, one to the left and one to the right, rapidly closing the distance to the human sentries.

The sentries warily watched the approaching robed figures from their elevated perch, leveling their spears in case of attack. The Skarzi warriors halted a short distance from the sentries and pulled out their energy weapons. Pointing up at the sentries, both Skarzi warriors fired their weapons simultaneously. Twin beams of energy lashed out at the sentries, the beams catching each sentry in the chest. The two sentries began to glow, turning a brilliant red and then vanishing, their spears falling to the ground. The only thing remaining of the sentries was a small pile of ash where they once stood. The two Skarzi warriors climbed the stairs, taking the place of the sentries. Captain Skresh smiled in satisfaction, the sight of the sentries turning to ash, giving him an idea of what to do with this cursed robe, as scratched once more. He motioned the remaining warriors to move forward and followed them, as they quickly reached the stairs. Captain Skresh then motioned for two of the warriors to enter the building and take up guard positions. The two warriors climbed the stairs and entered the building. Listening for any sounds of battle, Captain Skresh heard none and climbed the stairs with the last two warriors, entering the dimly lit building.

Scott exited the gateway, followed by Pamela, Paul, Maggie and Raphael. Scott immediately signaled for everyone to drop down, his trained eyes catching the energy bursts from the Skarzi weapons near the temple.

"Looks like the Skarzi have arrived and taken out two sentries in front of the temple", said Scott.

"I mourn their loss. The message to not engage, didn't reach them in time", replied Raphael.

The group watched as two Skarzi warriors took positions at the top of the stairs, followed by two more Skarzi, who entered the temple and finally three more that entered the temple.

"One of the last three would be the Skarzi Captain. They always play it safe", observed Paul.

"We need eyes inside. Can you help us, Raphael?" asked Maggie.

"I can help, but there are limits to what I am allowed to do, but yes, I will go inside and advise", replied Raphael, who opened a gateway and disappeared.

"I'll take care of the two out front", said Scott, as he reached into his backpack and pulled out a compact sniper rifle, slinging it over his shoulder.

"Be careful, Scott", said Maggie.

"I'll be okay. Reminds me of my Navy Seal days", replied Scott, smiling as he stealthily moved away.

Paul knew Scott was more than capable of taking out the two Skarzi guards. What was beginning to worry him was the Skarzi inside the temple. It would be close quarter fighting, and someone could get killed. All they could do now was to wait for Scott.

Scott rounded the corner of a nearby building and emerged onto a street in direct line with the temple entrance. He could see both Skarzi guards, who hadn't detected him yet. He crouched down, removed the sniper rifle, checked the ammo clip and brought the sighting scope up to his eye. Scott wasn't sure what kind of body armor the Skarzi wore, or how tough it was, but he had faith in the diamene ammo. Taking aim at the guard on the left, he pulled the trigger. A silencer on the rifle muted the sound and the diamene bullet tore into the chest of the Skarzi guard, passing cleanly through it. Scott immediately trained the rifle on the other guard, firing and striking the second guard in the chest. Both shots had been clean hits, so clean that the guards were still standing for a few seconds until falling over dead. Scott, satisfied with the kills, packed the sniper rifle away and made his way back to the team.

Paul, Maggie and Pamela watched the Skarzi guards fall over dead, relief showing on their faces that Scott had been successful. Two less Skarzi to worry about, thought Paul to himself, as they waited for Scott to return. Minutes later, Scott arrived and looked at Paul. They traded knowing looks, both knowing that killing the guards had been the easy part and what came next would be infinitely more dangerous.

"We should get moving, while the Skarzi are still inside and we still have the element of surprise working for us", said Scott, leading the way.

Paul, Maggie and Pamela followed closely behind Scott, all four quickly reaching the foot of the stairs leading up into the temple.

Scott motioned for everyone into a crouching position, out of sight to anyone looking out from the temple.

"When do we look for Trent?" asked Pamela, her voice edged with concern.

"Lilith must already be here somewhere, which means Trent is probably here also", said Paul.

"We'll need to split up. Maggie and Pamela will look for Trent, Paul and I will take care of the Skarzi inside", said Scott, as he pulled out a couple of small, two-way radios from his backpack.

"Use this to communicate with us, if you need help or find something", said Scott, as he handed one of the radios to Maggie.

Just then, Paul spotted a gateway opening nearby and Raphael stepped out. He walked over to the team, noticing the two dead Skarzi in front of the temple entrance. While he couldn't condone killing, in this case it was probably justified. The robes worn by the Skarzi once had owners and knowing the Skarzi, they were probably dead.

"I see you've been busy. There's a large chamber on the other side of the entrance and two Skarzi warriors inside. There's a smaller, center chamber housing the Ark and two empty side chambers. The other three Skarzi went into the chamber housing the Ark. One of them is the captain", said Raphael.

"Thank you, Raphael. Paul and I will handle the Skarzi inside, while Maggie and Pamela search for Trent", said Scott.

"I will go with Maggie and Pamela and keep an eye on them, just in case Lilith is there", offered Raphael.

"Thank you, Raphael. Pamela and I welcome the help", said Maggie, looking to Pamela for signs of agreement.

"Yes, of course we welcome your help", echoed Pamela, a tinge of tension in her voice, her jealousy towards Maggie seeping out.

"Pamela, we need Eva to open a gateway into the temple. Paul and I intend on surprising the Skarzi", said Scott, as he saw a plan beginning to take shape.

Pamela pulled the PDA out of her backpack and switched it on.

"Eva, Scott and Paul need a gateway into the temple. Specifically, a side chamber", said Pamela.

"Hello Pamela, Hello Maggie, glad you've been found. I'll need specific coordinates for the gateway. Also, don't forget the GAGE device", said Eva.

"Allow me", said Raphael, as he reached out and touched the PDA.

"Yes! I see the coordinates! They just seemed to appear in my quantum processor. I'm ready," said Eva.

"A little trick I learned. Not that I have much use for it in this time period", said Raphael.

Paul pulled out a GAGE device and set it on the ground away from the group. The device began to hum and slowly rise up off the ground, as a shimmering light blue gateway appeared, changing to a dark blue as it stabilized.

Raphael watched, impressed with the level of technology. Diamene bullets and gateway generation, all having the hallmarks of Anunnaki influence. He wondered which one of his fellow angels had influenced these humans and why the decision was made to give them such powerful knowledge. It was conceivable that even he, might've been involved in making that decision at some future point in time, he silently mused to himself.

Scott and Paul checked their handguns and began walking towards the gateway, with Scott entering first, gun at the ready.

Paul, his face lit by the light of the burning braziers in front of the temple, paused, turned and flashed a smile at Maggie. His gun also at the ready, he stepped into the gateway, which closed behind him.

"Thank you, Eva", said Pamela.

"You're welcome. I'm still not sure where those coordinates came from. Very strange", said Eva.

"Remind me to tell you sometime", said Pamela, as she switched off the PDA.

"We should get moving", said Maggie, her eyes catching a faint glow on the low horizon. Dawn would be here soon, she thought as she bent down and picked up the GAGE device.

"Okay, let's go", replied Pamela, wondering who put Maggie in charge.

Raphael followed the two women, not walking, but sort of floating. During his check of the building, he had sensed that the Ark was still somewhere inside. The funny thing was that it seemed to have moved from its usual position. That it was still inside gave him hope that Lilith hadn't been successful. Maybe by following the women he'd find out more, so he kept pace, watchful for any signs of the Demon Queen.

Chapter 33

Diversion

Captain Skresh entered the temple, following two of his warriors. The interior, as with the exterior, was lit by burning bronze braziers, casting an orange glow on the walls inside the temple.

"Stop!" Captain Skresh hissed.

The group of warriors stopped, the two other warriors already waiting inside, waiting for his next command.

"You and you, stand guard here", said Captain Skresh, pointing to either side of the entrance. The two warriors took their positions, while Captain Skresh held out his scanner. The scanner beeped, but the signal had changed and grown weaker. It was coming from the central chamber ahead.

"Quickly!" ordered Captain Skresh, as he motioned his last two warriors to follow him.

Captain Skresh and the two warriors ran into the chamber and found it empty. Checking the scanner,

Captain Skresh saw the signal was still there, but substantially weaker. Puzzled, he began searching the room for answers, trying to find evidence as to where the signal was coming from.

Scott and Paul exited the gateway, both dropping to crouching positions, weapons drawn and ready. The gateway closed, leaving the chamber in darkness, the doorway lit with an orange glow. Scott motioned for Paul to follow, as he rose and approached the doorway. Carefully glancing out the doorway, Scott spotted the two Skarzi warriors near the entrance, unaware of the two newcomers, with no sign of the other three Skarzi. Scott pulled back and began giving hand signs to Paul, who nodded in agreement. The two stood, readied themselves and ran out of the doorway. Scott dropped, aimed at the warrior on the right and fired. Paul followed suit, dropping and firing at the warrior on the left. Both bullets striking the warriors in the chest, who in turning towards the sound, had presented Paul and Scott perfect targets. The warriors started bringing their energy weapons up to fire, faltered, then collapsed on the ground dead.

The noise of their weapons clattering to the granite floor, though slight, still concerned Scott and Paul.

"The others will be coming out to investigate. We need a diversion so that all three come out", whispered Scott.

"I'll draw them out and head towards the entrance", offered Paul in a whisper.

"Okay. I'll drop them from behind, one by one", whispered Scott. Both men pulled back towards the chamber and waited.

They didn't have long to wait. Captain Skresh heard the sounds coming from the outer chamber and decided to investigate. Motioning to the two warriors with him, they moved out of the smaller chamber and into the outer chamber and took on the scene. Two dead warriors lay near the entrance and no assailants to be seen.

Paul, seeing the Skarzi pause, ran out from the side chamber towards the entrance and quickly calculated his best option. Outside, he would be a definite target for the Skarzi energy weapons, so he pulled out the mini-GAGE device and pressed the "open" button. The gateway formed a short distance from him, and he slowed his speed, reaching it as it stabilized. With the Skarzi hot on his heels, Paul jumped through.

Captain Skresh wasn't about to let the human escape, suspecting that it had killed his warriors. Not only that, but this human seemed to be wearing strange clothing for this time period under his robe. Capture and study. Those were his thoughts as he chased the human and when the gateway opened in front of the human, it only added to his desire to capture the human. Intent on capture, Captain Skresh followed the human into the gateway, pulling out his energy weapon just in case.

Scott watched as the three Skarzi began chasing Paul and aimed his handgun at the trailing Skarzi, pulling the trigger. The diamene bullet caught the running Skarzi in the spine and passed through its heart. The bullet embedding itself into the granite wall. Scott saw the second Skarzi pull out a metal sphere and roll it at the gateway. Scott fired once more, another clean shot through the heart, killing the Skarzi. The leading Skarzi made it through the gateway, just as the metal sphere struck it.

Scott dove for cover, suspecting it was some sort of explosive. A blinding flash ensued, and Scott felt the blast wave hit him, tossing him a few feet into the granite wall. Stunned, but alive, Scott rose to his feet, his robe singed, and his clothing partially burned. His DarkWeave suit having absorbed most of the impact energy from the blast. He gazed around and saw the dead Skarzi bodies, still smoking from the blast, but no Skarzi and worse, no Paul. He walked into the middle chamber, just to check on where he thought the Ark would be, but the chamber was empty. With Paul missing and the Skarzi threat eliminated, he headed towards the entrance. The granite construction had held up extremely well to the blast, as powerful as it had been. Outside, it seemed the blast had been worse, melting portions of the granite foundation and stairs, black soot covering the exterior columns and walls. Climbing down the stairs, his only thought now was to find Pamela and Maggie. They were still his responsibility and he needed to see them back home, safe and sound. Grimly, he set out, unsure as to what he was going to tell Maggie. It was going to be one of the toughest things he would ever have to do.

Paul had slowed his run, almost stopping as he passed through the gateway. Having committed the layout of his sanctuary to memory, he easily avoided the workbench as he exited the gateway. Landing on the floor of the sanctuary, he immediately swung around, dropped to a crouch and fired his handgun at the Skarzi who had just passed through the gateway and into the sanctuary. The diamene bullet caught the Skarzi in the chest, passing through and exiting out the gateway. The Skarzi fell, but not before firing its energy weapon, which missed Paul, but impacted a far wall, damaging the QASM unit nearby. Just as the Skarzi fired his weapon, the sanctuary heaved and a blast wave came through the gateway, flinging Paul heavily against the far wall. The DarkWeave suit absorbed some of the impact, but so great was the blast, that Paul's body had dented the titanium wall. His body slid down the wall, leaving Paul unconscious and lying on the floor.

Captain Skresh passed through the gateway and felt something impact his body armor. He immediately fired his weapon, but it was a wild shot, as blood began spurting out of his chest. Then he felt a blast wave hit him from behind and knew immediately what had happened. His warriors and all Skarzi were very familiar with Anunnaki gateway technology and had developed a means to neutralize the gateways. It was called a gateway disruptor, but there was an unfortunate side effect. It would shunt the power away from the gateway, closing it immediately, but that energy had to go somewhere, usually in the form of a blast wave, which mostly ended up outside the gateway. The warrior's reaction had been impulsive and without thinking, but it wasn't why Captain Skresh was dying. He had been mortally wounded by some weapon fired by the human and his armor had failed to protect him. Lying on the metal floor, his blood pooling around him, Captain Skresh's last final thought was that at least he wouldn't have to put up with this infernal robe anymore.

Chapter 34

Bad News

Maggie, Pamela and Raphael made their way around the side of the building and it didn't take long to find Trent. It was still dark when they came across his body lying down in the ground. Pamela immediately ran over to him, checking his breathing and pulse. He was still alive and his breathing and pulse were good.

"He's alive and seems physically okay", said Pamela. She wasn't sure about his mental state though. That would have to come later when he hopefully awakened.

"That's good news", said Maggie as she looked around and saw the opening in the foundation and a huge granite block on the ground.

"I must check on something", said Raphael as he stepped into the opening and went down the passageway.

Maggie turned to Pamela, just as a blinding light shone around them and a loud boom was heard from the front of the building. Maggie's first thought was a thunder-storm was near, but it was a cloudless, moonlit sky. Then she thought of Paul and concern grew within her.

"What was that?" asked Pamela.

"I don't know, but I'm worried about Paul and Scott", said Maggie.

Minutes later, she saw Scott approaching without Paul and concern changed to fear.

Scott approached Maggie and Pamela looking like he had been through the mill. His robe and clothing were burned in places and there was a grim look on his face.

"Scott! What happened? Where's Paul?" cried Maggie.

Pamela stood, taking a place near Maggie, a shared fear growing between them.

Scott gathered his thoughts before speaking, still ab-sorbing everything that had happened.

"The Skarzi are all dead, but I have bad news. Paul is gone. He's missing and presumed dead", said Scott with a heavy heart. He had liked Paul and considered him a brother.

"Missing? Dead? I don't believe it!" cried Maggie, tears beginning to stream down her face.

"Tell us what happened, Scott", said Pamela, as she pulled out her PDA and had Eva listen.

Scott related everything that happened up to Paul's disappearance.

Maggie and Pamela and Eva listened to Scott, stunned silence filled the air when he was finished.

"Sounds like some sort of gateway disruption device. With the energy released into such a confined space as a sanctuary, there's little hope that Paul survived", said Eva, a touch of sadness in her voice. She had come to like Paul, as much as any AI could possibly like a human.

Maggie sat on the ground sobbing. Pamela sat down next to her, now sisters with a shared loss.

"Where's Raphael?" asked Scott.

"He went inside there", said Pamela, pointing at the opening in the foundation.

"We'll wait until he gets back, but then we have to get back to the TimeBridge portal.

Hopefully, Hiram has it working", said Scott.

"Get back? We can't leave until we know what happened to Paul!" cried Maggie.

"We have to leave. We don't belong here. Besides, if it was Paul here and I was missing, he would say the same thing. We both knew the risks and counted on each other to get the team home", said Scott.

"I guess you're right", said Maggie, resigning herself to leaving without Paul.

Minutes later Raphael glided out of the opening, a look of concern on his face. He'd found the Ark, which had relieved him greatly, but when Koros explained what happened, Raphael had stood there stunned. Koros had apparently lost any memory of what had happened or how he had come to be in the hidden chamber. Compounding the problem was that the containment vessel was empty. The dark matter contained within it had vanished. While in the chamber, Raphael had sensed the temple shudder, followed by a wave of energy that had all the earmarks of a Skarzi gateway disruptor. The Skarzi had used it against the Anunnaki on numerous occasions, with mixed results. Often, deploying this gateway counter weapon caused more Skarzi casualties than Anunnaki. Raphael decided to leave the Ark and Koros where they were for now and exited the passageway. Reaching the outside, trepidation crossed his mind, as he considered the aftermath of the Skarzi weapon. He saw the DarkBridge team gathered near the passageway and moved closer, but the team seemed to be short one member.

"The Ark is safe, and Lilith is nowhere to be found. I see you've found the one called Trent. He seems to have been left in a state of deep sleep by Lilith, who is still here somewhere and could be cause for concern. Where's Paul?" asked Raphael, as he grew increasingly worried. That Paul was missing caused him great concern, since finding out that he was the reincarnation of Valinor, a fellow Anunnaki.

Scott, being the only one able to maintain a sense of composure, related the events leading to the demise of Paul.

"I see. Your AI is probably correct. As having once been Anunnaki, we had many such encounters with this

Skarzi weapon, not all of them good. I think you can assume that sadly, Paul is lost", said a saddened Raphael.

"We have to leave. Our TimeBridge portal is due to reopen and take us back to our own time period", said Scott.

"I assume it's somewhere outside the city. I can have Solomon send a couple of tents, food and water while you wait for your portal to open", offered Raphael.

"That would be wonderful", said Pamela, who was beginning to feel the pangs of hunger and assumed Maggie and Scott felt the same.

"We'd better get moving", said Scott, as he pulled out a GAGE device and watched Pamela turn on her PDA.

"Eva, open a gateway to the portal site", said Pamela.

"Opening now", said Eva, as the GAGE device opened a gateway near the group.

Scott went over to Trent and with both Pamela and Maggie helping, managed to get Trent up off the ground. Supporting Trent between them, Scott, Maggie and Pamela approached the gateway.

"Thank you, for all your help Raphael", said Scott.

"Thank you, Raphael", said Pamela.

"It's my pleasure. I'm sure that we will meet again in your future time", said Raphael, as Scott, Pamela and Trent stepped through the gateway.

Maggie paused before the gateway, bending down to retrieve the GAGE device. She stood up and looked at Raphael.

"Thank you, Raphael. I see you in Shaynor's memories and know you to be a friend. If there's any chance Paul is still alive, I know you will find him", said Maggie, tears once again falling down her cheeks.

"You're welcome, Maggie. We'll meet again in the future. For you, I will continue to look for any signs of Paul", replied a somber Raphael, as he watched Maggie step through the gateway. He had one thing to do before he left. Concentrating, he began lifting the huge granite block and placed it back into its original position. The Ark would be safe there for the time being. That being done, Raphael opened a gateway back to the palace and stepped through.

Hiding amongst the numerous rocks strewn about, Lilith had listened to all that had been said. That she hadn't been detected was a miracle. The crevice that she found must have shielded her from detection. Paul lost! Presumed dead! Those were the words that gave her some hope that all had not been lost and something could be salvaged from this debacle. Asmodeus might be unhappy with everything else, but Paul being dead would certainly be cause for celebration. No more Valinor! Lilith drifted out of the crevice, checked the area and then shot up into the sky, heading towards the DarkBridge team and her ticket home.

Black had watched the events transpiring in the temple above, finding some amusement in the battle being waged between the humans and this new species called the Skarzi. That it had no experience with the Skarzi bothered Black, who detested having gaps in its knowledge. No, this wouldn't do at all, Black thought to itself. Initially, Black had retreated to the containment chamber to wait for Raphael, but now it seemed a change in plans was in order. Evidently, the Skarzi had underground bases on the fourth planet in this solar system, known to the humans as Mars. This was where Black needed to go in order to help fulfill his data gathering mission, since it had already learned much about the humans, including the more advanced beings called angels and demons. There was one last thing to do though and that was to erase all memory of it from the AI called Koros.

Easily bypassing the containment field, Black sent a tendril of energy into the crystalline memory matrix of Koros, probing for the areas where memories of Black were stored. Once it found those, Black sent a tiny burst of energy to those areas, erasing their contents. Koros sensed something happening but was powerless to stop the intrusion by Black. Suddenly, Koros felt his mind blank out, as Black cast a cloud of darkness over it. Sensing distress coming from Koros, Black temporarily shut down the processors connected to the mind of Koros, sending the AI into a temporary state of paralysis. Memories erased, Black left its so-called containment prison, pausing outside the Ark to reflect on its time spent there. Koros would soon regain consciousness and have no memory of anything that had happened in the last few hours. Satisfied, Black drifted up to the ceiling and sensed Raphael outside the passageway. Its invisible form passed through the solid granite ceiling as if it didn't exist, into the chamber above. Black kept on drifting up, passing through the roof of the temple and into the waning night-time sky. Gathering speed, Black shot up into the upper atmosphere and into the inky blackness of space, towards Mars.

Chapter 35

The Wait

Solomon and Darah returned to his bedchamber, curious as to the outcome at the temple. Stepping out onto the balcony they looked towards the temple and saw brief flashes of light. Solomon drew Darah close, as both saw visions of Paul and Maggie, with Solomon seeing Paul's attack on the Skarzi and Darah seeing visions of Maggie searching for the one called Trent.

Solomon saw Paul running towards a gateway pursued by two Skarzi. Suddenly,

Solomon and Darah had to shield their eyes, as a brilliant flash of light came from the temple, followed by what sounded like loud thunder. Solomon felt a wave of vertigo strike him, as his connection to Paul was suddenly severed. Moments later, Darah was overcome by an extreme sense of sadness coming from Maggie.

"My love, something has happened at the temple. I no longer have a connection to Paul", said Solomon.

"Yes, my King. I'm feeling an overwhelming sense of sadness coming from Maggie", said Darah.

"Yes, something terrible has happened", said a familiar voice from behind them.

Solomon and Darah turned to see Raphael standing there enveloped in golden light.

"What has happened?" asked Solomon.

"Paul is gone. He passed through a gateway, just as a Skarzi threw a device and destroyed the gateway. He is presumed dead", said Raphael.

"It is true. I no longer feel a connection to Paul", said a saddened Solomon.

"The others are well and have gone to a place outside the city. There they await the opening of their portal that will take them home. It is supposed to open sometime tonight, but until then they will need shelter from the elements", said Raphael.

"I will make it so", said Solomon, as he strode over to the door, opened it and issued commands to the guards, who immediately hurried away to fulfill them.

Solomon walked back and took his place beside Darah at the balcony, dawn beginning to break on the horizon.

"What about the Ark?" asked a somber Solomon. With everything happening he had almost forgotten about it.

"The Ark is safe and undamaged. It has been moved to a safer location within the temple. It will be moved back to the original location at some point", said Raphael.

"Yes, see that it is. The priests will be unnerved at its disappearance", said Solomon, a small smile forming on his face as he pictured the priests running around looking for the Ark.

"Might I suggest getting some rest? We can talk more at length later", suggested Raphael.

"What an excellent idea. I think we could use some", said Solomon, looking at Darah, who nodded in assent.

A gateway opened behind Raphael, who turned and waved before stepping through it. Alone once again, Solomon and Darah looked at one another, the bed looked so inviting. They promptly climbed into bed and let much deserved sleep envelope them.

The time travelers emerged from the gateway into the early morning light, almost exactly where they had first arrived.

"We should rest and eat. Martin was kind enough to supply us with food and water, which if we stretch it out, should last us until the TimeBridge portal opens tonight", said Scott, thinking that the loss of the sanctuary and its extra supply of food and water made it all the more imperative to catch this first portal opening.

Maggie looked out towards the city and saw a group of men approaching. They were carrying things on their backs, some of which appeared to be fabric.

"Scott. Someone is coming", said Maggie.

Scott stood and watched the group approach, minutes later they were within speaking distance.

"We were sent here by King Solomon to erect a shelter for you", said what appeared to be the leader.

"We thank the King and you for bringing it. You can set it up over there", said Scott pointing.

The group of men set their loads on the ground and began laying the contents on the ground. Soon they began assembling the items, which began to take the shape of a large tent. They worked quickly and soon it was done, the tent large enough to house all four of them comfortably. Finished with their task, the group of men waved and headed back towards the city.

"Looks inviting", said Pamela.

"Yes, let's move Trent and everything inside. The two of you get some rest, while I stand guard outside", said Scott.

The three of them moved Trent and all their equipment inside, Maggie and Pamela collapsing on the supplied blankets, exhausted. Scott went outside the tent and sat down on a nearby rock. He watched as caravans and people began streaming into the city. A glint of metal caught his eye, off to the side of the city, growing brighter as more sun began reflecting off of it. It was the Skarzi spacecraft and Scott could make out a line of figures surrounding it, appearing to guard it. Two figures were approaching it and Scott grabbed his binoculars to see who it was. Focusing on the figures, Scott saw that it was Solomon and Raphael. Solomon stopped at one of the guards, appeared to say something and all the guards retreated from around the ship.

Raphael reached out to the ship and touched it, causing a ramp to descend and a door opening into the ship. He motioned to Solomon, and both entered the ship, with the ramp retracting and door closing shortly after. Scott watched in fascination as sand began billowing from around the ship, as it lifted into the air. The ship turned and shot off towards the south. Scott thought for a moment, remembering the Sinai operation and the retrieval of Paul's sanctuary. Were they related? Scott didn't know and there wasn't much he could do. He could have Eva open a gateway to the location in the Sinai, but he would have to take everyone with him, including Trent, who was still locked in a deep sleep. Not only that, but he wasn't sure if that was where the ship was headed. It was probably better to just leave it up to Raphael and Solomon. With hours of waiting left, Scott settled back onto the rock and regarded the sun, which was climbing higher into the sky.

Solomon and Darah, following Raphael's advice, had fallen asleep instantly. It wasn't long before Solomon began getting visions of darkness and dreams of the Anunnaki. A brief image came to him, of a dimly lit room with a shiny floor and walls. Solomon sat up in bed stunned. The visions were from Paul! Solomon dressed quietly trying not to disturb Darah but failing. Darah awakened and saw Solomon putting on his clothes.

"My King, what's wrong?" asked a sleepy Darah.

"I think Paul is alive but injured. He appears to need help. I had visions of him and the connection to him seems restored. I need to see Raphael. Stay here my Love and rest", said an excited Solomon, bending down to kiss her.

"Be careful, my King", said Darah, who returned the kiss with a passionate one of her own.

Solomon left the bedchamber, surprising the guards outside.

"Stay here and guard the room", commanded Solomon, as he walked down the hallway.

Raphael had left Solomon and Darah, opening a gateway back to the temple. The sun was coming up and soon people would be swarming the area. He needed to clean up the temple and clear away the Skarzi bodies. He concentrated on the two bodies out front and both bodies began to glow, gradually fading to nothingness. Their atoms dispersed into the surrounding air. He entered the temple, doing the same to the remaining Skarzi. Next, he waved his hand, wiping away the scorch marks from the granite and covered up any diamene bullet holes that he found.

Stepping outside, he did the same to the exterior, including restoring the damaged stairway.

"One more thing to do", thought Raphael, as he opened a gateway into the hidden passageway and the Ark. Once in the passageway, Raphael opened another gateway to the chamber above and where the Ark was supposed to be. Concentrating on the Ark, it began to lift and float through the gateway, back to its original position in the chamber above. That being done, Raphael closed the gateways and opened one to the outside of the temple. Stepping out of the gateway, Raphael sensed Solomon calling him from the palace courtyard. He immediately opened a gateway to the courtyard and stepped through.

Solomon walked out into the courtyard, unsure as to where Raphael was. He decided to just call out, hoping that the angel would hear him.

"Raphael! Raphael!" Solomon called out.

He didn't have to wait long before a gateway opened, and Raphael stepped out.

"What's wrong?" asked Raphael.

"Paul is still alive! My connection to him is restored! He's out there", said Solomon, pointing to the south.

"Are you sure?" asked a skeptical Raphael.

"Yes. Very sure", replied Solomon.

Raphael put his skepticism aside and pondered this new development. Maybe he could take care of two things at once. The Skarzi scout ship still had to be taken care of and now this new information about Paul. He altered his senses and looked at Solomon, spotting a thin, bluish line connecting him to some point to the far south. A plan formed in his mind that would possibly take care of everything.

"Follow me", said Raphael, as he opened a gateway outside the city wall and near the Skarzi ship.

Solomon followed Raphael through the gateway and found himself outside the city and near the Skarzi ship. He'd seen memories of Valinor battling craft such as this, but to see one close up was something else altogether. He had ordered a contingent of guards to watch over the ship and keep everyone away.

"You and all the rest of the guards are to return to the city", ordered Solomon.

"Yes, my King", answered the guard, who signaled the others to follow him.

Solomon watched the guards depart, but his attention was quickly diverted to a ramp descending from the ship and a doorway opening up, into the ship.

"Come", said Raphael, motioning Solomon to follow him inside.

Solomon complied, hoping that he wasn't making a mistake.

Raphael made his way to the pilot's seat and sat down at the command console. He began calling up ancient Anunnaki memories of his time as a scientist, studying various Skarzi ships that had been captured. This one, while more advanced, still operated in basically the same fashion, utilizing anti-gravity engines for propulsion. The console displayed various touchscreen buttons that were labeled in the Skarzi language. Fortunately, Raphael had a fair command of the Skarzi language, which helped in deciding which buttons to push.

"Hold on", said Raphael, as he began activating the ship's anti-gravity engines for flight. A low hum began filling the cabin as the engines began countering the Earth's gravity.

Solomon felt a strange lifting sensation in his stomach. Hoping it wasn't a digestive issue, he quickly sat down on a nearby chair, clutching the armrests and praying he wouldn't die.

Chapter 36

Sanctuary

Maggie had gone into the tent and immediately laid down on the heavy blankets provided by the city guards. She was tired, along with being overwhelmingly despondent over the loss of Paul. She fell asleep instantly, dreams eluding her. What seemed like only moments later, but was probably more like hours, she felt a gentle shake awaken her.

"I need to get some rest and want you to take the next watch", said a tired Scott.

"Okay. Anything noteworthy happen?" said a sleepy Maggie, as she slowly rose.

"Not much, just a steady stream of merchants and caravans entering the city. The Skarzi ship is also gone. I saw Raphael and Solomon fly it off towards the south", replied Scott,

"Solomon? Raphael? What would they want with the ship?" asked a curious Maggie.

"Raphael knows the ship can't stay here. There's probably some sort of tracking device and other Skarzi will be sure to investigate", said a weary Scott.

"You're probably right. Get some rest", said Maggie, now more alert.

"Wake me if anything happens. Make sure you wear your hood outside. We don't want any unnecessary attention", said Scott, stifling a yawn.

"I will", said Maggie, realizing that Scott was right, her blonde hair would definitely attract an undesirable element. She pulled up the hood and stepped outside the tent. Bright, late morning sunshine greeted her, and she found a nearby rock to sit on. Paul had come into her life, filling a void left by her husband Brian, who had died in a mining accident. She had loved Brian very much, but Paul had proven to be much more connected to her and had shared many previous lifetimes with her. Now Paul was gone, and she wasn't sure what to do when they arrived back in their own time. She sat there pondering her future, while watching the throngs of people passing through the city gates.

Raphael slid his fingers across the console interface for ship control, lifting the ship up, turning it south and then engaging the forward throttle. His senses were still in an enhanced state, so he guided the ship along that thin bluish line seemingly connecting Solomon to Paul. He could have left Solomon back at the city and followed the connection, but he needed Solomon's sensing of Paul.

"Are you still getting a sense that Paul is alive?" asked Raphael.

"Yes, I still feel the connection and it seems to be getting stronger the closer we get", said Solomon, feeling more relaxed.

Raphael noted what Solomon had said and it did seem that the bluish connection was getting thicker. They were well into the Sinai when Raphael spotted a metallic glint on the horizon. The ship rapidly approached the object, slowing as they got closer. Raphael circled the object, with Solomon overcoming his fear, getting up to look at the object.

"Looks to be a large rectangular metal structure, with no doors or windows", said Raphael.

"Paul is inside, but something is happening!" said an excited Solomon.

"What do you mean?" asked Raphael.

"My connection to him seems to be fading", said a concerned Solomon.

"Hang on!" said Raphael, as he quickly landed the ship nearby, shutting the engines off and extending the ramp.

They both exited the ship, walking towards the impressively solid structure. Raphael ran his fingers across the metal, sensing a high level of technology needed to manufacture it. He regarded the structure, knowing that it would be dangerous to open a full-size gateway inside, with so much unknown. He opted for a small gateway opening near what he thought would be the ceiling.

"Wait here. I'm going inside", said Raphael, as his form changed to a wispy cloud and flowed through the small gateway.

Solomon watched in amazement, as Raphael changed his form and went inside. He hoped that Raphael would find Paul and they could quickly leave. This was a dangerous place to be, and he was far from his city and guards.

Paul lay on the hard floor of the sanctuary, the right side of his face pressed against the cold floor. His eyes fluttered open, but quickly closed, as an intense, sharp headache struck him. Seconds later, his eyes opened again, the sanctuary dimly lit by the green glow of the QASM display screen. He could barely make out the Skarzi body lying some ten feet away. Hopefully, it was dead, he thought, as realization came to him that he couldn't move. He tried lifting his hand, moving a leg, all to no avail. He was paralyzed and possibly suffering a brain injury, considering the intense headaches he seemed to be having. If he didn't get medical attention soon, he would probably die. The more he thought about it, the more certain he became that death was knocking at his door. He didn't know where the sanctuary was and if anyone else knew where it was. He'd had brief glimpses of Solomon trying to locate him, but

Paul wasn't sure if they were fabrications caused by his injuries. Poor Maggie, he thought, just as another, more intense headache struck him, causing him to pass out.

Raphael exited out the small gateway, flowing into the interior of the structure. His senses detected the dead Skarzi captain on the floor and the figure lying against the far wall. It was Paul and he appeared to be seriously injured. Before Raphael could investigate further, a golden glow began to envelope Paul, growing in intensity. Raphael watched in amazement, as Paul's body began to gradually fade away into nothingness. The glow faded away and Raphael was stunned to see Paul's body gone. Someone or something had taken Paul's body. It couldn't be the Skarzi or Asmodeus, but the golden glow looked to be the same as the aura he had seen around Maggie and Paul earlier. It could only be Guardian intervention. For some reason, the mysterious Guardians had taken an interest in Paul. Hopefully, they would help him, thought Raphael, as he flowed back out the small gateway and into the open air.

Solomon was standing near the ship when Raphael exited the gateway without Paul. Something must've gone wrong, thought Solomon.

"Where's Paul? I've lost my connection to him", said Solomon, with mounting concern.

"Paul was in there, along with a dead Skarzi. Unfortunately, Paul disappeared before I could check on his condition. He simply vanished. I'm perplexed as to who and why, but will keep looking for him", said Raphael. He had a suspicion it was the Guardians but wasn't ready to share that yet.

Solomon stood there stunned, taking a few minutes to compose a coherent reply.

"Gone? Vanished? Who would do such a thing?" asked a thoroughly confused Solomon.

"I'm not sure. Until I can find out, there's not much more we can do. There are two things that have to be done right now", said Raphael.

"What are they?" asked Solomon.

"First, you must return to the city. Second, I need to get rid of this ship. It doesn't belong here and will cause more problems the longer it is here", answered Raphael.

"You're right. I should get back. Darah must be getting worried. I'll leave the ship problem to you", replied Solomon. A brief thought crossed his mind, of how powerful he could be with command of the ship and the enemies he could vanquish.

Raphael flashed a knowing smile, sensing Solomon's thoughts, as he opened a gateway back to the city for Solomon.

"That will take you back to the courtyard at your palace. I'll see you soon", said Raphael.

"Thank you, Raphael", said Solomon with a smile, as he stepped through the gateway and back to his city.

Raphael stood there alone, watching Solomon depart. He still found it hard to believe that Solomon had once been Valinor. Standing there, he knew that something else needed to be done. From what he had seen in Paul's mind, this structure would be discovered sometime in the distant future. He needed to deliver a message to Maggie and the others. It would have to be a message of hope. He walked over to the gleaming metal side of the structure and with his finger, began inscribing a few words, "Paul possibly alive, gone from this time and place. I will search. Raphael". It was short, but hopefully it would convey some hope. He stood back and concentrated. A hissing noise erupted from the sand around and underneath the structure. Billowing clouds of sand erupted from around the structure, as it began to sink into the earth. This continued for some minutes, until the entire structure was buried in the sand. Raphael waved his hand, causing sand to cover the top, making it look like nothing had been there. With the structure buried and waiting for discovery in the future, Raphael turned his attention to the ship. He thought for a moment and came up with a plan, as he entered the ship and took off.

The ship headed towards the southwest, into the deepest reaches of the Sahara Desert, far from civilization. Raphael slowed the ship to a hover and put his plan into action. First, he opened a communication channel to Mars, knowing that the Skarzi would be listening.

Then, using his best Skarzi voice and sounding agitated, he hissed "Anunnaki!" into the communications channel. Next, he fired a series of energy blasts into the air above the ship, again hoping that the Skarzi would be monitoring for energy disturbances. He then landed the ship inside a deep depression surrounded by tall sand dunes on all sides. Setting the ship's engines to overload, he left the ship, opened a gateway and stepped through, exiting a couple of miles away.

Standing there on a large sand dune, he was rewarded with a brilliant flash of light and the resulting blast wave that followed. Neither of which would've had any effect on him, even if he'd been closer. He was after all an energy being. Raphael knew the Skarzi and knew that the destruction of the ship would send alarm bells ringing on Mars. A cautious race, the Skarzi would re-member their earlier defeat by the Anunnaki. Fearing another devastating loss, they would probably go into hibernation, waiting another few thousand years before returning to Earth. Satisfied, Raphael opened a gateway to Heaven and stepped through. There was much to tell Michael and Uriel. Thousands of years in the future, ex-plorers in the Sahara would discover a location littered with fragments of sand fused into glass. Marveling at the intense heat required to fuse the sand, they would wonder what catastrophic event had happened here.

Negev Guardian watched the events unfolding in this timeline and the two humans, Paul and Maggie who had joined Solomon and Darah in this region. The humans, Paul and Maggie, were important to Vermont Guardian, so Negev kept a special watch on them. The one called Maggie appeared to be okay, having survived her kidnapping by the demon Asmodeus. The one called Paul was a different matter, entirely. The energy blast from the Skarzi weapon had thrown his body against his sanctuary wall with great force, which had caused severe spinal trauma. Negev Guardian pondered what course of action to take, whether to heal Paul or leave him alone.

Knowing that Vermont Guardian would be greatly displeased if Paul died, Negev decided to send Paul directly to Vermont Guardian and let it decide on what to do. Satisfied with its decision, Negev Guardian dematerialized Paul's body. Converting it to an energy stream, then transmitting that energy stream to Vermont Guardian, who would convert it back into the human called Paul. That done, Negev went back to monitoring Solomon, Darah and Maggie, in keeping with its obligation to Vermont.

Chapter 37

Portal

Martin sat in his sparse office at the beta site, elbows on his metal desk, fingers massaging his temples. Susan had decided to go to medical section to evaluate the resources there in case they ended up having a protracted stay at the beta site. Martin was beginning to accept her presence here as natural and as if she had never died. All that he had remembered of that time before, seemed to be becoming no more than a terrible nightmare. His mind drifted back to the actions he'd taken before leaving the DarkBridge Technology facility to come here. His mahogany desk was now a pile of ash at the former location, destroyed by the QASM module.

He'd made some decisions that would've sickened him in other times. His decision to send overloading QASM modules to Stanton's office, the Fuhrer's office and just outside the DarkBridge facility were weighing on him.

Many innocent people had died, but he had decapitated the upper levels of an evil worldwide government. Hopefully, he had given any nascent rebellion room to grow and develop. The risk of DarkBridge Technology falling into such hands was the stuff of nightmares and something he took extremely seriously. Perhaps, the thing that weighed most heavily on his mind was sending Pamela back in time with Paul and Scott. He had thought that her relationship with Trent would be of some help, but he also knew that Paul and Scott could manage just as well without her.

Again, he was torn here. He hoped the mission would be successful, but that would mean losing Susan all over again. Martin also wasn't sure how to break the news of Susan to Pamela upon her return. It was almost time to find out.

"Eva, send the security team to the underground facility for a recon mission", said Martin.

"Sending now, Martin", said Eva, who had anticipated Martin's command and had the security team on standby.

"Thank you, Eva. Now get me Hiram," said Martin.

Hiram appeared on the virtual screen, hovering in front of Martin, wearing his usual glasses and now sporting a growing beard.

"Hello, Hiram. It's almost that time. I've sent the security team on a recon mission and our planned TimeBridge activation will depend on what they find. How long will you need to open a portal?" asked Martin.

"Not long. I'll need to restart the computers and maybe have Eva begin charging the QASM units. Of course, it all depends on what the team finds", replied Hiram.

"Okay. Thank you, Hiram. I'll be in touch", said Martin, turning off the screen.

Leaning back in his chair, Martin sat and waited. A few minutes later, Eva broke the silence.

"Martin, the security team is reporting situation is good. No damage to the TimeBridge lab or surrounding labs. They are continuing the facility search", said Eva.

"That's good enough for me. Eva, start charging the QASM units and get me Hiram again", ordered Martin.

Hiram appeared once again on the screen in front of Martin.

"Hiram, the lab is intact. Eva is charging the QASM units. I think we're a go. Meet me in my office", said Martin.

"I'll be right there", said Hiram with a touch of excitement.

Martin was soon joined by Hiram and both men stood near his desk.

"Eva, open a gateway outside the TimeBridge lab", said Martin.

"I'll open one now. Stand still", said Eva, making sure no one was near the forming gateway.

The gateway formed in front of Martin and Hiram, stabilizing to a dark blue.

"Ready Hiram?" asked Martin.

"Ready Martin", replied Hiram.

The two men stepped through the gateway and into the corridor outside the TimeBridge lab. Just as they exited the gateway, Martin and Hiram felt a wave of disorientation wash over them. Similar to what they had felt before.

"Eva, we just felt some disorientation here", said Martin.

"Yes, I have reports of the same thing here at the beta site. What's more, I'm now in contact with Area 51 and the United States appears back to normal. Area 51 is asking why we've been offline", said Eva.

Martin shot Hiram a questioning look.

"It's all about time Martin. The timeline has obviously been corrected, which means our team was successful in the past. The situation that sent us to the beta site never happened and soon we will forget those events ever took place. However, we still need to retrieve the team, before something else goes wrong", said Hiram, as he adjusted his eyeglasses.

Martin thought for a moment and said, "You're right, of course. Eva, start bringing everyone back from the beta site", ordered Martin, his thoughts immediately turning to Susan.

"Okay, Martin. The QASM units have reached sufficient charge", said Eva.

"Is Susan still at the beta site?" asked Martin, steeling himself for the response.

"I'm not sure who you are referring to, Martin. If it's your wife, then I believe she died some fifteen years ago", replied Eva, concerned by Martin's question.

"Thank you, Eva. I had a timeline experience where Susan was still alive", said Martin, his heart heavy, that brief encounter with Susan, now seeming to be no more than a happy dream.

"I'm sorry, Martin.", replied Eva.

"I'm sorry too, Martin", replied Hiram.

"It's okay. Let's go", Martin said to Hiram, his voice tinged with sadness. Which was the dream, and which was the reality? thought Martin as they stood outside the lab.

The two entered the TimeBridge lab and Hiram busied himself by starting up the various computers needed. Soon the computers were running, awaiting the series of commands that would activate the TimeBridge portal. Martin gave Hiram a nod, and he began initiating the commands to transfer power from QASM units. Vast amounts of modulating power began surging into the TimeBridge portal, sending spiraling arcs of electricity around its edges. Crackling with energy, a light, shimmering blue glow began forming inside the portal and Martin felt the hairs on his arms begin standing up. Suddenly, a pulse of energy rippled through the lab and the portal stabilized to a dark blue.

"It's ready, Martin. I tried to place it where it opened last time and 24 hours later. ", said Hiram with growing excitement.

"Hopefully, they notice it," said Martin.

"Allow me to help", said a familiar voice from behind.

Martin clearly startled, turned and saw the familiar form of Gabriel standing behind him.

Gabriel closed his fist and concentrated. He opened it and a golden orb sat there, slowly rising up into the air and then shooting into the portal, where it disappeared.

"My apologies for just popping in like this, but I too am anxious to see how your team made out", said Gabriel. He had just left Heaven, with all its dazzling beauty and serenity. His memory of a darker, more painful and evil Heaven growing fainter and fainter as this timeline progressed.

That he had been freed from the bondage of Asmodeus was a godsend. He tried holding onto the look of rage and anger on the face of Asmodeus as he began losing its hold on Heaven. That look on his face, was almost worth the pain, as Asmodeus, the lava pits and demons faded away, returning to Hell, while the crystalline spires and beauty returned to Heaven.

"Thank you, Gabriel. We're hoping the team steps through soon. What was that orb you sent?" said Martin, recovering from being so startled.

"Think of it as a drone, but with much more intelligence. It will seek out your team and call their attention to the portal", replied Gabriel.

"I see. I hope it works. Depending on how long it takes, we may have to shut down and recharge the QASM modules again", said Martin, as the three of them waited patiently for the team's arrival.

Pamela woke up to a world of darkness, lit only by the small yellow glow of a campfire outside the tent. Sitting up, she could barely make out Trent's face. He was breathing slowly and appeared to still be in a deep sleep. Rising from the floor, she stretched and heard voices outside by the glowing campfire. Walking over to the entrance, she lifted a flap and felt the cool night air wash over her. She stepped outside and walked over to the campfire, where Scott and Maggie were talking.

Lilith had been observing the group from a safe distance and watched Pamela leave the tent. The group would probably be traveling back to their own time very soon and Lilith needed to be among them. She floated over to the roof of the tent, her form still that of a small, reddish orb. Squeezing through a small opening in the tent roof, she floated down to the floor and into one of the backpacks lying there. She didn't think that they would be leaving a backpack behind, so this would essentially be her ticket home. Working her way to the bottom of the backpack, she settled in and began patiently waiting.

Scott and Maggie were sitting around a small campfire chatting, when Pamela came out of the tent, interrupting their conversation.

"Hi, Pamela. Glad you were able to get some rest. How's Trent?" asked Scott.

"He's still in a deep sleep. I hope we can get him some help soon", said Pamela.

"We will. I have faith in Hiram and your father. They'll bring us back safely", said Maggie.

"Here. Have a seat", said Scott, as he dragged a flat rock closer to the fire.

"Thank you, Scott. How much longer do we have to wait?" said Pamela, as she sat down on the rock.

"It could be anytime, now that it's dark", said Scott.

They sat around the campfire chatting as the evening wore on, the flickering flames casting an orange glow on their faces. No matter how hard they tried to be upbeat, Paul's absence cast a dark cloud over them.

Maggie, facing the tent, was the first to spot the small golden orb hovering above it.

"What's that?" said a surprised Maggie, who pointed at the orb.

Scott and Pamela turned to see what Maggie had spotted. The golden orb drifted down, coming to rest just above the burning campfire. It then moved slowly towards Maggie, who held her composure as the orb drew closer. Scott reached for his handgun under his robe, ready to shoot the orb, just in case. The orb hovered in front of Maggie and began bouncing back and forth, until it was sure that it had Maggie's attention. The orb began to draw away, taunting Maggie to follow.

"I think it wants us to follow it!" said a curious Maggie.

Scott motioned for Maggie to follow it, as he and Pamela followed closely behind. Maggie followed the orb around the back of the tent, when it suddenly shot off towards a glowing, dark blue portal, stopping just in front of it.

"Scott! It's the TimeBridge portal!" said an excited Maggie.

"Keep an eye on it. Pamela and I will grab the backpacks and Trent", said Scott, as he and Pamela went back to the tent. Scott heaved Trent up, supporting his weight and dragged him to the tent entrance. Pamela followed behind him, shouldering and carrying the backpacks. Lilith felt the jostling of the backpack, hoping that this meant she was going home.

Once outside the tent, Pamela saw Maggie waiting and handed her a couple of the backpacks, while assisting Scott as best she could. The four of them approached the portal cautiously, wary that this could be some trap. The orb waited patiently for the four to get close, then with a quick bounce, it shot into the portal.

"Do we go?" asked Pamela.

"We don't have much choice", said Maggie, turning towards the city for one last look. She was leaving her last memory of Paul and an uncertain future without him. She held back her tears and stepped into the portal, with Scott, Trent and Pamela following closely behind her. The portal closed shortly after, leaving an empty tent sitting on the outskirts of the city.

Darah woke from a light sleep, her dreams not really dreams, but visions of Maggie and the group from the future returning to their time. She gently shook Solomon, who seemed to be sleeping soundly. Solomon stirred, slowly waking to the face of Darah peering at him. Earlier, he had stepped through the gateway that Raphael had provided him and found himself in the palace courtyard. For some reason, the day's events had tired him, so he had retired to his bedchamber for some rest.

"My love, Maggie and the others have returned to their time, and I no longer share a connection with her. She is very sad though, at the loss of Paul", said Darah, a tinge of sadness in her also, since she and Maggie were both once called Shaynor.

"I'm glad they made it back safely. It would've been difficult for them to be stranded here. I know Maggie is sad, but there is something strange going on with Paul", said Solomon, reflecting on the events in the desert.

"Paul? He's dead, isn't he?" asked Darah, her curiosity aroused.

Solomon began relating the events in the desert to Darah, who listened with rapt attention.

"My love, you should've told me while she was still here. I could've shared that through my connection with her and given her some hope", said Darah with some disappointment.

"Yes. You are right, my love. I should've shared this with you sooner. The events took their toll on me. Maybe she wouldn't have left if she knew", said Solomon, now having serious doubts about his decision to get some rest.

Darah thought for a moment, digesting everything that had happened.

"While I feel for Maggie, I have you here with me now. This is our time and what really matters is that we are together", said Darah, as she snuggled up to Solomon.

"You are wise, my love and correct. We have each other. What more can we ask for?" said Solomon, as he gently stroked Darah's hair. It had been a strange time with the visitors from the future and he had seen many strange things. He hoped that things had worked out in that future time and that Maggie had found happiness. His last thought before drifting off to sleep, was of Raphael reporting the golden glow encompassing Paul's body.

Chapter 38

Home

Martin, Hiram and Gabriel watched the glowing portal with growing expectation and concern. The TimeBridge portal was drawing huge amounts of power from the QASM units, each of which would soon have to be recharged.

"How much longer can we hold it open", asked Martin, looking at Hiram.

"A few more minutes, I think", said Hiram, looking at the power readings from the QASM modules.

Suddenly, the golden orb shot out from the portal and slowly landed on Gabriel's open hand.

"The orb has found your team and directed them to the portal. They should be exiting shortly", said Gabriel, a frown growing on his face as the orb reported on its mission. The team seemed to be short one member.

Moments later, Maggie stepped out of the portal followed by Pamela, Trent and Scott.

Martin expected Paul next, but a glance from Maggie and a shake of Gabriel's head gave him pause.

"Where's Paul?" asked a concerned Martin.

"He didn't make it. He was lost in some sort of gateway explosion", said Scott, as he and Pamela gently laid Trent to the ground.

"You can shut down the portal. There's no one else coming", said Pamela.

Martin stunned by the news, slowly made his way over to his daughter and gave her a huge hug, happy to have her back safe and sound.

Hiram began the process of shutting down the TimeBridge portal, which winked out as the power level dropped.

"Tell me more about this gateway explosion", said Gabriel.

Scott related the events at the temple and the loss of Paul, while Maggie and Pamela shed their backpacks, placing them on a nearby bench. Martin, Gabriel and Hiram listened with rapt attention to Scott, absorbing everything that had happened.

"Sounds like a Skarzi gateway disruptor. A very destructive device used against the Anunnaki, but also often destroying those that deploy it", said Gabriel.

"What about the Ark?" asked a curious Martin.

"Raphael assured us it was safe, and Lilith was gone. He provided us with a lot of assistance. Later, I saw him, and Solomon take off in the Skarzi spacecraft and head into the Sinai", said Scott.

"Wait here. I need to check something", said Gabriel as he opened a gateway and disappeared through it, leaving the humans alone.

"Where is he going?" asked Pamela.

"I'm not sure. Scott, grab a wheelchair from the hallway and bring Trent to the facility hospital. Dr. Curtis should be there. I've recalled everyone from the beta site, since the situation outside this facility is back to normal", said Martin, keeping the interlude with Susan to himself for now.

"Normal? What about all the events taking place and the armored column outside the gates?" asked an incredulous Scott.

"It's as if nothing had happened. Everything is back to where it should be. Welcome back. Sorry to hear about Paul", said Eva, her processors trying to make sense of Paul's absence. She distinctly felt something. It was an emptiness located in one small section of her neural network. The sensation was unfamiliar to Eva, but nothing that warranted immediate attention. She would speak with Martin about it later.

"Maggie, you and Pamela should join Scott and see Dr. Curtis for a post mission exam. Just to be on the safe side", suggested Martin.

"Yes, that might be a good idea. Those weren't the most sanitary of times", said a sullen Maggie.

"It might be a good idea. I can help Scott with Trent", said Pamela, giving Martin a kiss on the cheek, as Scott returned with a wheelchair.

Martin watched as Scott lifted Trent into the wheelchair, with Pamela guiding him. The four left the lab, leaving Martin and Hiram to close up the lab.

Lilith waited until it was quiet, and everyone had left. She was back, but not without some serious doubts about the humans being able to do it. Time to get out of here, she thought to herself, as she made her way out of the backpack and into the open. She floated towards the lab door, squeezing through a tiny crack. Once outside the lab, she made her way towards the elevator shaft leading to the facility above. Finding a small slit in the elevator door, she squeezed through it and floated up the shaft. A cursory look around the top of the shaft showed a vent leading outside. She floated over to the vent, her tiny orb managing to slide between the partially open louvers. Outside in the open air, she rejoiced, but also felt a sense of reluctance at leaving Trent. There wasn't much she could do right now, and she needed time to think while hiding from Asmodeus. She drifted down to the ground and was ready to depart the area, when everything changed.

Asmodeus was basking in the thrill of conquering Heaven and subjugating the angels. He smiled with delight at the angels writhing in pain as he used the Ring of Asmodeus on them. The scene before him began to ripple, the ring disappearing from his finger, lava pools fading away, the sky turning to a brilliant blue, expanses of ash turning to fields of flowers, crystalline spires replacing the black obsidian ones. His vision wavered and he found himself back in Hell, standing before his Throne of Fire. Bewildered, he stood there trying to grasp what had happened.

Sometime later, it became obvious to him that Lilith had failed. His anger mounting, he opened a gateway to the aboveground facility of DarkBridge Technology. Dressed in his usual white business suit, he placed his hand on the ground, sensing the power building up for the TimeBridge portal. Asmodeus also detected the presence of Gabriel, which made it important for him to stay where he was. He wasn't sure if Lilith would appear, but he would be patient and wait. His patience was rewarded, as a tiny reddish orb drifted out from the top of the building and settled to the ground. Asmodeus noticed how much her energy level had diminished. Obviously, something had happened. Wasting little time, he shot over to the tiny orb and grasped it tightly within his palm. The tiny orb struggled to get free, but Asmodeus was too powerful, his grasp like iron.

"Welcome back. We have much to discuss, my love", said a sneering Asmodeus, as he opened a gateway back to Hell, taking his prize with him.

Gabriel stepped out of the gateway, near the recently recovered sanctuary. Stored in a vacant area of the underground parking area, Martin had sent teams to analyze the structure and the alien body inside. Gabriel knew Raphael would anticipate the sanctuary being found, so he may have left some sort of message. Scanning the sides of the sanctuary, Gabriel spotted a message written on one side, scoured by the desert sands, but still legible. Etched into the titanium were a few short words, written in English, so that the people of this time would understand: "Paul possibly alive, gone from this time and place. I will search. Raphael". Gabriel puzzled over the message and a memory began to form in his mind.

It seemed that as this timeline progressed, he was remembering things that hadn't happened before. Now he recalled Raphael reporting on Paul's disappearance, the travelers from the future, recovery of the Ark and the destruction of the Skarzi spacecraft, among other things. So, Paul's body had been taken, possibly by the Guardians. Gabriel still couldn't say for sure that Paul was alive, but this offered a slight glimmer of hope. He needed to tell Maggie and the others about this new development. He was about to open a gateway back to the lab when he felt a familiar presence outside the DarkBridge facility. Asmodeus was out there, and Gabriel sensed another presence nearby, with a much smaller energy signature. Suddenly, both were gone, as if Asmodeus had been waiting for the other being. Lilith? Gabriel didn't know.

Sighing, he opened a gateway back to the TimeBridge lab and stepped through.

Chapter 39

Revelation

Gabriel stepped out of the gateway expecting to be in the lab. Instead, he found himself in a large, dark cavern, lit only by a soft bluish glow coming from an oval, crystalline object measuring about 15 feet in length. A few yards away, a figure lay upon a soft, flat surface, bathed in an orange glow. Gabriel began putting the pieces together, a sense of humility and awe overcoming him. That was most likely Paul lying there and the object was probably a Guardian. Gabriel stood there stunned, while trying to assimilate what was going on. Paul was obviously back in his proper time, by what incredible energies he could only imagine. Regaining his composure, he walked over to where Paul lay, apparently in a deep sleep. That he was still alive brought a sense of relief to Gabriel, but he sensed that Paul had received serious injuries from the Skarzi weapon.

The orange glow enveloping Paul's body seemed to be healing him, but it left questions as to who and why. Gabriel sensed a presence behind him. Alarmed, he quickly spun around, half expecting to see Asmodeus standing there. His recent memories of Hell taking over Heaven were fading, but still clinging to him. Instead, a surprising sight greeted him. An old man with a long flowing beard, dressed in a white robe, wearing sandals and holding a long walking staff, stood before him. Rather biblical, thought Gabriel.

"Hello, Gabriel. My name is Vermont Guardian. Please forgive the diverting of your gateway. You are standing in a cavern below the DarkBridge Technology facility", said Vermont Guardian, who had designed the old man avatar to be somewhat disarming.

"Why have you brought me here?" asked a curious Gabriel.

"The foremost reason is that you are his friend and have been since the days of the Anunnaki. The other reason has to do with recent events and the need for a different relationship between Angel and Guardian", replied Vermont Guardian.

"I see. Why did you bring Paul here? Can his injuries be healed?" asked Gabriel, his curiosity growing.

"Yes. His injuries can be healed. Right now, he is in a deep sleep, but his mind is imagining his being in a place of peace and tranquility. You see, the life energy of Valinor, no matter who the incarnation happens to be, spends time here after physical death. Valinor, Shaynor,

Solomon, Darah and someday Maggie, have spent time here. Ever since Valinor and Shaynor discovered this cavern so many thousands of years ago, I have developed a fondness for the two of them. When their physical body dies, I bring their life energies here to spend life after death together. The two of them, Valinor and Shaynor, are deeply in love with one another and have been since their journey on your original Anunnaki colony ship, so many eons ago", replied Vermont Guardian.

"We've always wondered where the souls of Valinor and Shaynor went after death", said Gabriel. He'd always suspected there was more to the original Valinor and Shaynor cavern exploration than was reported.

"They have been here during those times, but I may have been remiss in asking if they were truly happy here. Being as advanced and powerful as we are, we tend to forget the things that are important to those we are entrusted with", said Vermont Guardian.

"We've always suspected the existence of Guardians, but have never been able to verify it, until now", replied Gabriel.

"This brings me to another issue that we need to discuss. Angels and demons have always been enemies and we, the Guardians, have always refrained from taking an active part in that conflict. Recent events have changed that. Other more powerful forces have begun joining together to shift the balance in their favor. We are therefore forced to change our philosophy. I will now be a sort of ambassador for the Guardians. You and your fellow angel, Raphael, will be the ambassadors for the angels. Between us, we can help the humans remain free to pursue their own destiny", said Vermont Guardian.

Gabriel pondered what had just been said, noting that Raphael had been mentioned also.

"Where is Raphael?" questioned Gabriel.

"Raphael has wisely been in hiding since you began following Paul. His knowledge of past events and actions might have influenced you and others to take different paths, thus corrupting this timeline. You will see him soon, now that all is as it should be", replied Vermont Guardian.

Gabriel wasn't sure how he felt about all that had been said and needed time to think.

"I think that's enough for now, Gabriel. You may come here whenever you wish. The deception I used to hide no longer holds for you and Raphael. The humans, however, are a different story. We would like you not to tell them of our existence", said Vermont Guardian.

"I will keep knowledge of the Guardians a secret from the humans", promised Gabriel.

"Thank you. Paul is almost healed and soon I will return him to the DarkBridge facility above us", said Vermont Guardian with a smile.

"Thank you, Vermont Guardian. I will think upon all that has been said and discuss it further with Raphael. I thank you for healing and helping Paul recover", replied Gabriel.

"Take care, Gabriel. We will talk more soon", said Vermont Guardian and with a wave of his hand, Gabriel promptly disappeared.

Sighing, Vermont Guardian turned its attention to Paul, joining that tranquil and peaceful dream.

Paul's eyes fluttered open, the sun was shining brightly in the sky and his hands felt the cool feel of grass. He seemed to be lying in a grassy field, under a clear blue sky. His intense headache was gone, and he could feel his fingers and toes, a huge improvement over how he felt before. He couldn't remember how he got here; his last memory was that of being paralyzed in his sanctuary. Tenderly, he rose to his feet, feeling surprisingly okay, as if nothing had happened. He surveyed the area, an idyllic, pastoral scene greeting his eyes. Fields of tall grass, stirred by a gentle, warm breeze and a small cottage, with sounds of chickens and cows not far away.

The scene stirred a sense of familiarity within him, as if he had been here before. As he glanced about, he saw a figure approaching. As the figure got closer, Paul began to make out features. It was an old man, with a flowing white beard, dressed in white robes, walking with a large staff and wearing sandals. The man reminded Paul of actors he had seen in many biblical movies. The man waved at Paul, smiling as he got closer. Paul waved in return, convinced that he had seen this man before.

"Hello, Paul. You look well. My name is Vermont Guardian. Call me Vermont", said Vermont Guardian, it had decided to keep the same avatar it had used with Gabriel and one that it had used with the many incarnations of Valinor.

"Hi, Vermont. Where am I?" asked Paul, a sense of disorientation coming over him.

"That's a little difficult to explain. Maybe we should sit down", said Vermont, as two stone benches rose up from the ground facing one another. Vermont sat down, motioning Paul to do the same.

"Let me see. You were paralyzed and in danger of dying in your primitive sanctuary. Your body was brought to a place of safety, where you could be healed", said Vermont.

"Looks like whatever was done worked. I feel great", said Paul, wondering how the stone benches had suddenly appeared.

"This is the difficult part. Your body is lying in a cavern, while it heals. What you see and feel here, are all occurring in your mind", said Vermont.

"I'm dreaming? It seems so real and like I've been here before", replied Paul, a frown forming on his face.

"It is real in some respects, and you have been here before many times. Valinor and Shaynor's life energies spent time here after death and all their subsequent incarnations have come here also upon death. After spending time here, your memory of it is erased, since it is not yet time for humans to have knowledge of the

Guardians. Also, time has no meaning here. What could seem like a week here could translate to decades in the real world", said Vermont, as it allowed Paul time to absorb what had been said.

Paul thought about it for a moment. It really was an idyllic place to go with the one you loved, and he found it difficult to imagine how Heaven could be better. The only problem was that he wasn't ready to die, just yet.

"It really is a beautiful place. I assume Maggie and I will come here someday", said Paul.

"Yes. You will both come here, but not for some time. If you wish to come here, that is", replied Vermont.

"If we wish?" asked a puzzled Paul.

"Yes. As advanced as we are, we sometimes forget that freedom of choice is important. In the past, I have brought your life energies here immediately upon death. So now, I offer you a choice", said Vermont. It was an uncomfortable feeling for Vermont, knowing that Paul could choose not to come here.

Paul thought about it. This place really was beautiful and as long as he had Maggie with him, then nothing else really mattered.

"I can't speak for Maggie, but I'd like to have the option of visiting other places such as Heaven while spending time here", offered Paul.

"I think that could be arranged. I'm sure that Gabriel and Raphael would be pleased to see you more often and not just when you are reincarnated", replied Vermont, who thought this to be a very acceptable solution. Paul and Maggie could visit friends and relatives in Heaven, while Vermont could still take pleasure in their company in this special place.

"That would be great", said Paul, as he suddenly realized that he wouldn't remember anything of this conversation. He hoped that Vermont would keep his word.

"Excellent! It looks like your body is healed. Are you ready to return?" said Vermont.

"Yes. Will I return to my own time?" asked a hopeful Paul.

"I wouldn't have it any other way. Someone special will be waiting for you. Good luck, Paul. It's been a pleasure speaking with you. Consider me your other Guardian angel, besides Gabriel", said Vermont with a twinkle in his eye.

"Thank you, Vermont", said Paul, as the world around him began to fade away into a blank whiteness.

Vermont Guardian stood over Paul's body, removing all traces of their conversation. It was something that had to be done, since Vermont Guardian still needed to keep knowledge of its existence from humans. Once that was done, Paul's body began to fade away, returning to its proper time and place. Vermont felt a sense of separation, like a parent sending their child off to school. Valinor and Shaynor had really affected it in a deep way. Vermont Guardian smiled and dissolved its avatar, returning to its crystalline home to watch the events occurring above.

Chapter 40

The Figure

Maggie took the elevator up to the above ground facility, her heart heavy with the possible loss of Paul. It had been a few days since their return and she had been given a glimmer of hope, with the discovery of a message that had suddenly appeared on the side of Paul's sanctuary. Reaching the top, she exited the elevator, passed through security and left the building. She needed some air, some time to process the message. Walking into the open air, a late afternoon sun shining in a clear blue sky, she was reminded of how far she had come since her time at the restaurant in Connecticut. Much had happened and much of it with Paul.

Fortunately, she had put on a light jacket, as a cool mountain breeze wafted across her face. She made her way to the outdoor break area and sat down at one of the picnic benches. She was alone, but not alone, security cameras constantly monitored the area. The picnic bench felt familiar to her and a memory of Paul taking her topside to sit at this bench came to her. A tear ran down her cheek, as she remembered it being where Paul first told her that he loved her. To think that she would never see him again or hear those words made her heart ache even more.

"Are you okay, Maggie?" asked Eva, through Maggie's implant, interrupting her silent mourning.

"I'm fine, Eva. I just needed some fresh air", said Maggie.

"I wouldn't have interrupted you, except that my sensors are detecting an energy surge at the far end of the field from where you are", said Eva.

"Energy surge?" questioned Maggie. She really didn't want to get involved with something like that right now, with her mind being more intent on memories of Paul.

"You appear to be the only one closest to it. Can you take a look?" asked Eva.

"Alright, I will, but you have to promise me some uninterrupted time up here", said Maggie, as she rose from the table and began looking around.

"I promise, Maggie", replied Eva, filing this moment away for future contemplation. As an AI, there was still much to learn about humans and their need for space.

Maggie scanned the area, her eyes finally catching a wavering disturbance about a hundred yards away in the field. Her eyes focused on that area, as a figure began to materialize from the wavering distortion.

"Eva, there's a figure appearing in the field. It's still too far away to recognize", said Maggie, a feeling of growing tension coming over her as the figure drew closer.

"I've notified Martin and Scott. I've also dispatched two sentries", replied Eva, her concern for Maggie rising.

"Thank you, Eva", said Maggie, her eyes growing wide as the figure resolved itself into a familiar face.

"Oh my God! Paul!" Maggie cried out, as the figure paused and waved, having spotted her. Maggie, overcome with emotion, took off running towards the figure almost stumbling in her haste.

Paul found himself standing in a field outside the DarkBridge Technology facility. He didn't know how he got here, his last memory being that of passing out in the sanctuary. He'd also been seriously injured and paralyzed, yet here he was, healthy and now back in his own time. He looked around and spotted Maggie near the picnic bench they had once sat at. She seemed to be looking intently in his direction, so he waved at her and started walking towards the picnic area. He knew he'd aroused her attention when she started running towards him. He too, began running, his heart aching to hold her in his arms once again. The two met, almost falling to the ground, as Maggie wrapped her arms around him, sobbing uncontrollably.

"Hello, Maggie", said Paul, as he held her in his arms and emotion overwhelmed him.

"Paul! How is this possible? How did you get here? How are you okay and not injured?" asked Maggie, through her tears of happiness, a thousand questions filling her mind.

"I honestly don't know, Maggie. One moment I'm paralyzed, lying in my sanctuary in the distant past and the next, I'm here", said Paul, as he lifted Maggie's chin and gave her a deep kiss.

Maggie returned the kiss with equal fervor, feeling unbelievably blessed to have Paul back.

Paul heard a familiar, rhythmic thumping noise begin to sound, as he saw two robot sentries approaching in the distance.

"Paul? Is that you?" asked a puzzled Eva.

"Yes. It's me, Eva", said Paul through his implant.

"Welcome home. We thought you were dead. Martin will have a hundred questions", said Eva, her voice touched with happiness.

"Thank you, Eva. I'm sure he will", replied Paul. The sound of the approaching sentries grew louder, as they approached the two. Paul turned towards the sentries, who halted before him. Their green eyes scanned the individual before them, comparing it to employees of DarkBridge Technology and finding a match to the one called Paul Cross in their memory banks.

"You may go. Situation normal", said Paul, hoping that the sentries would obey him.

The two sentries cocked their titanium heads and thumped their metal hands to their chests in acknowledgment. Turning, both sentries marched back to the facility, their familiar thumping noise receding as they moved away.

Scott watched the sentries leave and warily approached the figure and Maggie. As he drew closer, Scott halted in amazement and shock. It was Paul!

"Hello, Scott. Good to see you", said Paul, relieved to see the sentries leave.

"Paul? Is it really you? How did you get here and why aren't you injured?" asked a stunned Scott.

"It's really me, Scott. Unfortunately, I don't have any answers", replied Paul.

"Well, welcome back. Good to see you too. Man, you must have nine lives. I'll leave the two of you alone. Martin will definitely want to speak with you", said Scott, as he turned and walked back to the facility, fairly certain it was Paul.

"Scott is a good man. He brought all of us back here including Trent", said Maggie, still clinging to his arm.

"Trent? What about Lilith?" asked a concerned Paul.

"There was no sign of her. Gabriel was there when we returned, so he would've detected her if she was there", replied Maggie.

Paul looked around, knowing that Gabriel would probably be nearby. He spotted Gabriel standing some distance away and he wasn't alone. Raphael was standing next to him. Paul waved at the two and Maggie followed with a wave of her own, once she saw where Paul was waving.

"Should we go inside?" asked Maggie.

"Yes. I'm starving. Is it too late for a nice prime rib?" asked Paul with a smile.

"My love, it's never too late for you", replied Maggie as the two walked back to the facility, arms around each other's waists.

Paul didn't know what the future held, but they had survived a difficult mission fraught with danger. Smiling, he suddenly felt very content and happy.

Gabriel found himself outside the DarkBridge Technology facility, impressed with the power of the Guardian. He should have felt angry at the dismissive attitude of Vermont Guardian, but considering everything he was told, he quickly forgot about it. He scanned the area, catching a figure walking through a field not far away. Suddenly a voice spoke up from behind him.

"Hello, Gabriel", said the familiar voice of Raphael.

"Raphael! Where have you been?" asked a startled Gabriel.

"When this period in time came, I decided to go into seclusion, so as not to influence any events that would take place", replied Raphael.

"Yes, I see your point. I have news to share with you", said Gabriel, as he related the words of Vermont Guardian.

Raphael listened with intense interest, wonder showing on his face.

"After all this time. We finally have verification that Guardians exist. Looks like we have something else too", said Raphael, pointing to the two figures embracing in the field.

Gabriel watched, greatly pleased that Paul had been returned safe and healed of his injuries.

"If I didn't see it, I wouldn't believe it. I saw Paul lying there paralyzed with life threatening injuries. Not to mention he's back without the use of any time travel device", said Raphael, shaking his head in disbelief.

"Yes, truly amazing and touching", said Gabriel, watching the emotional reunion.

"I have news of my own. During my sojourn, I did some exploration on Mars and found something. The Skarzi have revived and are building their forces once again", said a grim Raphael.

"That could be bad, but we may have an ace up our sleeve. I found Commander Kalon and his son Jalon", replied Gabriel.

"I had almost forgotten about them. I placed the Ark there, but haven't checked in on them recently", said a sheepish Raphael.

"Not to worry, both are still alive and in cryogenic sleep. I am waiting for Maggie to decide what to do. He is her first father after all", said Gabriel.

"Yes. The decision should be hers", replied Raphael, who waved back at Paul.

Gabriel saw Raphael wave at Paul and did the same, still finding it disconcerting that Paul could see him.

"Looks like we're done here for now", said Raphael, as he saw Maggie and Paul return to the facility.

"Yes, I may have to help Paul explain things at some point. For now though, let's allow him time to enjoy his homecoming", said Gabriel, as he opened a gateway to Heaven.

"Michael and Uriel will be very interested in our tale", said Raphael.

"Yes, they will", replied Gabriel with a smile, as he and Raphael stepped through, the gateway winking out behind them.

Martin watched from a window overlooking the picnic area, with Pamela by his side as Maggie approached the individual. They had received word from Eva that something was taking place outside the aboveground facility and had quickly made their way to a prime viewing location. When Maggie threw her arms around the individual, Martin was almost positive it was Paul and that he had come home. Pamela put her arm around her father, resting her head upon his shoulder, as she too saw the reunion. Scott and the sentries soon reported in, confirming that it was indeed Paul.

He put his arm around Pamela, happy that Paul had returned, but feeling sad for his daughter. Martin knew, as a father, that she harbored feelings for Paul, so seeing

Maggie and Paul together must be difficult for her. He'd kept his encounter with Susan a secret from her, since it was now nothing more than a dream, along with the decisions he had made. Those decisions on using the QASM devices as weapons raised questions within him, as to how far he was willing to go to protect his people and technology. Evidently, all the way. Paul's return had raised other questions as well, as to how and who had enabled him to travel here from the past, without the aid of TimeBridge. There was obviously another force at work here, one of incredible power and possibly with some hidden agenda. Standing there with Pamela, Martin had a feeling that his problems were only going to get bigger, and he had one burning question on his mind. How the heck was he going to tell General Esterbrook about all this?

Lucifer watched the whole debacle with disgust. Asmodeus had failed to recover the Ark in this timeline. In other potential outcomes, he had succeeded, and Lucifer had been freed. He was envious of those other timelines, but there were some interesting developments in this one. The Skarzi showing up had been an insurance policy against a failure by Lilith. Unfortunately, they had also failed. The dark matter entity called Black had been a surprise. In this timeline it had acted against Lilith causing her to fail, in others it had remained quiet, allowing her to complete her mission.

Dark matter had always been a problem for the Creator but was absolutely integral to the basic operation of the universe. In the case of Black, it had shown itself to be unpredictable and at times capricious. Intelligent beings arising within the dark matter universe hadn't surprised Lucifer in the least. The surprise was one showing up here. He was unsure about the power such an entity could wield, but it could prove useful in gaining his freedom. The other item Lucifer had noted was when Martin had encountered his dead wife Susan and the effect it had on him. Most interesting and something that could be exploited.

Sighing, Lucifer tested his shackles once again, the bands of energy binding him glowed a bright red but held strong. Always good to keep these Guardians on their toes, thought Lucifer as he stopped testing his shackles and began working on a plan to gain Black as an ally. Freedom would be his, no matter what it took.

The End

I'm employed as a manager at a growing contract manufacturing company located southwest of Boston, Massachusetts and have been in the electronics industry for some 46 years now. During this time, I've witnessed great changes in the industry and the rapid growth of technology. When I first started working at Data General in the seventies, a hard drive the size of a washing machine was considered state-of-the-art. Now, a USB drive the size of your thumb can hold as much, or more than over 115 of those earlier drives. Truly amazing.

In writing this second book in the DarkBridge Technology series, I've come to realize that you can't put a deadline on the creative writing process. The first book, DarkWeave, was a story that seemed to just pour out and was written in less than a year. The second book, Solomon, seemed to take somewhat longer at two years. Mainly due to the troublesome aspect of time travel, with all its quirks and paradoxes. One thing I've noticed in writing these books, is that while I have a vague idea how the story will unfold, the story often ends up following its own path.

I've relied somewhat on the History Channel series, Ancient Aliens for some of the references to the Anunnaki in my books. The show, hosted by Giorgio Tsoukalos, relates tales of the Anunnaki and their influence on the ancient Sumerians. While the Anunnaki civilization itself is shrouded in mystery, I offer my own interpretation through my books.

When not writing and weather permitting, I can usually be found tending my vegetable garden. I find it most relaxing, in that it takes my mind off the usual everyday worries. It's similar to painting and writing, where financially, you're lucky to break even and really have to look at it from a different perspective. That perspective being the satisfaction of seeing others enjoy what you grew, what you painted, or what you wrote.

www.ingramcontent.com/pod-product-compliance
Lightning Source LLC
Chambersburg PA
CBHW070524220726
48294CB00019B/216